CRITICAL ACCLAIM FOR RABBI DAVID SMALL

"If Agatha Christie's Miss Marple and Hercule Poirot had had a son who naturally became a detective, sharp as Marple on murder, wise as Poirot on plotting, he would be known as Rabbi David Small."

Vogue

"A rousing toast should welcome the advent of Rabbi David Small, whose Talmudic training makes him a master of detectival disputation."

The New York Times

"First-rate."

The New Yorker

"Delightfully different."

Cleveland Plain Dealer

"A winner all the way...sensitive...with fine comic relief."

Saturday Review

"This Jewish Sherlock Holmes is not only as brilliant and perceptive as his British counterpart, but in time very likely will surpass him in exciting adventure."

Detroit News

Also by Harry Kemelman
Published by Fawcett Crest Books:

Thursday
The Rabbi
Walked Out

by

HARRY KEMELMAN

FAWCETT CREST • NEW YORK

Once again
to the new generation:
Nina, Jennifer, Jared Rooks,
and
Jonathan, Micah, Joab Kemelman,
and
the new member, Murray J. Rossant

1

When her husband was preparing a sermon, Miriam was careful to stay out of his way, not for fear of disturbing his train of thought, but lest she give him an excuse for interrupting his work. For David Small, the rabbi of Barnard's Crossing Conservative Temple, did not like to prepare sermons, or for that matter to preach them. He had begun as usual by laying out paper, sharpening pencils, adjusting the lamp—all to postpone the agony of beginning. He was thin and pale, and sitting over his desk, his shoulders had a scholarly stoop. His thin hair, which was beginning to gray at the temples, did not make him more distinguished-looking, only older. He wrote a few words, peering down at the page nearsightedly through thick-lensed glasses. He crossed them out, drummed his pencil on the desktop, and then began to doodle, the sermon forgotten as he became completely engrossed in working out a complicated design of straight lines and loops, of circles and squares joined by cross-hatching. He

7

was delighted when the doorbell rang. "I'll take it," he called out from his study.

Hurrying in from the kitchen, Miriam said, "Don't bother. It's probably the newsboy come to collect for the week." But when she opened the door, it was to the pleasant ruddy face of Hugh Lanigan, Barnard's Crossing's police chief.

From behind her, the rabbi greeted him cheerfully. "Come in. Come in, Chief. Miriam was just going to make some coffee. Weren't you, dear?"

Dutifully, Miriam said, "Yes, I put the perc on. Do come in." She could not refrain from adding, "David is working on a sermon, and I knew he'd want an excuse for stopping."

Lanigan smiled. "What's the matter, David? Having tough going with this one?"

"David has tough going with all his sermons," said Miriam tartly. She was small, and in sweater, skirt and loafers she might have looked like a teen-ager were it not that her face with its pointed chin showed maturity and determination. Her mass of blond hair piled on her head, as though to get it out of the way, almost seemed to overbalance her trim little figure.

"That so? I would have thought you'd enjoy it," said Lanigan. "You can bawl them out and they can't answer back. It's a captive audience."

The rabbi grinned. "I don't care too much about bawling out people, especially when I'm all too conscious of my own shortcomings. Besides, it doesn't do any good. The serman is just a kind of entertainment the rabbi provides to help pass the tedium of the service. Actually, it's not even his traditional function. In the old days the rabbi didn't do it."

"You mean when a synagogue engaged a rabbi, they didn't expect him to preach?"

The rabbi shook his head. "It wasn't the synagogue that engaged him. It was the town or the community. And they engaged him to act as a judge and settle questions of law when they arose. The rest of his time he was supposed to devote to study."

"They'd pay him just to study?"

"Why not? Universities subsidize scholars. Why shouldn't a community?"

"I suppose. And he didn't have to preach at all?"

"His contract called for two sermons a year, on the Sabbath before Passover and on the Sabbath before the Day of Atonement. But they weren't really sermons as you think of them. They were dissertations, like the lectures of a law professor. He didn't exhort the congregation. The kind you're familiar with, against sin, was usually given by an itinerant preacher called a maggid. Of course, nowadays, the rabbi, like the priest and the minister, is expected to give a sermon every week. Some rabbis like the idea. I suppose they have a knack for it. The poorest student in my class at the seminary now has one of the most prestigious pulpits in the New York area on the strength of it. He has a wonderful baritone voice and can bring tears to your eyes just—just reciting the alphabet. We called him The Voice."

"Reuben Levy?" asked Miriam. "The one who explained about the parables?"

The rabbi laughed joyously. "That's the one." To Lanigan he explained, "We were sitting around once, a bunch of seminary students and their wives, talking about sermons, because at the time we were being sent out to small communities for a Sabbath. Levy explained that in preparing a sermon he didn't search for examples and parables to illustrate some point he was planning to make. He worked it in reverse. When he heard a good story, he'd keep it in mind and then build a sermon around it."

"Like the fellow who got a reputation as a crackshot by firing first and then drawing a target around the bullet hole?" suggested Lanigan.

"Exactly!" said the rabbi.

As Miriam went out to the kitchen for the coffee, the rabbi went on. "My own sermons are always of the dissertation type. You see, three times a week we read portions of the Pentateuch, so I tie in my sermons with the portion of the week."

"Then you always have a subject," said Lanigan. "That should make it easy."

"True, but after all these years, I begin worrying that I might be repeating myself."

"Ah, well," said Lanigan as he accepted the coffee cup from Miriam, "have you ever thought that your congregation might not be listening anyway?"

The rabbi smiled sourly. "Thanks."

"No, but seriously, you've been here ten years now?"

"Twelve."

"So, if you were to give some of your old sermons, the ones you gave when you first came, who'd know the difference?"

"I'd know," said the rabbi.

"But look here, you say your sermons are like a professor's lectures. Well, *they* give the same lectures year in and year out, don't they? I mean, a new class comes in and they have to cover the same ground. Now, I'll bet that in the twelve years you've been here, a pretty fair hunk of your original congregation has gone—died, moved away, retired to Florida. And a lot of new folks have come into town. So if what you told your original congregation was important for them to know, it's just as important for the new ones to know."

The rabbi nodded. "That's true enough. It happens gradually, so you hardly notice it, but it's true; there aren't many of the original members left."

"And a lot more of your people have moved into the area," Lanigan pointed out.

"We have almost three hundred families now," said Miriam.

"Three hundred?" Lanigan repeated. "I would have thought there were more than that in town."

"Oh, there are—in town," the rabbi agreed. "Maybe another couple of hundred families, but they're not members of our temple." He smiled. "If Henry Maltzman, our president, has his way, they'll all join up. He's very strong for building up the numbers." He laughed. "He's always talking about finding the right gimmick to do the trick."

"Well, why aren't they members? Now in our church when someone moves into the parish, the pastor or one of his curates calls on him. And if he doesn't show up, they keep after him. I'll bet there aren't a dozen Catholics in town who aren't connected with the church one way or another."

"Your religion is church oriented," said the rabbi. "It's built around the Mass and Communion and Confession, and these involve a priest in a church. Our religion is primarily centered in the home. The Sabbath is celebrated in the home. The Passover Feast takes place in the home. Besides, the financial structure of the two is different. Ours is based on membership, and the annual fees of necessity come to several hundred dollars a year. That's a lot for a young married couple, and that's what most of the new people are. They came because they got jobs in the research labs and automated plants on Route 128."

"And a lot of those are cutting back," Miriam observed, "and some may go out of business altogether."

"You thinking of the Rohrbough Corporation?" asked Lanigan.

"There's been talk of it," said Miriam. "I know some of the wives are worried."

"I saw an article in the Sunday papers," said her husband, "about some big Chicago outfit taking it over."

"The Segal Group?" Lanigan shook his head. "They're not likely to be of much help. The article was mentioned at the selectmen's meeting last night, and Al Megrim who is a stockbroker and ought to know said they were a financial outfit, not an operating company. They trade corporations like kids trade baseball cards. They take over a

company and milk it, manipulating the stock while
they liquidate the assets, and then move on leaving
a bunch of empty buildings." He put down his
coffee cup and sat back in his chair. "Did you hear
anything about the meeting?"

The rabbi shook his head.

Lanigan shifted uncomfortably in his chair. He
cleared his throat and said, "Well, they voted to
reconsider setting up the traffic lights near the
temple."

"But they approved it unanimously last week,"
said Miriam, dismayed.

"After spending weeks discussing it," added her
husband. "Did anything happen to change the situation? We have children going to the religious
school every afternoon and—"

"I know, I know, David. It's probably just
routine," said Lanigan.

"Routine to pass a measure one week and reconsider it the next?"

"Well, Ellsworth Jordon—know him?"

The rabbi shook his head.

"He owns some land down there. Hell, he owns
land all over town. But that makes him an abutter.
He wrote them that he hadn't been notified. So
Megrim asked for reconsideration, and the rest of
the board went along out of courtesy to him."

"So what happens now?" asked Miriam.

"Oh, they'll take it up again next week," said
Lanigan soothingly. "And I expect they'll pass it.
But I'd plan on being there," he added.

"How about a delegation?" asked Miriam.

Lanigan hesitated. "No-o, I don't think so. They

might feel you were trying to pressure them, and they might resent it. This is New England after all, and the selectmen are all conservative Yankees. They can get stubborn, not to say mulish, against pressure. That's just my opinion, you understand."

She looked questioningly at her husband.

"I think the chief is right," said the rabbi. "But I'll talk to Henry Maltzman. He's coming here tonight."

As Miriam cleared the table of cups and saucers, the rabbi walked their guest to the door. "What's really behind this vote for reconsideration?" he asked. "Is it just that this Jordon is indignant that the selectmen failed to notify him?"

Lanigan halted on the threshold. "In a town this size, you hear things about all kinds of people. And I listen because I find it comes in handy sometimes in doing my job. I have the feeling that he did it because he doesn't like you people."

"Doesn't like—"

"Jews."

2

Henry Maltzman was a big man. Although he had developed something of a paunch since the days when he had been a captain in the Marines in the Korean War, he still kept his head erect, with the chin in and shoulders back as though on parade. While at fifty, it seemed a little unnatural, like a fat man at the beach sucking in his belly at the approach of a pretty girl, it was generally agreed that he was a fine figure of a man, even handsome, with ruddy cheeks and close-cropped crinkly hair. It was rumored that he had an eye for the ladies, and vice versa. And perhaps there was some indication of his appeal in the very fact of his election to the presidency. For he had been a rank outsider in the temple organization, having served only one term on the board of directors before running for the presidency after the bylaws had been changed to permit women to vote and to hold office.

Maltzman's bulk loomed large as he looked down at the Smalls. He had little blue eyes, which normally sparkled with friendliness, but which could also turn steely when he was crossed and which seemed to protrude dangerously when he was angry. His eyes were friendly now as he shook hands with the rabbi, and he favored Miriam with the warm smile that came automatically for women as she took his coat to hang in the closet. He took the seat to which the rabbi motioned him, but he immediately rose again when Miriam returned from the hallway.

"Oh, you are probably going to talk temple matters," she said, "so I'll leave you."

"I wish you would stay, Mrs. Small," he said. "It's about the temple, of course, but it concerns you, too. At least, I think it does. It's the place of women in the temple service I want to talk about, Rabbi."

"Wouldn't you like some tea or coffee?" asked Miriam.

"No, really. Nothing."

"David?"

"Nothing for me, Miriam."

Maltzman waited until she was seated before sitting down himself.

"Now that we have women on the board," he said, "there has been considerable pressure to have full equality in the services. And, of course, something like this can't be decided by a simple majority vote of the board. We'd have to have a referendum, or hold a general meeting, to decide on something as basic as that."

"I agree that it isn't anything that should be decided by the board alone," said the rabbi. "So why not hold a general meeting?"

"Because the other side won't abide by the vote," said Maltzman, showing annoyance. "Kaplan, who represents the Orthodox element, as much as told me that if we made the change and permitted women to be part of the minyan and called them to the Reading and all the rest of it, he'd pull out. He and his group would leave the temple."

The rabbi nodded. "Yes, I expect he would. I don't know how many would go along with him, but if there were enough to get another synagogue started, I imagine others would follow."

"That's the way I see it," Maltzman agreed. "So it seems to me that this is the time to show some leadership. Now if the rabbi of the congregation were to push for equality, give sermons on it—"

"Don't count on me, Mr. Maltzman," said the rabbi quickly.

"You mean you're against it? But why?" Maltzman was honestly perplexed.

The rabbi smiled. "Put it down to a natural traditionalism, if you like. If we make so drastic a change, other effects follow, quite unforeseen effects, and some of them undesirable. It's a basic sociological law that you can't change just one thing."

"Then you mean you'd be opposed to any change at all?"

"No, I'm not opposed to change as such. But I'm opposed to unnecessary changes. It seems to me that this particular change is part of the present ferment of the Women's Lib movement, and as happens in the initial stages of any movement, you get all kinds of exaggerated reactions. A men's club must admit women, or it's sexist. You mustn't say

'Chairman,' you now have to say 'Chairperson.' I was present at a lecture when the speaker used the phrase 'every man for himself.' He was challenged by a woman in the audience and had to say 'every man or woman for himself or herself.' Ridiculous! Look here, we are an institution going back several thousand years. Are we to change because there has been a sudden shift in fashion? Would you have us change the traditional Kol Nidre chant because the musical fashion is rock and roll?"

"But there *have* been changes, Rabbi."

"Sure, when it was practical and necessary. The prosbul of Hillel changed the laws of the sabbatic year when it was necessary to carry on the commerce that had developed at the time. Rabbi Gershom changed the marriage and divorce laws. Not to mention the many laws we changed when they became moot with the destruction of the Temple in Jerusalem. Our own Conservative Movement was launched and developed to meet the challenge of the American experience. Changes were made when needed. But only when needed."

The rabbi paused and when Maltzman didn't respond, began again, his voice rising, "They want to be part of the minyan? Why? The minyan is for the purpose of public prayer. It requires a minimum of ten adult males. If any others want to join, men or women, they are more than welcome. But we just barely make our ten every morning, and it is Kaplan and his group of Orthodox whom we count on. No matter what I urge or what the board of directors decrees, if they don't see ten adult males, they will not regard it as a minyan and they won't participate in the service.

"As for the honor of being called to the Reading, that's what it is—an honor. Only a handful at any service are called. Does that mean that the rest of the congregation are discriminated against? It's really more of a social than religious honor, and there are people who have never been called all their adult lives."

"What if the congregation as a whole votes for it?" asked Maltzman.

"Ah, that's something else. If a sizable majority of the congregation wanted it, it would indicate that a major sociological change had taken place in the community and that this was an expression of it."

Maltzman looked uncertainly from the rabbi to his wife and then said, "How do you feel about it, Mrs. Small?"

Miriam laughed. "To tell the truth, Mr. Maltzman, there have been some terribly cold and snowy days in the winter when David has gotten up early and gone to the temple to insure the likelihood of a minyan; I remember snuggling deeper into the bedclothes and thanking God that I had no such obligation."

Maltzman grinned. "Yeah, I suppose. All right, I'll tell them how you feel about it, Rabbi." His grin broadened. "And how you feel about it, Mrs. Small. It won't end the matter—"

"I know," said the rabbi. "My calendar shows a meeting with a delegation from the Sisterhood." He turned to Miriam. "Perhaps now Mr. Maltzman would like a cup of tea. I would."

She looked questioningly at Maltzman, and after a moment's hesitation, he said, "Well, all right. Yes, I think I'd like a cup now."

Miriam immediately left the room and Maltzman said, "You know, Rabbi, I don't agree with you. I don't agree with you at all on this matter. Other congregations, and Conservative congregations at that, have women participating in the services. They've got rabbis, too, so I suppose there are arguments, I mean rabbinic arguments, on the other side."

"It's a matter of where you want to put the emphasis," Rabbi Small agreed affably.

"Well, with me, the emphasis is on membership," said Maltzman. "I see a lot of our people in the community, and they are not members of the temple. This could be just the gimmick that would get some of them to join."

"Would more join than we'd lose if the Orthodox pulled out?" demanded the rabbi.

"It's a consideration," Maltzman admitted.

Miriam came in with the tea, and as she handed Maltzman his cup, she said, "Did you hear what happened at the selectmen's meeting last night? Was it reported to you?"

He listened intently as the rabbi told of Lanigan's visit.

"Oh, that sonofabitch, that dirty anti-Semitic sonofabitch—I'm sorry, Mrs. Small, but—"

"You mean, Megrim, the selectman?" asked Rabbi Small.

"Oh no, Megrim is all right. I was referring to Ellsworth Jordan."

"Why do you call him anti-Semitic?" asked the rabbi.

Maltzman glared. "What other reason is there for him to oppose the traffic light? He's against it because we're for it. Let me tell you something about Jordon, Rabbi. He owns land all over town and I'm in the real estate business, so I have some sort of contact with him. And not once have I been able to deal with him. He owns land under various titles—Jordon Realty, Ellsworth Estates, E. J. Land Corporation—"

"E. J. Land Corporation?" Miriam echoed.

Maltzman nodded. "That's right, the company that owns the land near the temple, that we've wanted to buy for the new religious school. I wrote E. J. Land Corporation, asking the price of the lot. And I got no answer, no answer at all. So after a while, I asked my good friend Larry Gore at the Barnard's Crossing Trust, because you write to E. J. Land Corporation care of the bank. I asked him what gives. And he tells me the land is not for sale. So what is it for? Jordon is crazy about paying taxes? He's planning to farm it?"

"Maybe he's planning to build," the rabbi suggested mildly.

"Practically next door to the temple? Nah. He's crazy but not that crazy. Besides, he hasn't built in twenty years. Back then he put up some houses— he's an architect or an engineer of some kind—and sold them at just the right time. Then he bought up a lot of land, planning to build lots of houses, big housing projects. But he got sick and didn't go ahead with it. Well, just about then, land values began to climb. They'd built the bridge and the tunnel, so getting into Boston was a matter of thirty or forty minutes, and the town became suitable for all year round living instead of just a summer vacation place for the rich. Land values climbed, and he had acres of it. Some of it could be sold for more than ten times what he paid for it. He's a crackpot and a nut but—"

"That doesn't sound like a nut," Miriam observed.

"Oh, I guess he's shrewd enough in money matters. But he's still a nut." He began to laugh. "Last year I was collecting for the United Appeal and I drew his name. He lives in this old ark of a house all boarded up—"

"On a hill?" asked Miriam.

"That's right. It's a great big lot of land with an iron fence all around."

"The children called it the haunted house," said Miriam. "Remember, David, when we drove by there? But it's all boarded up. I didn't think anybody lived there."

Maltzman nodded. "That's because of the trees, but as you come up a long driveway, you see that it's only the top two floors that are boarded up. I drove up and rang the bell. From inside somebody shouted, 'Come in, come in.' So I pushed the door open and found myself in this big room lit by one ceiling light with maybe a twenty-five-watt bulb. Then I hear a voice that says, 'What is it, young man? What do you want? Speak up, young man. State your business.' Well, I look around and don't see anyone, and for a minute I thought the voice was coming through a loudspeaker, like in one of those spy films. Then, I saw a couple of feet waving in the air, it was him. He was standing on his head in a corner of the room! Now, is he a nut, or isn't he?"

"Lives alone, does he?" asked the rabbi.

"Uh-huh. Maybe has a day woman come in to cook and clean for him."

"And he has no family?"

Maltzman shook his head. "So I understand."

"Then that accounts for it," said the rabbi. "He doesn't have anyone he's responsible to so he doesn't have to worry about embarrassing anybody. He can say anything he likes, or wear any kind of clothes, stand on his head when he feels like it. Poor devil, I feel sorry for him."

"But if he's an anti-Semite, David," said Miriam.

"What's this," sneered Maltzman, "turning the other cheek?"

"Not at all," said the rabbi. "If it is anti-Semitism, it's irrational, and sometimes an irrationality can take hold of a man's mind if there's no one to oppose him or contradict him or that he has to explain to and then it's like being possessed by devils. A man shouldn't be entirely alone. Yes, I'd say he was to be pitied."

"You mean, if he had a wife or kids, then he'd have to behave himself? Maybe. But it's been my experience that an anti-Semite is an anti-Semite is an anti-Semite. The only difference is that the one with a family and kids is apt to infect them, too. Right now, the question is the traffic lights."

"Maybe if I went to see this Jordon," the rabbi began.

"No! I'll take care of Jordon and that's an order."

The rabbi colored at the peremptory tone, and Miriam lowered her eyes in sympathetic embarrassment. Maltzman noticed and promptly sought to make amends. "What I mean is that a man like Jordon takes a man like me to handle. I mean, it's a political matter and it takes political experience. Besides, I'm president of the temple, so it's my baby."

When Maltzman left, Miriam said, "I don't think he likes you, David."

"Really? You mean you think he dislikes me?"

She nodded.

"He seemed friendly enough." He colored and then smiled. "Except at the end there when he gave me my orders. And that was just a manner of speaking with him. I don't think he really meant it."

"Oh, he was respectful enough—the way the army officers were always respectful when they talked to the chaplains. He thinks of himself as very much of a he-man. You're a scholar, and it's something he doesn't understand, and he's wary of it—and hostile."

"Well, that's not unusual, his hostility, I mean," he said philosophically. "I've had it from previous presidents, and other members of the congregation, too. Doctors, lawyers, successful businessmen. I suppose they wonder why anyone would become a rabbi. 'Is this a job for a Jewish boy?' " He laughed. "Maybe they're right."

"He could make trouble for you," she observed.

"Of course he can. Other presidents have. From my first year. But it's twelve years now, and I'm still here."

"But it's different now, David."

"Why is it different?"

"Because there are new rules now. The board consists of only fifteen. It's like an executive committee. Eight members could vote you out, and they could do it just like that." She snapped her fingers. "Because all you have is a one-year contract."

"It's the way I wanted it," he said stubbornly. "I don't ever want to stay longer than I'm wanted."

"I know, and I understand, but it makes it a little hard to plan ahead."

3

Slouched down in his recliner, one long chino-clad leg crossed over the other, a worn laceless sneaker dangling from the upraised bony foot, Ellsworth Jordon reread with satisfaction the report on the selectmen's meeting in the local newspaper.

"But can I make it stick?" he asked of the empty room. "Or will they vote on it at the next meeting? I think, maybe, I can get Al Megrim to hold. I'll talk to him about it next time I see him at the club. But he's only one vote." He tossed the newspaper on the floor and made a tent of his hands by pressing the fingertips together. "Let's see, there's Sturgis, he'll vote against almost anything that'll cost the town money. Same as Blair and Mitchener will vote for it," he added angrily. He got up and began to pace the room. "So that leaves Cunningham. He's the swing vote." He faced himself in the wall mirror. "He's the key. You realize that, don't you? All right." Satisfied that he had convinced the image in the glass, he resumed his pacing. "So what do we know about Cunningham? He's retired, but he gets an occasional commission as the agent for the Steerite Boat Company of Long Island. And the president of that company was here last summer and was crazy to buy my land on the Point." Once again he stopped in front of the mirror and looked sharply at his image. "Now, what if I were to go down to New York and drop in to see him accidental-like, and mention I might be induced to sell that piece of land if I weren't so upset about his Mr. Cunningham planning to vote for some unnecessary traffic lights. . . . How do you suppose he'd respond to that?"

The wrinkled face with the scrawny neck in the mirror smiled back at him. Then the pale blue eyes narrowed as he thought of what the trip would involve. He'd have to dress up in a regular suit—with a tie, and shoes. He'd have to pack a bag and drive out to the airport, unless maybe Billy could take the morning off from the bank. But then he'd have to arrange to be met on his return. And what would he do in New York after he'd seen his man—what was his name? Leicester? Yeah, what would he do after he'd seen Mr. Leicester?

The usual was out of the question since Hester was in Europe. So he'd have to sit in his hotel room and watch TV. Hell, he could watch TV at home. Besides, Leicester might be out of town. "It's not worth it," he announced, and resuming his seat in the recliner, he picked up his newspaper. "Maybe I'll just talk to Cunningham," he said.

In recent years, Ellsworth Jordon did not get to New York too often, but whenever he did, he tried to arrange matters so that he would spend some time with Hester Grimes whom he had first met in the fifties when she was twenty-two and studying at the Actors' School. He was working for the prestigious architectural firm of Sloan, Cavendish and Sullivan, and though almost forty, his rank was still that of junior architect. She was Esther Green in those days, thin with jet black hair and large dark eyes, intense, serious, determined that someday she would play the great female dramatic roles—Nora, Lady Macbeth, Joan of Arc.

He was tall and blond and handsome, for all that his hair was beginning to thin and he was beginning to put on middle-aged weight. He treated her with a kind of whimsical gallantry which she found all the more attractive because it was not common in the Bohemian circle in which she moved.

In spite of the disparity in their ages, they had been very much in love. For the six months or so that it lasted, it had been a hectic affair, marked by frequently violent quarrels followed by teary reconciliations. Then his big chance came. He was to be sent to Berlin on a major project which would take several years to complete. He wanted her to go with him.

She demurred. She had her own career to think of. And besides, although neither religious nor in any way connected with the Jewish community except by accident of birth, the thought of living in Germany was repugnant to her. The discussion quickly degenerated to an argument, and then, as happened frequently with them, to a quarrel. Annoyed by her resistance, he was led to minimize the importance of her ambitions and then even to disparage acting itself as a valid art. "While I admit that it might be a legitimate way of earning a living," he declared loftily, "it is essentially one that appeals to a childish urge to show off." As for her reluctance to live in Germany, he felt that it showed that she still retained the paranoia of her race and that it proved that she was still bound by a narrow ethnic parochialism.

It ended as so many of their quarrels did with his agreeing with her that they were no good for each other and leaving, as always, presumably never to return. Shortly after he went abroad, she discovered she was pregnant.

Had he still been in the city, she would no doubt have arranged to get word to him, even if she would not herself have called him. And of course,

he would have come, and of course, there would
have been a reconciliation, and of course . . . But
he was not in the city; he was three thousand miles
away. Had she had family, or if her friends and associates had been of the middle class in which she
had grown up, she probably would have undergone
an abortion, even if it would have involved the
services of some quack in a sleazy tenement. Or she
might have gone out of town and had her baby in
secret and then given it up for adoption. But her associates were all Bohemian and long on ideals, especially where the necessity of living up to them
was someone else's. When she suggested that
she had even considered having the baby and bringing it up by herself, they immediately hailed the
idea and warmly applauded her resolution. She *did*
change her name to Hester Grimes, but that was for
professional reasons.

It was almost two years before Ellsworth Jordon
saw her again, and then it was on the TV screen.
He had just returned from Berlin and was in his
New York hotel room watching the late night Damon Parker Talk Show when she appeared, dressed
in a low-cut, skintight evening gown to sing a blues
ballad in a deep throaty voice. Afterward she offered her cheek to be kissed by the master of ceremonies and took her place on the dais with the
other guests to spend the rest of the hour in idle
chitchat. From Damon Parker's questions about the
progress of her career, it was obvious that though
not a "regular," she had appeared on the program
several times before. Later, she told an amusing
story of the party she had held the day before her

son's first birthday. Although her appearance on the screen had excited him, Jordon told himself firmly that he must close the door on the past and make no effort to see her. But the story of the birthday party made him change his mind. Why, on the basis of simple arithmetic, the boy must be his!

Although she agreed to meet him, it was more to test herself than because she felt any desire to see him. And when he appeared at her apartment, she noted dispassionately that he was far less attractive physically than she remembered him. The skin at his throat sagged and he looked old.

"You've lost some weight, haven't you?" she remarked.

"That's right. I was sick—a mild heart attack. They wanted me to lose some weight and take it easy."

"I'm sorry." She was not really concerned, only polite.

"The boy—he's mine, isn't he?" he asked eagerly.

"No, Ellsworth. He's mine."

"You know what I mean—"

"Yes, of course."

"Why didn't you let me know? Why didn't you get in touch with me? You could have got the address from the office here."

"What for, Ell?" She laughed. "So you could come back and marry me to give the baby a name? Or would you have insisted that I join you in Germany and have my baby there, or have it aborted there?"

"But dammit, Esther—"

"It's not easy having a baby, Ell, especially when you have to have it all alone. But once you live through it, then it's not so bad. From what I hear from some of my friends, there's a lot to be said for bringing up a child without the interference of a father."

He thought she was trying to hurt him, and he felt he had to retaliate. "That's the Jew in you," he said spitefully. "You enjoy suffering for the pleasure of making us feel guilty."

If his words cut, she did not show it. She shook her head. "No, you're wrong. There's no pleasure in suffering. Not for me there isn't. But it doesn't last forever." She smiled. "And as it turns out, having Billy all by myself was the making of me."

"It gave you new depths of feeling, I suppose," he sneered.

She chuckled. "No, it was just that because of him, I got my chance. I had got a job in this little nightclub. It didn't pay much, but then I wasn't very good. I'd sing a little, tell a few jokes and do a couple of impersonations. But one night Damon Parker came in with a party, slumming, I suppose. After my act, he asked me to join the party, and I told him I had to beg back for Billy's night feeding. He's an emotional, sentimental guy, and he got all worked up when I told him that I was bringing up the baby myself. He saw me as an original—the New Woman. And he invited me to appear on his show. Well, with the exposure I got, I was made."

"So I and the baby were just stepping-stones to your career."

"Something like that."

"All right, what about now? And the future?"

"What about it?"

"I have a share in the child. Billy is my son as much as he is yours."

"No, Ell, you have no share in him at all. What do you want to do? Contribute to his support? I don't need it."

"I mean share in his upbringing, in his education. A boy needs a man to look up to, an image to model himself after. All the psychologists agree on that."

"Just the men psychologists, I expect," was her comment.

"Even if we don't get married, you could come down with him to visit with me at Barnard's Crossing. Then when he gets older, he can come down on his own summers."

"No, Ell. I don't want him to know that you are his father."

"But sooner or later, you'll have to tell him. He'll ask. He'll want to know."

"Of course. And I've prepared for it. I've worked up a perfectly wonderful father for him, an idealist, a soldier who went off to war—"

"Which war?"

"Well, that was a problem, of course, because there haven't been any wars recently. At least, none that we've been engaged in. There are always military actions of one sort or another that mercenaries take part in. But I didn't want that for him. And then I thought of the Suez action of Britain, France and Israel. It was over before Billy was born, or conceived, but there's still a lot of unofficial fighting going on over there in the Middle East. So I worked up a young Israeli who came here to study. We met and we fell in love. Then he had to return to Israel. I was to follow and we were to get married there."

"But he gets killed in some military skirmish?"

"Exactly. So I stay here to have my baby."

Thinking it over afterward, and in his loneliness in Barnard's Crossing, he thought about it a good deal, it sometimes seemed to him that she had not been unconcerned and indifferent; that on the contrary, she had been vindictive and had gone out of her way to hurt him. And he was inclined to interpret her attitude as an indication that deep down she still cared for him, that she had perhaps hoped to provoke him into a quarrel that would lead to a reconciliation. The thought was in back of his mind the next time he came to New York and arranged to see her. And it was never totally absent each of the times he saw her over the years.

But there were also times when he brooded over her coldness, her lack of feeling. It was then that he thought she was trying to avenge herself, and that her consenting to see him whenever he came to New York was so she could enjoy the satisfaction of seeing his hurt.

On the other hand, Billy was obviously always pleased to see him. Of course, it might be because he always brought a gift. But he was sure the boy really liked him.

Whenever he tried to involve himself in Billy's development, she brusquely brushed him aside and refused to accept his advice or recognize his concern. And that hurt. She might talk about the boy's progress at school, or problems that had developed, but it was as she might to a casual acquaintance and not as to one who had any involvement in the matter.

It was on Jordon's most recent visit, however, that she seemed inclined to admit him to a share of their son. There had evidently been some crises, and her confidence in her ability to cope had been badly shaken.

"He refuses to go to college," she announced tragically.

"Well, that's not so terrible," he remarked. "What's he want to do instead?"

"Nothing. He has no plans. He's not interested in anything. He doesn't read. He doesn't do anything. He just mopes."

"I expect he's tired, tired of school and study. You've probably been pushing him hard to make good grades so that he can get into a good college, and he's just sick of books. Why not let him take a year off?"

"To do what?" she challenged.

"To work. Let him get a job."

"What can he do? He's not trained for anything."

"Well, it doesn't have to be a big executive type of job. Any job will do where he's kept busy and makes some money."

"And if he works for a couple of weeks and then quits?"

"Then insist that he get another job."

"But I won't be here. My agent has arranged a European tour for me."

"Oh, I see. What you're really interested in is having someone keep an eye on him. Tell you what, let him come and visit with me for a while."

Instantly she was suspicious. "So you can tell him you're his father and try to take him away from me?"

He laughed. "Oh no, I'm not that much of a damn fool as to think I could compete with an Israeli war hero."

"Then why do you want him?"

"Well, because I *am* his father and I feel some responsibility and it might be kind of nice to have a young person around. I had another heart attack last year. Nothing serious, but it's probably a good idea that I have someone in the house with me in the evening and at night. The housekeeper usually leaves right after she does the dinner dishes."

"You mean you want someone to look after you?"

"Oh no, I don't need any looking after. It's just that it would be nice knowing someone was in the house at night. If anything were to happen, he could call a doctor."

"And what would he do all day long?"

"He'd work, of course. I could get him a job of some kind. I'm pretty well-known in town. He's eighteen? nineteen?"

"Eighteen."

"I've got it," he said triumphantly. "I could get him a job in a bank. Larry Gore would do it for me. He's president of one of the banks in town. He handles all my investments and is a distant relative of mine, the only one I have. But more than that, he'd do it for me if I asked him."

She looked at him uncertainly. "But—I don't know—Billy might not like it, and yet wouldn't say anything. He's sensitive. I'd hate to think that he might be unhappy and yet—"

"Look," he said firmly, "I'd have him write to you regularly. You'd get a letter from him every week. I promise you. If he didn't like it, he wouldn't mind telling you, especially in a letter. And then you'd call or write me and I'd ship him home. I'm going home tomorrow morning. Say the word and I'll start the ball rolling."

They discussed it at length. She was uncertain and raised many objections, which he answered skillfully as the consideration moved from her interests, to Billy's, to his own. "Oh, he won't be any bother to me. Quite the contrary. It will be nice having someone to talk to at the dinner table. And I'll feel better knowing there's someone in the house at night."

When Billy came home, she broached the idea.

"Mr. Jordan has invited you to come and visit with him while I'm abroad."

"You mean the whole time?"

"That's right," said Jordon. "And after, till you get around to go to college, if you like."

"Well, gee, it's a small town where you live, isn't it?"

"It's a small town," Jordon admitted, "but it's a nice town, right on the seashore. There's swimming and sailing. And you're only about half an hour from Boston."

"But what would I do all day long?"

"You'd get a job," said Jordon promptly.

"What kind of a job?" asked the young man cautiously.

"Maybe in a bank."

"Hey, that's kind of cool."

Despite the lateness of the hour, Jordon chose to walk back to his hotel rather than order a cab. He exulted in the thought that his son would be living with him. He was a boy, and he would make a man of him.

He heard the grating of a key in the front door lock. He called out, "Is that you, Billy? Come in, come in, boy, the door's unlocked." He rubbed his hands and smiled as the young man entered. "How'd things go at the bank today? All right? Anything unusual happen?"

"Unusual? No, sir."

"Well, that's the best way, I guess. The regular routine. Oh, case I forget, tomorrow when you go in, would you look up Johnny Cunningham's account and let me know how it stands."

4

"Oh, Ben, I love it. I simply love it." Mimi Segal whirled around like a ballerina pirouetting, her arms outstretched, her head lifted, her blond hair flowing in the crisp autumn breeze. She squinted against the reflection of the sun on the dancing wavelets. "There's a sign there on the beach that says Private. Does that mean it's a private beach?"

"I should think so," said her husband. "The lot goes down to the beach so the beach must be part of it. Those houses on either side, they each have paths leading to those little landing docks, so I guess these lots include the adjoining part of the beach."

"How did you find it? And how do you know it's for sale?"

He smiled fondly at her. "While you've been going in to Boston shopping, I've been wandering around the area." He was a good bit older than she, fifty to her thirty-eight, so there was a touch of the avuncular in his affection for her. "I saw this place when I walked out to the lighthouse yesterday."

"But how do you know it's for sale?" she persisted.

"Anything is for sale if the price is right." He turned to where the car was parked and called out to the chauffeur. "Hey, you know who owns this land?"

The chauffeur, who had been provided along with the car by the Rohrbough Corporation, shook his head. "I don't know, sir."

"Well, they'll know in town," Segal said to Mimi. "Let's walk along the beach and see what it's like." He put his arm around her waist, and because she was taller than he and was always worried that he might be self-conscious about it, she bent her head to rest on his shoulder. He was of average height, but she was tall for a woman, like a fashion model. It was her second marriage, and she had met him shortly after she had managed to free herself of an alcoholic husband. She had had doubts when he had indicated that he wanted to marry her, mostly because at forty-seven, he was still a bachelor. What was wrong with him? Why hadn't some woman grabbed him up long ago? He was not bad-looking. In fact, she decided she liked his sharp, intense face, with its sensitive mouth and long thin nose. With his shock of iron-gray hair, she thought he was even distinguished-looking. So she had agreed—and had no regrets.

"Are you sure this is what you want, Ben?" she asked anxiously.

"About building a house here?"

"About that, and well, everything, leaving Chicago, giving up finance to go into production—"

He halted in his stride, the better to explain. "You plan and you maneuver and you finally bring it off and make a lot of money. But even more, there's tremendous satisfaction in it. The second time, there's satisfaction, but it's not such a big deal. And then after a while, it becomes just another business. Because, you see, you know how to do it now. It becomes routine. Sure, there's a lot of money to be made, but that's all."

"Most people would say that's enough."

He nodded. "Sure. But if you use it just to make more money, there's no sense to it. I couldn't spend it; I never learned how, not the kind of money I was making. So I used it for leverage to make more deals—"

"But what do other businessmen do?" she asked.

"Some of them make things, or transport them, or distribute them so people have access to them. That seems more worthwhile."

"You do the same thing Bert Richardson does, and you've always admired him tremendously."

"You bet. And do you know what he told me? That he felt the same way. But what keeps him going, he told me, is that he's got three sons, and he hopes maybe they'll be able to make better use of his money than he has. Then I began thinking, there's one thing I could buy with my money. I could buy a new lifestyle. A lot of men have that idea when they get to my age. Doctors want to become businessmen, lawyers want to become college professors, businessmen want to become artists or actors. Not many of them do. Most of them feel they can't afford it, or they're afraid to take the chance. But here I am with plenty of money and sick of just putting deals together. Why shouldn't I try something else? So I started to look around, and when this Rohrbough proposition came up, I thought I'd like to try operating it."

"I'm glad you told me, Ben," she said. "I was afraid you were doing it for me because of what I said once about wanting to live a normal life and be a part of a community."

"Then you don't mind?" he asked.

"Mind? I love it, Ben."

"And you don't miss your friends in Chicago?"

"We have no friends in Chicago, Ben. Just business associates. You can't make friends when you live in a hotel, not even in a big suite in a residential hotel. You're always just a transient. Oh, Ben, I'm so happy. Let's celebrate."

"You're on," he said. "But look, I was planning to drop in at one of the local banks. They do the payroll for Rohrbough, and I wanted to size the place up. I'll have the driver drop me off there, and you'll go on to the hotel. We'll get together around noon."

"How are you going to find out who owns it?"

"No problem there. I'll ask at one of the local realty offices. They'd know. Or I could ask at the bank. Look, baby, I'll pick you up afterward, and we'll drive up the coast and have lunch at some restaurant where they specialize in fish and seafood. I've been hankering for it since we came. How about it, baby?"

"Swell. But the car will be parked at the hotel, so why don't I plan on picking you up?"

"I'll give you a call."

5

Lawrence Gore, president of the Barnard's Crossing Trust Company, smiled appreciatively as Molly Mandell, his secretary, his executive secretary he would say, entered his office, a sheaf of papers in her hand. She was so brisk and efficient, so interested and willing, so sympathetic and understanding, that it was a pleasure to have her around.

An attractive woman of thirty, she was neat and tidy in her navy blue suit. Her wavy brown hair was cut short and brushed back from her wide forehead. She had large dark eyes that were eager and alive. She had a no-nonsense mouth and a rounded chin which emphasized the oval of her face. And she was small. He liked small women because he himself was so cruelly short. Sitting behind his desk, his body visible only from the waist up, he seemed a large man. The long, narrow head with its thick blond hair and keen blue eyes was supported by a muscular neck rising from wide shoulders. It was something of a surprise when he rose and one saw that he was only a couple of inches more than five feet tall.

His eyes focused on the large plastic button pinned to her blouse. On it, in bold letters, was printed Women's Lib.

"Something new in costume jewelry, Molly?"

A sidelong glance at her bosom. "Oh, the state legislature is debating the Equal Rights amendment. The girls are wearing these to remind them where the votes are." She placed the papers on the desk before him, and then taking the visitor's chair, she watched him read the letters she had composed and typed for his signature.

Teetering gently in his swivel chair, he read each in turn carefully, and then as he reached for his pen, he said, "These are exactly right, Molly. You got just the tone I wanted."

"You mean the ones about the silver? Well, I don't have the same appreciation for Peter Archer silver that you have, of course, but I think the idea of the exhibition at the Boston Art Museum is wonderful, and I think it's doing the bank a lot of good, too."

"Think so? How about the display out front?" he asked. "Are people taking notice?"

"Oh sure. It's been getting a lot of attention." She flipped the pages of her notebook. "A Mr. Dalrymple asked me if you'd be interested in looking at a vinegar cruet he has. He's not a depositor. He just came in because he heard you had some pieces on exhibit in the bank."

"A vinegar cruet, eh? Yeah. We've got about

half a dozen so far, but if he has a real good one, I'd like to see it."

"I'll get in touch with him. And Mrs. Gore called. She asked if she could have her check earlier this month. She's going down to Florida to visit her brother. I said it would probably be all right."

He nodded curtly.

"Nancy asked if she could have Friday off. I told her we'd be shorthanded because Pauline wasn't due back until Monday."

"Quite right."

"She was a little put out."

"She'll get over it, I expect."

She closed her notebook. "Henry Maltzman was in to make a deposit, and he asked me what action we were taking on his request for a loan."

"What did you tell him?" he asked quickly.

"Just that I'd mention it to you."

He tapped the desktop with his fingers. "Graham says it's out of line with his statement."

"Graham is a Scotchman," she said scornfully. "He always says the loans are too big. If it depended entirely on him, we'd never make any."

He chuckled. "You've got a point there."

"And Henry Maltzman has been a good friend of the bank. He's touted a lot of business our way," she went on.

"You're right," he said. "One hand washes the other. If he should come in again today, tell him you think it's all right. Don't tell him I said so, because I don't want him to think it's official just in case the loan committee takes the bit in its teeth and decides to overrule me. But you can kind of hint—well, you'll know what to tell him."

"I'll manage," she said confidently.

"I'm sure you will. And now is there anything else?"

"You asked me to remind you of the Jordon report," she said coldly.

He noted the abrupt change in her manner and thought he knew the reason for it and was sympathetic. "Has he said anything—uh—nasty to you?"

"Oh, it's not what he says. It's just that—he's a dirty old man."

He was shocked. "You mean he—uh—made a pass at you?"

"I mean he brushes up against me, touches me—accidentally on purpose. Is he very important to the bank?"

"Just our biggest account and a director."

"Well, one day you're going to lose him—or me."

"Maybe if I talked to him . . ."

She laughed. "Don't bother. I can take care of him. I stood for much worse when I was working in Boston and riding the subway every day."

He grinned. "I can imagine. Well, try to stay out of his way. And now, how about the Cavendish report?"

"I was planning on working on it all day tomorrow."

"Hm." He drummed a rapid tattoo on the desktop with his fingertips. "He called earlier and said he was coming in around noon tomorrow and asked if he could go over it with me at lunch."

"I could take it home and work on it tonight," she suggested.

"Could you? Gee, that would be swell. You're sure your husband wouldn't mind? How is he, by the way?"

"Herb's fine. He won't mind. He's going to a meeting of the executives of the temple Brotherhood tonight anyway." She laughed. "It's my mother-in-law who might object."

"Really? Why should she object?"

"Oh, she objects to anything I do," she said lightly. "From her point of view, all my time outside of work belongs to her precious son, even if he's not there." She sat back and went on conversationally, "What really burns her up is seeing Herb setting the table and starting dinner. But he gets home from school at three o'clock, and I don't get home until a couple of hours later. He doesn't mind, but it burns her up."

"I suppose he has papers to correct, lessons to prepare?"

"He does it all in his free periods and study periods. It will be all right."

"Well, I sure appreciate it. And look, you can take time off in exchange."

"Oh, there's no need, really." She hesitated. "But next Wednesday there is a meeting and—"

"And you'd like to go. Plan on it. Take the afternoon off. Take the whole day off if you like."

There was a timid knock on the door.

"Come in," he called out, and the receptionist, a young girl with a ponytail and wide innocent eyes, sidled in, shutting the door firmly behind her.

"Oh, Mr. Gore, there's a man out there who's just hanging around. I asked him if I could help him, and he said, no, that he just wanted to look around. I mean there's nothing to see in a bank—"

"Maybe he came in to look at the Peter Archer silver," Gore suggested.

"No, he just glanced at it."

"He may be a dealer, Elsie. They don't like to appear interested."

"Well, I thought where there was that bank robbery over in Scoville—"

"You thought he might be casing the joint?" He laughed. "What's he look like?"

"Well, he's an older man. I mean his hair is like gray. . . ."

Molly had risen and opening the door had craned forward, the better to see into the lobby. She came back and with suppressed excitement said, "I think I know who it is, Larry. There was a picture of him the other day in the *Boston Jewish News* that my mother-in-law subscribes to. It's Ben Segal of the Segal Group of Chicago, the ones that are taking over the Rohrbough Corporation."

"You think so?" He got out from behind his desk and went to the door. Over his shoulder, he said, "There was a picture of him in *Business Week* a month or a month and a half ago. See if you can find it in that pile on the table."

Molly began flipping through the magazines and almost immediately called out, "Here it is."

He came back and studied the picture for a moment. "It's him all right." He said to the receptionist, "You're a good girl, Elsie." Then he strode through the office to where Segal was standing and said, "Welcome to Barnard's Crossing, Mr. Segal."

Segal turned and stared. "You know me?"

"Only from your picture in *Business Week*." He held out his hand.

"But that was a month ago," said Segal.

"Sure, but it spoke of your interest in the Rohrbough Corporation, and anything to do with Rohrbough concerns us. I'm Lawrence Gore, the president of the bank. We do the Rohrbough payroll, you know."

"I know."

"I'd like to talk to you about it if you've got some time. Look, it's about noon. How about discussing it over lunch."

"Well, I promised to take Mrs. Segal to some nice seafood restaurant."

"Splendid. We could pick her up wherever she is, and I'll take you to the Agathon, the best seafood on the North Shore. How about it?"

"Sounds good," said Segal. He nodded at the silver display in the wall case. "Do you sell the stuff?"

"The Peter Archer silver? Are you a collector? Do you know silver? No? Well, Peter Archer was a colonial silversmith whose shop was right here in Barnard's Crossing. He's practically unknown, except for collectors of course. Paul Revere is the name everybody knows. Now some of us think—I think—that Archer was a better craftsman and that Revere's reputation is due to his connection with the Revolution, Paul Revere's ride and all that sort of thing. So some of us"—he smiled self-consciously—"well, I guess it was my idea. Anyway, we thought we ought to do something about it. I approached the people at the Boston Art Museum, and they agreed to a Peter Archer exhibit if I could come up with a decent representation of his work. Those pieces in the bank are on loan from people from all over the area. It's all in the spirit of the Bicentennial. But, of course, we're hard-headed Yankees around here, so I was able to get as much as we have, and it's still coming in, by pointing out to the owners that having pieces exhibited at the Boston Art Museum will increase their value."

"Sounds like good business, Mr. Gore. Mrs. Segal is at the hotel. Maybe I ought to call her and tell her we're coming over."

"Sure. Use this phone." Gore reached for the phone on the receptionist's desk and slid it over.

"Where did you say you were taking us, Mr. Gore?" asked Segal as he lifted the receiver.

"The Agathon Yacht Club."

"A yacht club? Sounds kind of grand."

"This is sailing country, Mr. Segal, and the yachts are small sailboats mostly. It's the oldest club on the North Shore, though, and over the years it has developed into quite a place. Besides the regular docking facilities, we've got tennis courts, the only grass courts around. Costs a fortune to maintain them, but I suppose it's worth it—and a driving range, and a pistol range. But the nicest thing is the dining room. It's right on the water. I mean it's right over the water on pilings. You can actually hear the waves under you. It's like eating on the deck of a boat."

"Sounds nice. Mrs. Segal will like it."

6

"Why it's like being on the water!" Mimi exclaimed as she sat down at the table near the window that Lawrence Gore had selected.

Her husband said, "Nice."

Gore beamed. "Right now, since the tide is in, you *are* on the water. This room is cantilevered over the water, but only when the tide is high." He laughed. "It would have to be about a hundred yards long to make it when the tide is out."

"And there are so many boats!" Mimi observed.

"Not half as many as there are during Race Week," said Gore. "The harbor is really crowded then. It almost seems as though you could cross it on foot, jumping from deck to deck."

"Very nice," said Segal. "All the members own boats? They all interested in sailing?"

"Oh no. Some had them and gave them up. There's a lot of work involved in owning a boat, and a big expense, too. Some never owned a boat, but crew occasionally for their friends. And then there are some who aren't the slightest bit interested."

"And you?"

"I used to be pretty keen. But nowadays the only facility I use is the pistol range." He smiled shyly. "I'm the club champion."

"Pistols, eh? I don't believe I've ever fired one."

"Oh, it's really a lot of fun. Would you like to try it—after lunch, I mean?"

"No, I think I'll pass it up," said Segal, smiling.

The waiter approached and they ordered. There were not many dining, and they were served quickly—fish chowder, and then broiled mackerel. They ate slowly and Segal obviously enjoyed it. "They do you very good here," he remarked. "This fish, and the chowder—excellent."

"Delicious," murmured Mimi.

"Well, we've got a good chef. And the fish was probably caught this morning. That's the advantage of living on the coast."

"I like fish," said Segal. "Only members allowed to eat here?"

"And their guests, of course," said Gore.

"What's involved in becoming a member?"

"The usual," said Gore. "A member sponsors you. Your name is posted, and then the membership committee votes on you. You pay your fees and that's it."

"Oh, Ben, wouldn't it be nice to come here for dinner whenever we wanted a seafood meal," said Mimi.

"Yeah. Suppose you put my name up for membership," Segal suggested negligently.

"I'd be happy to," said Gore. "But you know I

could always fix you up with a guest card for a few days whenever you come down."

"Thanks, but we expect to be here more than just a few days every now and then. In fact, we're thinking of settling here."

"You mean right here in Barnard's Crossing? I'm glad to hear that. You'll like it here. It's really a wonderful old town." He hesitated. "Does that mean that you are planning on holding Rohrbough?"

"That's right. I'm going to operate it personally. That's confidential."

Gore smiled slyly. "Does that mean you want me to keep it a secret, or that you want me to leak it discreetly?"

Segal stared. Then he laughed shortly, a single explosive, Ha. "You're all right, young man. As a matter of fact, it doesn't mean a damn thing. It just came out—automatic, I suppose. We've got a controlling interest in the company, and I think it has good possibilities. No reason for keeping it secret."

"And you'll be living here? Have you found a place yet?"

"I suppose we'll build. As a matter of fact, Mimi and I have been doing some looking around. You know a good realtor?"

Because he had been talking about him with Molly Mandell earlier, and also because he thought Segal might appreciate his showing preference for a Jew, he said, "Henry Maltzman whose place is just down the street from the bank is a good man. He knows all the property in the area that's available."

"But we've already found a piece of land," said Mrs. Segal.

Segal showed momentary annoyance. "That's right," he said, "but I don't mind paying a commission. A good agent is worth it."

"You're absolutely right," said Gore. "There are a lot of local ordinances, and in an old town like this, there are tricky rights-of-way that you want to know about before you buy. A local agent can save you a lot of grief."

"Oh, I always make it a point to deal with local people."

The waiter brought their coffee and Segal lit a cigar.

"I'm glad to hear you say that," said Gore, "because we're local, too. The bank, I mean. Rohrbough started with us, and we did all their banking until they went public and got too big for us and had to go into Boston. But they continued to maintain their connection by having us do their payroll. I don't mind admitting that I'd hate to lose it. It's a great convenience to the people working at Rohrbough, and we like to be of service to our friends and neighbors."

Segal cocked a quizzical eye at the younger man. "You get something out of it besides the chance to be of service to your friends and neighbors, don't you?"

Gore laughed self-consciously. "Well, of course, there's our fee for the bookkeeping, and it means extra people, a lot of extra people, coming into the bank. It gives us a crack at them for Christmas

Club and personal loans and auto loans and occasionally a mortgage."

Segal smiled. "Not to mention the float on maybe a quarter to a half million dollars a week."

Gore grinned ingenuously. "Not to mention it. But it rarely goes up that high, especially these days. And while some deposit their checks in their own banks, so there's the delay of having it go through the Boston clearinghouse, and others maybe cash them at the supermarket, where it also has to go through Boston, an awful lot cash their checks directly with us the same day they get them."

"All right," said Segal. "I'll think about it. You won't forget about that membership, will you?"

"I'll take care of that right away."

7

"Why should you want to be included in the minyan?" asked Rabbi Small petulantly. He peered nearsightedly from one to the other of the three women seated in front of his desk in his study. "You're exempt from the commandment to recite the morning prayers. Why should you want to assume an unnecessary burden?"

"Like we used to be exempt from the burden of voting?" Molly Mandell shot back, her dark eyes flashing. "Or the burden of holding property?" She had an air of assurance, and it was obvious that she had no intention of being led by Mrs. Froelich, who as president of the Sisterhood was the head of the delegation. She was smartly dressed in a charcoal gray pantsuit. On her lapel she sported her large plastic Women's Lib pin.

Rabbi Small was taken aback both by the question and by the tone in which it was asked. It was not merely sarcastic; it was also hostile. He shook his head slowly.

"No, Mrs. Mandell. It's not like that, not like that at all," he said earnestly. "Look here, you know what a sin is. Well, what's the opposite? What's the antonym of sin?"

"Virtue?" Mrs. Froelich offered.

"A good deed," suggested Mrs. Allen.

The rabbi nodded. "It's both of those things in English, but in Hebrew we have a single specific word for it. The word is *mitzvah*, and it means a commandment. When we perform what has been commanded us, we have done a mitzvah. The important thing to keep in mind is that a commandment carries with it the implication of something that you would not ordinarily do of your own accord. We do it because it is commanded. The reason for some of the commandments are obvious. The commandment to observe the Sabbath as a day of rest is something that we can readily understand,

a day of rest once a week—that makes sense. You
might do it without a commandment. But you
might not be so willing to extend the privilege to
your servants. Hence, the commandment. The commandment that proscribes the mingling of linen and
wool in garments, *shatnes*, is harder to understand,
but devout Jews do it even though they can't see
the reason for it. Because it is commanded."

He paused to look at each of them in turn and
then went on. "The important thing to remember is
that while we are responsible for what is commanded, we get no extra points for doing what is
not commanded. We are commanded to recite
prayers three times a day, and there is no extra virtue in reciting them six times a day. In Christianity
there is. The priest may prescribe the recital of a
dozen Hail Marys as a penance. They have religious communities of monks and nuns who have
vowed to pray all day long. While a pious Christian
may spend a good deal of his time in prayer, it is
not so in our religion. In study, yes, but not in
prayer. Keep that in mind. It's important. If you recite the blessing on wine or bread, and then don't
drink wine or taste a morsel of bread, it is not a
mitzvah, but the reverse. The classic example is
that of the person who, while away from home,
hears fire engines and prays that it is not his house
that is burning. Such a prayer is considered sinful
for two reasons: because it implies that you want it
to be someone else's house that is burning; or because you are praying for an impossibility, that
something that has already happened will not hap-

pen. Do you understand?" He peered at them eagerly through his thick-lensed glasses.

"You mean," began Mrs. Froelich uncertainly as she tried to frame her thought, "that—I can understand the first reason, but—"

"Let me try to make it a little clearer," said the rabbi. "I have a relative, my cousin Simcha. Simcha the *Apicorus*, we call him in the family. An *Apicorus* is an agnostic, from Epicurus, the Greek philosopher, and a mistaken notion of his doctrine. Although Simcha is actually a pious and observant Jew, he has some queer notions about some of the commandments. For example, he does not consider chicken as meat in the context of the dietary laws. He argues that since the reason we do not mix meat and dairy foods is in elaborate adherence to the commandment, 'Thou shalt not seethe the flesh of the kid in the milk of the mother,' it does not apply to chicken, since chickens don't give milk."

"Say, that's cool," Mrs. Allen exclaimed.

The rabbi smiled. "He also refused to affix a mezuzah to his doorframe on the grounds that the commandment is 'To write them on the doorposts of your house,' and he argued that it wasn't his house, that he was only renting. Now, I grant you that that's a pilpul, a matter of splitting hairs, and pretty extreme at that, but it gives the general idea that a commandment is an obligation, not necessarily welcome, that one carries out because it is commanded. In the same vein, a famous rabbi said that one should not say of the foods forbidden by our dietary laws—pork, shellfish, and the others—that we will not eat them because they are unpleasant and unpalatable, but rather that they are tasty and even delectable, but we will not eat them because there is a commandment forbidding it. Do you get the idea? Now, women are exempt from the positive commandments that have to be done at a particular time, so they are exempt from attending the minyan for the morning and evening prayers."

"But why are they exempt from those commandments, Rabbi?" asked Mrs. Froelich.

"Because observing them would interfere with their more important work of managing the home and the family."

"Naturally," said Molly Mandell sarcastically, "the idea is to get as much work out of them as possible."

"No." The rabbi shook his head. "No, Mrs. Mandell. It's because with us, the synagogue, or as we call it, the temple, is not the center of our religion. With us, it's the home. It is there that the Sabbath is celebrated, there that the Feast of Passover, the most important liturgical ceremony in our religion, is held, there that the Succah is built. On the practical side, Mrs. Mandell, I can imagine a case in which a husband, overzealous in reciting the Kaddish for a dead parent, might insist on his wife accompanying him to the minyan to insure that there are the necessary ten, even if it means neglecting to prepare breakfast for the children."

Mrs. Froelich nodded vigorously. "When his father died, Harvey went to say Kaddish every single day, morning and evening, for a year. Before that he never went to the daily minyan, and he hasn't gone since. But he certainly was Old Faithful that year. And you know, he wasn't even close to his father. They never really got along."

"Sure, he had guilt feelings," Mrs. Allen offered.

"To hear you tell it, Rabbi," Molly Mandell said, "the whole Jewish religion is practically dedicated to making things easier for women. It sounds nice, but it's a crock, and I can prove it. Because in those daily prayers you say every morning, you start by thanking God for having been born a man."

The others were taken aback by her vehemence and looked at the rabbi to see his reaction. He had colored but he managed a smile. "I don't see how you can object to that particular blessing, since it is in such complete agreement with the thinking of your movement."

"What do you mean?"

"Well, your Women's Lib movement maintains that life is easier for the man than it is for the woman, doesn't it?" he asked.

"Well sure, but—"

"So why shouldn't men thank God for it? And is it wrong for them to try to equalize the differences a little by according women special privileges?"

8

Laura Maltzman was not a pretty woman; in fact, she was plain. She was tall and angular with square shoulders. She had a long face with a square chin, which seemed a little off center, as though she had just been struck a blow, or was on the point of turning her head. But her eyes were large and kindly and understanding. As her husband, rubbing his hands in satisfaction, came into the living room from the hallway, where he had been on the phone, she looked up inquiringly.

"Just got word," he said, "that the loan is going through, pretty sure anyway."

"Oh? Who called?"

"Molly Mandell. She spoke to Gore about it, and she thinks he'll go along. She thought I'd like to know." He strode up and down the room and then stopped in front of her. "Look, this dinner you're having, how about calling the Mandells and inviting them?"

"But they're so much younger than the others," she objected.

"So what? I want her—them—to know that I'm appreciative—"

"You appointed Herb Mandell to the board last week."

"Yeah, but he's active in the Brotherhood, so she might think it was for that. I want *her* to know I'm appreciative. See? She's got a lot of influence in the bank. And she's been friendly to me, like this phone call tonight. That can be pretty important, having someone you can count on right there in the bank. So I want her to know—"

Laura dropped her eyes to the knitting in her lap. "You think she's pretty?" she asked.

Instantly he was wary. "Well now, she's no cover girl, but yeah, I think she's kind of cute. She's eager and alive and fresh—"

"I guess she's fresh all right. Lillian Allen was telling me that she was with the group that went to see the rabbi, and she was pretty fresh to him."

"Oh, Lillian Allen! What did she say?"

"She said that Molly said the whole Jewish religion was sexist and she practically called the rabbi a male chauvinist pig."

"Did she?" He chuckled. "Well now, that's not what I would've called him. I figure him for more the namby-pamby type. I mean, a real he-man wouldn't become a rabbi and spend his life praying. I know these guys. You'd think butter wouldn't melt in their mouths, but in their own quiet way, they screw up the works. So don't expect me to get uptight because Molly Mandell told him off. I intend to do a little of it myself if he gets in the way. The temple belongs to the members, and I and the board of directors are the people they elected to run it for them. The rabbi is just somebody we hire to do a job, and the sooner he realizes it, the better. Now, will you call up Molly Mandell and invite her?"

"If you insist."

His face got red and his eyes protruded. "Yes, Goddammit, I insist."

9

Ellsworth Jordon paced the living room of his old Victorian house, glowering at the clock on the mantelpiece each time he passed it. Billy was late getting home from work, and he was worried, and annoyed with himself for being worried. By the time he caught sight of him hurrying up the long driveway, his annoyance with himself had turned into anger at the young man.

"Where have you been?" he demanded. "You're late."

Billy was contrite. "Oh, I'm sorry, sir. I missed the bus and I decided to walk instead of waiting for the next one. It was so nice out."

"Don't you know Martha has an engagement for tonight and has to leave early? She mentioned it this morning."

"Gee, I forgot."

"And I am due at the Agathon."

"Gee, I'm sorry. But Martha can leave the dishes and I'll do them."

"Well, we'll see. Wash up now and let's not keep Martha waiting any longer."

They ate in silence. Normally, Billy would have prattled about his day at the bank, but having been reprimanded, he was reluctant to speak. Jordon occasionally shot furtive glances at the boy and wondered at his sullenness. He had reproved him for coming home late, which was his right and duty. But when he had told him to go and wash up, Billy should have realized that in effect his explanation and apology had been accepted. So why didn't he speak? Did he expect him, so much his senior, to make the overture?

Though he continued to glower over his plate, after a while, Jordon reflected philosophically that young people naturally lacked subtlety, that in the few months that Billy had been with him, he had adjusted quite well, that in the evenings and on weekends when they were together, the boy had even proved companionable, albeit in the gauche, awkward way to be expected in the young. To be sure, the boy was graceless and uncertain, but he presumed all young people of that age were. He didn't look you in the eye, and he slouched and was slovenly in his dress. His glasses kept sliding forward on his nose, and one of the bows was attached by a bit of wire. On the other hand, he was obedient, even docile, and thank God, his face was not pimpled. And, a positive plus—he seemed to enjoy his work at the bank, where he worked as a teller. Gore had even reported that the customers seemed to like him.

It had been no problem getting him the job. "I've got a young fellow coming to stay with me for a while, Larry. I've known his family for a long time. I'd appreciate it if you'd give him a job in the bank while he's here."

"How long is he going to stay?"

"Months. Maybe a year. Maybe longer. For some time I've thought I ought to have someone sleeping in."

Lawrence Gore smiled knowingly and nodded.

Jordon frowned. He had a reputation as a pinch-penny, and he knew what Gore was thinking—that rather than hire a companion, he was having Billy come for just the cost of his keep. But he didn't feel it necessary to explain. "And I'd consider it a personal favor, Larry," he went on, "for any kindness you can show him. I don't mean for you to grant him any special privileges that the other employees don't have, but you know, a friendly word of encouragement now and then. I guess he's something of a mama's boy and doesn't have the confidence—"

"Sure, I understand, Ellsworth. Tell you what. I'm starting a class of pistol shooting. He can join and I'll teach him how to shoot."

"Goddammit, Larry, this isn't the Wild West.

Use some common sense. Learning to shoot a pistol isn't going to help make a man of him—"

"That's where you're wrong," said Gore earnestly. "I was the runt in my class in high school. Most of the girls were taller than me. Once at a party they rigged it so I had to dance with this big, tall girl, Florence Richardson. My eyes were just about level with her breasts. God, it was embarrassing."

The older man grinned lewdly. "Your face right up against her tits, eh? That might not have been so bad."

Gore grinned back. "Yeah, nowadays it wouldn't bother me, but it sure did then." He shook his head in reminiscent reflection. "It wasn't just with girls, you understand. Being short makes some men assertive, but most people become shy and cautious and withdrawn. Well, in college you had to go out for some sport, and I chose the pistol team, figuring it was something where my being short wouldn't matter. And you know, as I learned to handle the weapon, I began to grow."

The older man looked down at him and said, "Not noticeably."

"Yes, noticeably. I didn't get taller, but feeling comfortable with a handgun gave me confidence in everything. It gives you a sense of power, and that makes you sure of yourself. When I won the intercollegiate Regional Championship, I was a giant. You leave the boy to me, Ellsworth. I'll make a man out of him."

Not until Martha came in to serve the main course did Jordon break the silence, and then it was to address her. "Big date tonight, Martha? Somebody special?" he asked jocosely.

"No, just a date," she said.

"Anybody I know?"

"I don't guess so. It's a feller from Lynn I met the other night when I went bowling."

"Well, don't worry. You'll get out in good time. Just leave the dishes and Billy will do them." There, he thought, I've called him by name. That should let him know that I'm not angry any longer. But the young man did not take the hint and kept his eyes on his plate and remained silent.

When Martha came in to serve the coffee, she was already in street clothes. "I'll be going now," she said. "I've stacked the dishes, and the soap powder and towels are on the drainboard."

"Okay, Martha, have a good time." Moodily Jordon sipped his coffee, his eyes abstracted. When he finished, he left the table without a word and went into the living room. Presently Billy joined him there, and Jordon looked up from his paper and asked, "Dishes all done?"

"Yes, sir."

"And put away?"

"Yes, sir."

"Well, that's good. That's fine. You written to your mother yet?"

"I thought I'd do that tomorrow."

Jordon's face darkened. "I promised your mother that she'd get a letter from you every week. I want you to do that right now."

"But I told Mr. Gore I'd be over to help him with the photos of the silver collection."

The answer infuriated the old man. "Well, your mother comes first. You go to your room right now and do that letter."

"Oh fish!" Billy muttered, but he went to his room and closed the door behind him.

Jordon followed him to the door. "And I'm locking you in till you finish," he called after him and turned the key in the lock.

Through the door he called, "And you'll stay in there until you've written that letter. I'm going to have my regular meditation now, so I'll thank you not to disturb me for the next twenty minutes. After that you can knock if you've finished and I'll let you out. But I'm telling you that if it's not done by then, I'm going to the club and you'll wait in there until I get back."

He listened for a moment, his ear to the door, but Billy did not reply. He sat down in his recliner for the Transcendental Meditation he was convinced was good for his heart. When the twenty minutes he allowed himself were up, he got out of his chair and tiptoed over to the door of the boy's room. He listened, his ear pressed to the door, but he heard nothing.

So be it, he thought. If this is going to be a test of willpower, we'll see who's the stronger. He went to the front door, opened it and then banged it behind him. Then opened it carefully once again and listened. Hearing no response, he eased the door closed silently and got into his car parked in the driveway.

10

The call came late in the afternoon. "Mr. Maltzman? Ben Segal speaking. I'm interested in buying some land. Mr. Gore at the bank suggested I call you. I wonder if we could meet with you—"

Ben Segal? Did he know a Ben Segal? Then it came to him. It must be the Ben Segal of Chicago. There were rumors that he was in town. He breathed deeply. "Where are you calling from, Mr. Segal?" he asked calmly.

"I'm calling from your local hotel, the Arlington Arms. We're staying here."

For a moment he debated whether to appear busy and then decided against it.

"If you're free now," he said, "I can come right over."

They sat in the gaudy, overfurnished sitting room of the only suite that the Arlington Arms afforded and which was intended primarily for business conferences. The Segals sat on a heavily brocaded sofa, Maltzman on the edge of a leather lounge chair,

uneasily balancing a coffee cup and the petit fours
that Mrs. Segal had rung for when he arrived.

"I'm interested in buying a piece of land," Segal
explained. He fished in his coat pocket and found
the match cover on which he had scribbled the
name of the street. "It's out on the Point, I think
you call it, on Crossland Avenue, just beyond Por-
ter Street."

"Yeah, I know it," said Maltzman frowning.
"But that's all residential land out there and our
zoning laws are pretty strict."

"Of course. I understand." He smiled. "I wasn't
planning on building a factory there, or a ware-
house."

"I mean it has to be a single family residence.
You can't just have a house that's used mostly for
executive meetings and dinners and maybe as a
place to put up visiting firemen. It has to be used
by a family as a regular residence. See what I
mean?"

"Oh yes, I understand," said Segal. "This is going to be just an ordinary house—"

"We're planning to live in it ourselves, Mr.
Maltzman," Mrs. Segal explained. "We're planning
to settle here."

"That's right," her husband added. "I'm going to
operate Rohrbough Corporation personally."

Mimi leaned forward eagerly. "You see, Mr.
Maltzman, we've lived in cities all our lives, both of
us. And in hotels at that. We have a large apartment in Chicago to be sure, but it's still in a hotel.
And we're fed up with the city. With the noise and
the dirt and the crime—being afraid to go out for a

walk in the evening. So we're planning to settle here. It means changing our whole lifestyle, becoming part of a community. That's what we want. It's that, I expect, as much as anything that decided Ben on operating Rohrbough personally."

"That's right," said her husband. "At lunch today, Gore was telling us about your town meeting that everybody goes to. Well, we'd like to go to that. And to the Fourth of July bonfire, and to the arts festival you hold in the town hall."

Maltzman nodded slowly. An idea was beginning to take shape in his mind. He directed his eyes to Ben Segal. "Are you still Jewish? I mean, you haven't converted or anything?"

Segal shrugged. "I don't practice it, but I've never denied it."

Mimi said, "His brother changed his name to Sears and wanted Ben to, but Ben wouldn't consider it."

"That's fine," said Maltzman, "but in a small town like Barnard's Crossing, people want to know where you stand. If you want to be respected and accepted, you got to be part of the group they associate you with. And here, that means joining the temple. You got to show that you're willing to stand up and be counted."

"But I'm not the least bit religious," Segal protested.

"So what? Most of our members aren't. We only get about a hundred at Friday evening service. I always go because I'm president of the congregation. Joining the temple is not a matter of religion, so much as a way of showing you feel you belong."

"But it's different with me," said Segal. "I honestly don't think I have a right to be a member of a synagogue. You see, I was never Bar Mitzvah. My folks were terribly poor when I was a kid, and they just couldn't afford it at the time."

"Oh Ben, dear, you never told me." Mimi was all sympathy. "But about Bar Mitzvah, I imagine you can have it anytime. Can't he, Mr. Maltzman? Seems to me I saw something on TV about a seventy-year-old man in California who just had one. His folks couldn't afford it either when he was a youngster."

"Say, I remember that," said Maltzman. "And in the *Hadassah Magazine* there was a story about a whole bunch of men, a club, or from the same synagogue, mature men, who went to Israel and had a group Bar Mitzvah at the Wall. Look here, Mr. Segal, if you're interested, I'll see the rabbi and arrange it." Then it came to him—the gimmick. "Tell you what, I'll put it up to the board, and if they see things my way, we'll have the temple sponsor it."

"Well, it seems to me there's quite a ceremony, isn't there? I mean, it's not just the party. I seem to remember kids my age who had to study up for it. Special prayers they had to learn by heart and—"

"Nothing to it, Mr. Segal," said Maltzman earnestly. "You're called up to the Reading of the Torah and you pronounce a blessing. The Bar Mitzvah kids chant it in Hebrew. But you don't have to chant it. Or if you were willing, I could arrange for the cantor to teach you. And even if you don't know how to read Hebrew, we have it transliterated in English. Or you could even say it in English. Then after the portion is read, you say another blessing, and we could work that the same way, and that's it. Of course, normally the Bar Mitzvah boy chants the portion from the Prophets, too. Hell, some of them run the whole Reading service. Kind of showing off, you see. But it's not necessary. Believe me, the whole thing's a pipe."

"Is yours the only synagogue in town, Mr. Maltzman?" asked Mimi.

"That's right, Mrs. Segal, and all Jews in the community belong, all that have been living here for some time. Of course, there are some families that are new, and maybe not a hundred percent sure they're going to remain on account of their jobs, but those who've settled here, practically all of them belong. You say the word, and I'll make arrangements with the rabbi and all."

Ben Segal looked doubtfully at his wife, and when she nodded brightly, he said, "All right. Count me in."

"Swell," said Maltzman. "And I'll get to work on that lot on the Point right away."

11

In the dining room of the Agathon Yacht Club, one could order a cocktail, but only with dinner. And while you could linger over coffee and a brandy afterward, the house committee did not like you to linger too long. During the sailing season, the dining room was busy and there were apt to be people waiting for a table. In the off-season, the waiters resented having to wait overlong to clean up.

There was the lounge, of course, but it was on the formal side—a room of long windows curtained and velvet draped, of rugs and carpets, of sofas and armchairs in satin and brocade, of highly polished mahogany tables, with silk-shaded lamps. It was where you met your guests and chatted for a few minutes, just long enough for them to be impressed, before ushering them into the dining room, or down to the dock to your boat. Mostly women sat there and had tea or coffee brought to them.

For serious drinking, or for the long pointless conversations that killed an evening, there was the bar, and it was masculine territory. It was not forbidden to women, but by tacit agreement they never went there. It was a bare room with glaring ceiling lights that cast pools of light on the bare gray battleship linoleum that covered the floor. The furniture consisted of half a dozen round cigarette-scarred wooden tables, each surrounded by several captain's chairs. Against the wall was a small bar, little more than a high counter, behind which were shelves of bottles, a small refrigerator and a sink.

The decor, or lack of it, was a holdover from Prohibition days. The feeling then had been that while it was not necessary that drinking be surreptitious, it would be brazen to do it in luxurious comfort. With repeal, and periodically since, there were suggestions that the room should be refurnished, something on the order of leather armchairs and knotty pine paneling and sporting or sailing prints, but the members who used it most resisted stoutly, perhaps through fear that if it were spruced up and redecorated, women might be attracted to it.

There were no waiters, only the barman. If it was not busy, he might in response to a nod bring over a refill, but usually you got your drink at the bar and carried it over to a table. Thursday was usually an off night at the bar, which is why Jordon chose it for his weekly visit. He did not like crowded bars, full of the boisterous din of well-lubricated good fellowship. He preferred the company of his old cronies, people he was used to, with whom he could talk sensibly, even seriously and philosophically, or sit with them in pleasant silence if the mood so moved them.

Although others would probably drift in later, only one table was now occupied, and as he waited for his drink to be poured, Jordon noted with satisfaction that of the four men seated around it, two were Thursday night regulars. There was old Dr. Springhurst, the retired rector of St. Andrew's Episcopal, silver-haired and distinguished-looking in his Roman collar and gray flannel suit. As an avowed atheist, Jordon got a special pleasure in arguing religion with him. The other was Albert Megrim, a stockbroker and one of the selectmen of the town, with whom he liked to talk politics. Megrim was a stoutish man, with a round face surmounted by thin hair precisely parted in the middle. He always wore a dark conservative business suit and a white shirt with a bow tie, even on hot summer nights.

The other two at the table, Jordon knew only casually. Jason Walters, a corporation lawyer, was a tall, craggy man, who went in for vigorous sports and made a fetish of keeping fit. Jordon noted that he was wearing a sweat suit and sneakers and was probably going to top off the evening with a fast game of squash. The fourth man, by far the youngest of the group, not yet forty, was Don Burkhardt, a partner in a firm called Creative Engineers Incorporated, which went in for such diverse things as designing office furniture and layout, work-flow analysis and even preparing the graphics for the annual reports of corporations. Him, Jordon eyed with distaste as he waited at the bar for his drink to be poured. He did not like his carefully tailored Eisenhower jacket and jeans of carefully faded blue. He did not like his blond Afro hairstyle, a halo of curls framing his narrow face. And most of all, he did not like what he regarded as his radical ideas, by which he meant that Burkhardt made no secret of voting Democrat, and considered himself a liberal Democrat at that.

As they saw Jordon approach carrying his drink, the four men shifted a little to make room for him to insinuate another chair.

"How are you keeping, Ellsworth?" Dr. Springhurst greeted him.

"Tolerable, Padre, tolerable."

"Gore is down at the pistol range, I suppose," remarked Albert Megrim.

"No, I came myself this time," said Jordon. "Larry is busy preparing for his Peter Archer silver exhibition. Why?"

"We were wondering about this new member he proposed. Is he a yachtsman? Has he got a boat?"

"Whatsat? New member? I'm on the committee and I don't know anything about any new member."

"His name has been posted, Ellsworth," said Jason Walters. "Name of Segal."

"It's Ben Segal of Chicago," said Megrim, "the one who's taking over the Rohrbough Corporation."

"Segal? Jew?" demanded Jordon.

Megrim smiled sardonically. "You can't always tell these days. He's not what I'd call a Jew, Ellsworth. I mean, he's a financier. There was a long write-up on him in *Business Week*. A man like that is not a Jew."

"I know exactly what you mean," said Walters.

"There's a private bank in New York that our firm has had dealings with for years, trust funds and what not. Well, one day I had occasion to call their president, and I was told he wasn't in. So I asked to be switched to the head of their trust division, and he wasn't in. So, kind of jokingly, I asked what was going on, was it some kind of holiday in New York? And the switchboard operator tells me it was Yon—Yom—"

"Yom Kippur," Don Burkhardt supplied.

"That's right, Yom Kippur. It's their very special holy day." He turned to the younger man. "How did you know?"

"Because my partner is a Jew, and a lot of my friends are."

"Oh! Well, anyway, the point I was trying to make is that all the years I had been dealing with them, it never struck me that they were Jewish. The whole firm is. At least all the top brass. What do you think of that?" He shook his head in wonder.

"You guys make me sick," said Burkhardt, pushing away from the table as if to give physical demonstration of his disgust. "You talk like a bunch of Ku Klux red-necks."

"You mean me?" Jason Walters was indignant. "Don't you try to make me out a bigot. I'll have you know our family physician is Dr. Goldstein here in town and we think the world of him."

"If you mean me, Don," Megrim drawled, "it's hogwash. My last year in college, I roomed with a Jew. He lives out in Detroit now, and whenever I get there on business, he's the first one I call on. We go to dinner and then maybe a show and afterward we might go to a bar and just talk. Why, there are things I tell him that I wouldn't tell to my brother, or my wife, either, for that matter. He's probably closer to me than—"

"And I might point out," Jason Walters went on loftily, "that a couple of years ago, instead of going to Bermuda or Palm Beach for our winter vacation the way we usually do, Grace and I went to the Holy Land, and I told everybody what a terrific job they were doing. Of course, they've got to do something about the Palestinian refugees, but on balance they've done wonders, and I said so every chance I got."

"You've got to understand, Don," said Albert Megrim soothingly, "that this is a social club. It's a place where you come to meet people. Naturally, you prefer your own kind because you're more comfortable with them."

"That's right," said Walters earnestly. "Look, my daughters go to the dances here. Well, naturally, I want them to meet their own kind of people. That doesn't mean I'm prejudiced."

"Sure," said Burkhardt scornfully, "everybody denies being anti-Semitic, but—"

"I don't," said Ellsworth Jordon.

"You don't?" The young man stared at him. "You mean you *are* anti-Semitic?"

"Certainly. All of us are. And you are, too, Burkhardt. You're ashamed to admit it because you have a lot of crackpot liberal ideas about how only the ignorant are prejudiced. But you are just the same. Having one as a business partner, or as a family physician whom you think the world of, or as a best friend proves nothing. Or, rather, to a Jew it proves you are anti-Semitic. That's a kind of inside joke among them. Anytime anyone says his best friends are Jews, they know it's an anti-Semite talking." He smiled broadly. "I know, because at one time some of my best friends were Jewish."

"But you just said—" Don Burkhardt was nonplussed.

"Oh, I can admit it because I know why we're anti-Semitic."

"You do? Why?"

"Because they make us feel uncomfortable."

"Why should they make you feel uncomfortable?"

"Because they're better than we are," said Jordon simply.

They stared at him.

"Hogwash! How do you mean, better?" demanded Megrim.

"Morally, ethically," said Jordon. "I guess they're just more civilized than we are. That's what makes us feel uncomfortable, and that's why we dislike them." He laughed aloud. "And the joke is that the buggers don't have any idea why they're disliked, not a clue. They just don't understand the psychology of it. They point out that they're good and loyal citizens with a low divorce rate and a low crime rate, that they're sober and industrious and ambitious. They're active in all kinds of worthwhile movements and reforms and are usually on the side of the underdog. But that doesn't get you liked, you know. Quite the contrary. They were the first to help the Blacks, for instance, and the result is that they are the ones the Blacks resent most."

"Yeah, but they helped the Blacks because they're both minority peoples," Megrim pointed out. "But you take in Israel, where they are in the majority—"

"They're making the same mistake," said Jordon promptly. "They set up a two-bit country on a two by four piece of land, and the first thing they do is to take in all their kinfolk from the Arab countries, the old and the sick, and not a dime among the lot of them. And they feed them when they themselves haven't got a pot to pee in. And there were almost as many of these refugees as the total population of the country at the time."

Jordon took a sip of his drink and continued, "On the other hand, the entire Arab world, about eighty million of them with Lord knows how many millions of square miles of territory, could not find room for a couple of thousand of their own kinfolk and left them in refugee camps to rot. And everybody like Jason Walters here says the Israelis have got to do something about their Palestinian refugees, the Israelis, mind you, not the Arabs."

"Yeah, they take care of their own," said Megrim. "Everybody knows that. But today—"

"Today they have the Good Fence over at the Lebanon border," said Burkhardt. "And those aren't their own they're giving free medical treatment. Any Arab who comes to the fence, Christian or Moslem, who needs help, gets it."

"Yeah, how about *that*, Padre?" Jordon jeered. "Those are Christians that are being slaughtered, and nobody in the Christian world lifts a finger or even protests, not the Pope, not your World Council of Churches, not the Christian countries. Only the damn Jews. It's downright embarrassing. No wonder that no one supports them in the UN. That's the point I was making. They make everybody uncomfortable, so everybody votes against them."

"The United States doesn't do much better there," Jason Walters pointed out. "And if you come right down to it, most countries hate us, too."

Jordon chortled. "Sure they do, and it's for the same reason. We're a little that way, ourselves."

"Hogwash! They hate us because we're rich and powerful," said Megrim.

"No, that's not it," Jordon asserted. "When you're powerful, you're feared. Sure you may be hated, but only as long as there's reason for being afraid of you. In World War II we hated the Japs and the Germans because we were afraid of them. We didn't hate the Italians because we weren't. And as soon as the war was over, we also stopped hating the Japs and the Germans. You want to know why America is hated today? Why all this 'Yankee, Go Home' propaganda? It's because we were guilty of perpetrating a terrible act of charity, the Marshall Plan. Never before in the history of the world had a conquering country set out to rebuild the countries it had defeated. We gave away millions, with no strings attached. And we've been hated for it ever since. And they'll go on hating us until the memory of that tremendous moral act is dimmed or forgotten."

"That's pure hogwash, Ellsworth," Megrim drawled. "The reason they dislike us is because we're brash and pushy when we're in their countries. Maybe it's because we're away from home, or because we don't know their language or their customs, so we feel a little uncertain and we cover up by being, well, assertive. And that's why we tend to dislike Jews—because they're pushy."

"I wouldn't say they were pushy," said Burkhardt. Now that the conversation was on a philosophical level, he could speak calmly. "I think they're a little more intense than we are. That's all. My partner, for instance, when he gets involved in a project, it's as though the whole world depended on it. The same when he tries to relax and play golf. He races through the course. It's as though everything he does is a little bit more, as though he's operating on a higher body temperature, if you see what I mean. And I've noticed it in others, too. It may be something in their genes. Stands to reason, with all the trouble they've been through, pogroms and what not, those living today must be the result of a special selection process."

"Not at all. It's their religion," Jordon declared flatly.

"They don't have any religion," said Dr. Springhurst, his interest stirred for the first time.

"Cummon, Padre, they invented it, the modern kind, I mean," said Jordon.

"They did. And for a while, they *were* a religious people. The Lord was close to them in those days and proved Himself with miracles." The old man shook his head lugubriously. "But the more He

proved Himself, the more they moved away from
Him. Imagine, after a miracle like the parting of
the Red Sea, they constructed the golden calf. Nevertheless they remained a religious people. It was
during the life of our Lord Jesus that the great
change came. He saw it and tried to prevent it.
That was His mission, to prevent the Scribes and
the Pharisees from turning the true religion into a
kind of practical ethical culture society. They don't
have a God, not one they can look to for salvation.
Their God can't be known, by definition, if you
please. He can't be seen. He can't even be imagined. He's like X in algebra. It enables them to justify any regulation or code of rules they wanted to
set up: 'Do it because it is commanded by the
Lord.' They don't demand faith. They have no
hope of heaven, no fear of hell, merely a code of
behavior justified only with 'Thus saith the Lord.'
See, that way they don't have to prove anything.
They don't have to convince their people that it's
right or worthwhile or intelligent or practical.
There's no argument about a different way or a better way by the opposition. Merely, this is the law
because God says so. Sure, they passed some good
laws, as any governing body would be likely to do,
and some damn silly ones, too. But that's not religion any more than the American Constitution is
religion, or the Code Napoléon. That's what our
Lord Jesus fought against. This wasn't the usual
backsliding that Moses had to contend with when
they turned away from the God of Israel to other
gods. But this was turning away from the basic
concept of religion, the relation of a man to God.

That's why they are disliked, Ellsworth. Because they are the one godless people."

"That puts them right in your church, Ellsworth," said Megrim, grinning. "They're a bunch of atheists according to the good doctor."

"Nah." With a wide sweep of his hand, Ellsworth Jordon made a gesture of dismissal. "You've missed it, Padre. We don't object to them because they're godless. I certainly wouldn't on that account. Maybe they did give up their religion for an ethical culture society. But not content with that, they then palmed Jesus on the rest of us. Remember, He's one of theirs. They foisted Him on us, and they slid out from under. They gave us a religion that nobody can follow—turn the other cheek and all that sort of thing, while they developed a system, a set of rules, if you like, that people can live with. That's what we resent, that they eased us into a religion that makes us feel guilty all the time."

"But you don't follow it," Megrim insisted. "You say you're an atheist, so I can't see how you're affected."

"Sure, I'm affected," said Jordon. "I grew up in it, didn't I? Once you're exposed to something like that, you can't ever get rid of it. It's what enables them to do so well at—oh, all sorts of things. Their minds are clear. They're not guilt-ridden. They're not weighted down with superstitions. Their mathematicians or doctors or physicists, nothing they believe conflicts with their science. They don't have to keep a portion of their minds in a water-tight compartment, the way we do. So they have a tremendous advantage over us. They function more efficiently, so it seems as if they are operating at a higher temperature.

"The Christianity they gave us consists of concepts that no one but a saint could possibly follow—and I've often wondered what *their* dreams were like. All this business of 'Turn the other cheek,' and 'If thine eye offend thee, pluck it out,' and 'Love thine enemy,' it's beyond the capacity of a normal human being.

"On the other hand, the Jews set up a religion, or a code of ethics or what have you, that a normal person can follow, like helping each other out, and respecting each other, and enjoying life by eating and drinking and having families. And what's the result? We don't follow our rules because they're beyond our capacity, and we keep only the irrational and the superstitious elements—the fear of going to hell, the guilt feelings we have when our minds perform their normal function of questioning the impossible. Whereas the Jews stick to their principles because they're well within human limitations. And sometimes they even manage to follow the Christian rules—when it's convenient, or good business, or reasonable, like in this Good Fence. But that's loving your enemy and turning the other cheek."

A thought occurred to him. "Hey, you guys want to know something? Theirs is the only Christian nation in the world today. How about that, Padre? Here your church has been trying for centuries to convert them, and in the meantime they've converted themselves, and you didn't even know it."

"Well, now that you've proved that Jews are

Christians, do you feel different about Segal's membership?" asked Megrim, grinning.

"Hell no," said Jordon. "I'm still going to blackball the sonofabitch."

"I—I don't understand," said Burkhardt.

"What don't you understand?" asked Jordon.

"On the one hand you claim that Segal is a better man than you are, and on the other hand, you say you're going to blackball him."

"So what? Suppose you're gaga over some woman, and you know she's mean and petty and downright nasty. Does that mean that you'll stop desiring her? Desire, or dislike for that matter, or any of the emotions, they have a logic of their own." He leered at the younger man. "When you're young, you tend to be careful what you think. Ideas come into your head, but if they're not the right kind of ideas, you push them away. Either you try not to think of them, or you twist them around to where they're respectable. You're afraid they'll annoy your family or your boss or an important customer or client. But when you get to my age, especially where you don't have a family or a boss or important customers, more particularly when you've been brushed by the wings of the Angel of Death as I have, then you don't have to worry about strange ideas that come into your head. You can face them and even think them through, and then go on and do as you damn please."

"And it doesn't bother you if you're inconsistent?" urged Burkhardt.

Jordon smiled broadly. "Not one damn little bit.

So I can say that the Jew is a better man than I am, and I still don't want him around."

"You know, Ellsworth," Megrim mused, looking up at the ceiling, "this young fellow you've got living with you, the wife saw him yesterday at the bank and was saying she thought *he* looked Jewish."

Jordon stared blankly. "Oh, my God, I forgot all about Billy. Look, I've got to run along." And rising hastily he left the room.

Although he believed in discipline, Jordon was no martinet. And in handling Billy, Jordon had been careful never to be too severe. After all, the boy was not really under his jurisdiction. He was free to go and might well leave if things got unpleasant. Besides, he wanted Billy to like him.

If he had thought that the boy was going to be so stubborn, he would not have locked him in his room in the first place. He had expected that Billy would certainly submit before it was time for him to go to the Agathon. When he did not, of course he had to carry out his threat, but he had intended to stay at the club only long enough for a drink and get back in half an hour at the latest. He had not intended to get involved in a long discussion, certainly not one that had lasted as long as this one had.

He shut the front door with a bang and waited for the boy to call out and ask to be released. There was no response. A little worried now, he went to the door of the boy's room and knocked. Then, his ear to the door, he listened intently. Still hearing nothing, he turned the key and flung open the door. The room was empty!

It was clear what had happened, the boy had climbed out of the window, no great feat since the room was just above ground level. The window was ajar an inch, obviously so that he could raise it easily and climb back in on his return. Nevertheless, he looked in the closet and was relieved to find that Billy's clothes were still there. Jordon began to chuckle. Then he slapped his thigh and roared with laughter. He left the room and locked the door once again. The boy had shown spirit and he liked that. What's more, he had got his own way, and without whining or arguing. And his way of doing it had meant that neither of them had lost face. He admitted that he was pleased at how it had worked out.

A thought occurred to him, and he reached for the phone and called Lawrence Gore.

"Is Billy there with you, Larry?" he asked.

"No, Ellsworth. He just left. Anything important? I could yell to him from the window."

"No, and I'd rather you didn't tell him I called." He chuckled. "I'll see you tomorrow at the bank and I'll tell you about it. By the way, what time did he get there? . . . About eight? What do you know?"

The boy must have left within minutes after he had been locked in. He rubbed his hands together gleefully. Wonderful!

12

With hat and coat on, Henry Maltzman took a quick look around the office, snicked off the lights and prepared to leave. Then the phone rang. It was Laura, of course. She always managed to catch him before he left.

"Henry? Would you stop by the market on your way home? I need a few things."

"Sorry, Laura. I'm not coming straight home. I've got to see the rabbi first. It's important."

"Well, couldn't you pick up these few things first and—"

"Nothing doing. I'll get stuck at the market, and then by the time I get to the rabbi's, he'll be getting ready to leave for the evening service."

"Then after you see the rabbi—"

"The market will be closed. No, Laura, you'll have to get them yourself or just manage without."

"But we're having people over tonight. Have you forgotten?"

"No, I haven't forgotten. But I can't help you.

Call the market. They sometimes deliver in an emergency."

In the rabbi's living room, half an hour later, Maltzman talked of his great coup. "Do you realize what it will mean for the temple, having a man like Ben Segal as a member?"

"What will it mean?"

"More members," Maltzman answered promptly. "Everybody likes to belong to an association—a club, a lodge, a temple, what have you—with a big shot. It's human nature. If it's a big, successful business tycoon like Ben Segal, maybe they figure his luck will rub off on them. Or maybe they hope to transact some business, or even get some advice on some stock they own. Mostly, it's just so they can do a little name dropping. 'I was saying to Ben Segal—you know, of the Rohrbough Corporation—he's a member in our temple—' That kind of thing."

"Well, I can think of better reasons for joining a temple, but I don't insist on them," said the rabbi good-humoredly.

Maltzman grinned. "Or we wouldn't have enough members for a minyan."

The rabbi grinned back. "All right, so did you sign him up?"

"Well, there's a little hitch, from his point of view."

"What's the hitch?"

"Well, see, when he was a youngster, his folks were awfully poor. They had this little store where he used to help out right after school. So at the time, when he was thirteen, they couldn't afford to have a Bar Mitzvah for him."

The rabbi smiled. "So?"

"So it bothers him. He feels he's not really a bona fide Jew. He's that kind of guy—awfully sincere. All the different cities they lived in—see, they moved around a lot because he'd take over a corporation, in Detroit, say, and they'd move there, and then they'd trade it for a corporation in Dallas, say, and they'd move *there*, living in hotels all the time—so in all these cities, he never joined a synagogue, mostly I guess because he never got around to it, and wasn't planning to stay long, in any case, but also because he felt he wasn't really a Jew, not having been Bar Mitzvah."

"But surely, you explained—"

"But here, he's planning to stay," Maltzman hurried on. "He didn't get control of Rohrbough to trade it. He's planning to run it, and he's planning on building a house in the area and living here. He wants to become part of the community. That's when I braced him about joining our temple, and he springs that Bar Mitzvah thing on me. I was just going to tell him it made no difference, when his wife tells how she heard about some old geezer of seventy out in California who just got himself Bar Mitzvahed, and why couldn't he do the same thing. And right then it came to me—the gimmick!"

"The gimmick?"

"That's right. Ever since I became president, and even before, I've been searching for a gimmick, the gimmick that would sell the temple. You got something to sell, you need a gimmick. In my line, when

I first started selling houses, it was tiled bathrooms with glass shower doors. You had a house that was built solid with nice large sunny rooms in a nice location, it didn't mean a thing without a tiled bathroom. It caught the eye. It didn't have a tiled bathroom, forget it. Well, after a while all houses had tiled baths, so you had to come up with another gimmick. So they came up with tiled kitchens. Then it was kitchens with wood cabinets. Then rumpus rooms. Then finished cellars with a bar. Get the idea? So when I became president of the temple, and decided that what we needed was more members, I tried to think of some gimmick that would bring them in. I've been racking my brains for a gimmick. And then Mrs. Segal tells about the old guy who was Bar Mitzvah, and her husband is interested, and right away I've got my gimmick. He wants a Bar Mitzvah? Swell! We'll give him a real one. We'll send out invitations to every Jew in the community, members and nonmembers. 'You are cordially invited to join with us in worship and attend the Bar Mitzvah of Benjamin Segal.' We'd do it up brown. He'd make the usual speech—"

"Today, I am a man?"

Maltzman grinned. "Sure, why not? I'll bet he'll go along. Then I'd make my little president's speech and give him a prayerbook like we give all the Bar Mitzvahs. And then you'd give him your blessing and make your little speech the way you usually do. Then we'd have a party in the vestry so he could get to meet everybody. I even had the idea we'd give him a bunch of fountain pens as a gag—"

"Fountain pens?"

"Oh, I guess that was before your time. But when I was a kid, a fountain pen was the most popular gift for the Bar Mitzvah boy. Not ballpoints, but the kind with a gold nib that you fill yourself from a bottle. See, the kid would be going on to high school where he'd need it. They cost anywhere from a couple of dollars to fifteen or twenty, so it was a pretty good gift, too. Gosh, when I was Bar Mitzvah, I must've got half a dozen. I wore them all in my breast pocket the next day, so I looked like the doorman at the Russian Samovar. Segal is my age, so he'll know about it and get a kick out of it."

"I see."

"So is it all set?"

"No, it's not all set, Mr. Maltzman. I certainly have no intention of going along with the gag. Mr. Segal was Bar Mitzvah when he was thirteen whether he knows it or not. There's no special rite or ritual required. It's automatic. It's not like baptism. It isn't initiation into the religion or the tribe. That's what circumcision is. If Mr. Segal feels that he wants to be rededicated to the religion of his fathers, it would make more sense if he had himself circumcised again."

"That's crazy!"

The rabbi nodded. "But at least it has some justification in logic. Bar Mitzvah, though, merely means that one is of age, old enough and presumably mature enough to take responsibility for one's own actions and sins. It's just like becoming twenty-one, or eighteen, or whatever the age is now where you can make your own contracts. No special ceremony is required, no party and no speeches. When you're twenty-one you can vote or make a contract. Well, that's all that Bar Mitzvah means, that you are of age."

"But you're called up before the Ark for the Reading in the Scroll."

"That's because, as an adult, you're now a member of the community. It's a courtesy we extend to any new person in the community, or to a stranger who happens to be present. In the morning services when we read from the Scroll, if there's someone present whom I haven't seen before, I always offer him the opportunity. You'd know that if you came to the minyan occasionally."

"But that old guy on the West Coast—"

"I can't be responsible for what happens on the West Coast."

"And in other places, too. In the *Hadassah Magazine* there was a picture of a whole group, all senior citizens, that went to Israel and had a mass Bar Mitzvah at the Wall." Beads of perspiration began to appear on Maltzman's forehead.

The rabbi shook his head. "I can't answer for the judgment of any other rabbi. I interpret the Law as I see it. I don't approve of changing the meaning or the interpretation of an old and treasured tradition. The whole business of ceremonies of confirmation and rededication, it's foreign to us. We confirm our faith every time we perform one of the command-ments, every time we recite our prayers or make one of the blessings or gain some new insight into our religion. The rabbis of old warned against making unnecessary vows. It suggests that we might be taking the name of the Lord in vain. In fact, on Yom Kippur, in the Kol Nidre prayer, we ask to be released from vows, rather than the other way around. Of course, if you want to throw a party in the vestry for this Ben Segal, I can't stop you, although I might question the propriety and the good taste of having a party to celebrate the signing up of a new member just because he's rich. But what happens before the Ark and the Scrolls of the Law is within my jurisdiction, and I cannot permit it."

Maltzman's eyes protruded dangerously and his face was flushed. He rose so abruptly that the chair fell over. He glared at the rabbi for a moment and then bent over and picked up the chair. Erect once again, he appeared to have recovered his composure. He even smiled. "We'll see about that, Rabbi." Then he turned and left the room.

13

The guests had all arrived by the time Henry Maltzman got home. His wife, Laura, could tell by the violent way he shrugged out of his topcoat that something was wrong.

"Did you see the rabbi?" she asked.

"Yeah, I saw him." He strode into the living room. "Hello you folks. Sorry I'm late. I had to see our spiritual leader."

His sarcasm revealed to his wife that he was angry and it worried her. "I think we can eat now," she announced brightly and led the way into the dining room.

She served the soup from a tureen on a side table and called out, "Don't wait. I always say soup should be piping hot."

"Needs salt," grumbled her husband.

"Delicious, absolutely delicious," said Mrs. Streitfuss. "It has a special taste. Lentils?"

"Lima beans," said Laura. "The big ones. I let them dissolve, and it gives a special flavor."

"You must give me the recipe."

"Now, that's what I call soup," said Allen Glick. "Why can't you make soup like that?" he asked his wife.

As Laura cleared the dishes for the next course, her husband, who had been silent till now, leaned back in his chair and said, "You people hear about the Segal Group taking over the Rohrbough Corporation?"

"Oh, that was reported in the papers last week," said Roger Streitfuss, "at least, that it was in the works."

"Well, it's all set," said Maltzman, "and what's more, Ben Segal, who heads up the Group, is going to run the place personally. He and his missus are in town right now. And—now get this—they're joining the temple."

"Hey, how about that!" exclaimed Herb Mandell.

"Imagine, a big shot financier like that comes to town, and first thing he does is want to join a temple." Allen Glick shook his head in wonder.

"Well, I wouldn't put it that way exactly," said Maltzman. "I mean, he's not one of those pious Jews who can't live without a synagogue. As a matter of fact, he didn't think of himself as a Jew at all. Oh, born one and all that, and not denying it, but he never had a Bar Mitzvah on account his folks were so poor at the time, so he didn't think of himself as a real Jew. See what I mean?"

"Well, I don't think—"

"In the *Hadassah Magazine*—"

"Seems to me—"

Maltzman held up his hand to still the babble. "I read that article in the *Hadassah Magazine*, too. It's the one about that group of old geezers from California who went to the Wall in Jerusalem to be Bar Mitzvah. Right? Well, I told him about it, and he was willing." He looked around the table to gather their attention. "Then I got an idea. You know, all along I've been saying we ought to do something to bring in new members. I figure there are at least a hundred Jewish families in town, maybe more, that don't belong to the temple. Maybe they're not sure they're going to stay on in town. Maybe they haven't been approached right."

"Maybe they don't want to join a temple where women are second-class citizens," said Molly Mandell.

Maltzman nodded. "Maybe. Anyway, I've always thought if we could get the right gimmick, we could sell the temple to these people. And I was sure this time I had it. Here's this big shot, and he's going to be running Rohrbough, and some of our people work there. Now, he feels funny about never having been Bar Mitzvah, feels he isn't really a Jew, and yet with a name like Segal, he feels he can't be anything else, unless he changes his name, and he wouldn't do that. So it came to me—the gimmick. I could kill two birds with one stone. Why don't we give him a Bar Mitzvah, the temple, I mean. And we send out invitations to all the Jews in town, whether they're members of the temple or not— 'You are cordially invited to join us in worship and the celebration of the Bar Mitzvah of Mr. Ben Segal of Chicago—' Get it?"

He could tell from their faces that they did, that they all thought it as wonderful an idea as he did.

"So I went to see the rabbi about it. That's why I was late getting home."

"And?"

"And nothing. He wouldn't hear of it. Said it was against our religion. That you're Bar Mitzvah when you become thirteen whether you want to or not. And he wouldn't have anything to do with it."

"Well . . ."

"Seems to me my father said that."

"I don't understand. Wouldn't they know in Jerusalem?"

"And the Hadassah people would know, wouldn't they?"

"I guess our rabbi knows better," said Maltzman bitterly. "He says he's not responsible for what other rabbis do. This isn't the first time—"

"Maybe he feels you're against him," suggested his wife, as she entered to serve the main course. "All the other presidents invited him to sit in on the board of directors' meetings and you never did. If he were at the meeting and something came up—"

Maltzman was exasperated. "I've explained to you that it's a different kind of meeting now. Until we reformed the bylaws, practically anybody could come to the meetings. There were forty-five directors plus all the past presidents. We held the meetings Sunday mornings when people came to bring their kids to the Sunday School, or when they came to the morning minyan. So those who were on the board, some of them would stay for the meeting. It was a crazy system. There'd be only about fifteen or twenty present at most meetings, but if something was proposed and somebody was against it, they'd spend the week calling all the members of the board, and the next meeting, when it was to be voted on, there'd be forty or more, and it would be voted down. You could never transact any business. Well, now we have a board of fifteen, and it's like an executive committee. And we meet in the afternoon. And it's every other week, instead of every week. It's a business meeting, not just a place where you come to chew the fat. Everybody who is supposed to comes. If someone stays away two or three meetings, he's dropped, and I'm empowered to appoint someone to take his place the way I appointed Herb Mandell here when Joe Cohen found he couldn't make it regular. So, even if I invited the rabbi to attend the meetings, he would be unable to come every meeting. He has a wedding or a funeral or some other kind of meeting he has to go to on a Sunday afternoon. And if he didn't come every week, we'd have to spend time when he did come explaining what the points at issue were."

"It seems to me," said Molly Mandell placidly, "the big mistake we made was in giving the rabbi a lifetime contract."

"We didn't give him a lifetime contract," said Roger Streitfuss. "We offered him one and he refused it. A couple of years back, I think it was. He's on a yearly basis. It was his own idea."

"That's right," said Maltzman. "It was the year he went to Israel. Maybe thought he might want to go back there and didn't want to be bound by a long-term contract."

"So how do you work it?" asked Molly, interested. "Do you meet with him on the terms every year and then draw up a contract?"

"Oh no. His salary is just one item in the budget. When the board votes the budget, the secretary sends him a letter telling him his contract has been renewed for the year. And that's it."

"And what would happen if you wrote him and said it hadn't been renewed?" asked Allen Glick. "I'm just asking, you understand."

"Gosh, I don't know. I suppose he'd—I don't know what he'd do," said Maltzman.

"I bet he'd resign," said Roger Streitfuss. "I know he's had trouble with other administrations, and he's fought for his job. But he's never actually had an official vote passed against him."

"You got a point there," said Allen Glick. "What else could he do but resign? Either that, or appeal to the board to reconsider. And he's too proud for that."

"With fifteen on the board, it only takes eight to vote the rabbi out," remarked Streitfuss and then added vehemently, "If the matter came up, I'd vote against him."

The others understood his feeling. They all knew about the rabbi's refusal to participate in a joint wedding ceremony with a Methodist minister when the Streitfuss girl had married a Gentile.

"And I would, too," Allen Glick said. "What about you, Herb? You're on the board now. You've got a vote."

"Oh, Herb would go along," said Molly before her husband could answer for himself. "The way I see it is if we hope to get equality for women in the service and make this a modern, up-to-date temple, we've got to get Rabbi Small out and get in a rabbi who'll push for it."

"So you've got three votes already," Streitfuss said. "All you need, Henry, is five more."

Maltzman's eyes gleamed. He rubbed his hands. "Yeah, I think we might be able to bring it off."

Smiles appeared on the faces of his guests.

"But we've got to be awfully careful about this," Maltzman went on. "It's got to be kept secret, because if the opposition gets wind of it . . ."

14

Stanley Doble, the janitor at the temple, was not the ideal employee. For one thing, he was unreliable. He had been known to interrupt a job of work, presumably to go for his lunch, and not return for several days because he had met someone who had suggested they drive up to Maine to bag a deer. Also, he got drunk on occasion, although, in all fairness, usually on his own time. On the other hand, he was an accomplished handyman, who could do a skillful job of carpentry, repair the

plumbing, maintain the heating and air-condition-
ing system and was knowledgeable about electric-
ity. While frequently exasperated by his lapses, the
temple authorities felt that on the whole, it was a
fair trade-off. Moreover, since the wages they paid
him were not high, they winked at the outside jobs
he took on.

Most of the time, he was dressed in a dirty T-
shirt and grease-stained overalls and sported a two
days' growth of beard. When shaved, and with hair
combed and wearing his "good clothes," however, he
was quite presentable. Although not tall, he was
powerfully built and carried himself with a kind of
truculence, as if to warn taller men that he was not
to be trifled with. His face was coarse and fleshy,
and his eyes small with the lids half-closed, as
though he were peering at the sun. The nose was
bulbous and a little askew at the tip, having been
smashed once in a fight. But while not an attractive
man, he was usually good-natured and friendly.

He was not wearing his good clothes when Martha Peterson bumped into him at the supermarket
downtown, and there was a smudge of grease on his
cheek, which was why she refused his invitation to
"come and have a soda" at the drugstore. But when
he asked for a date, she said, "Well, I'm free
tonight."

His face fell. "Aw, Marty, today's Friday, they
got a service at the temple tonight and I got to
clean up afterward. I was thinking about tomorrow
night."

Because she felt it was important for her to
maintain her status as the arbitrary, even capri-

cious, conferer of favors, she said loftily, "I'm sorry, but tonight is the only night I'm free."

And since the immediate was always more important to him than the responsibility of a later time, he said, "Okay, then. I guess I can make some arrangement at the temple. I'll pick you up at your place around seven."

"No, you pick me up at work."

"Why can't I pick you up at your place?"

"On account I don't want to go home by bus. I left my car to be serviced, so I won't have it to go home with."

"Aw, gee, Marty."

"What difference does it make to you?" she asked.

"Well, your boss, old man Jordon, him and me had a fight about some work I done for him, and I said I'd never set foot in his place again."

"You afraid of him?"

"Afraid? But where I said I wouldn't . . ."

"Well, if you can't, I guess there's other fish in the sea."

He looked at her calculatingly through slitted eyes. It occurred to him that in the light of the sacrifices he was making, she would feel obligated and make suitable recompense. "All right," he said decisively. "I'll pick you up at seven, but you be ready now, so when I ring the bell—"

"I'll be ready."

15

Lawrence Gore looked up inquiringly as Molly Mandell entered his office.

"I know you don't like me to bother you, but Mr. Jordon—"

"Was he in this morning?" he asked quickly. "Did he—er—try to annoy you again?"

She blushed. "No, he hasn't been in. But the report—"

He held up a finger. "Right. The Ellsworth Jordon quarterly report. It's due today. I haven't forgotten it. As a matter of fact, I spoke to him this morning." He tilted back in his swivel chair. "And he invited me for dinner tonight."

"So he can go over the report with you?"

"I suppose. And he's letting me have his Peter Archer soup tureen."

"So he finally decided to let you borrow it for the exhibition?"

"Oh, I think he was going to all along. It's just his way. But I called him this morning and told him I was taking the collection to the museum tonight

and it was now or never. So he said okay, I could
pick it up this evening and he invited me to dinner."

"How are you taking it in?" she asked curiously.

"In my beachwagon."

"You going alone?"

"Sure. Why not?"

"Because it's very valuable, isn't it?"

"It sure is."

"You ought to have someone with you. You
could get into an accident and—"

"You're right, Molly, as usual." He thought for a
minute. "I'll ask Billy. Have him come in, will you,
Molly."

When the young man appeared, he said, "I'm
taking the Peter Archer silver into Boston, to the
museum tonight. How would you like to come
along and ride shotgun?"

"Gee, that would be swell. Shall I meet you at
your house? What time?"

"Oh, I'm coming to your house. The old man invited me to dinner. I'm picking up his soup
tureen—"

"I knew he was going to let you have it. He had
Martha shine it up the other day."

"So it's all set. We'll go back to my place right
after dinner, and you can help me load the stuff in
the car."

Molly reminded Gore of the Jordon report again
at noon, and he said he'd get on it as soon as he returned from lunch. But he met some customers at
lunch and it was after two when he got back. When
she asked him about it once again, he said, "I've

been thinking it over. If I bring it with me, I'll have to go over it with him and discuss it item by item. I could be there till midnight. I'll tell him I'm sending it by mail."

"But he's such a stickler for getting his reports on the day they're due. And it's due today."

He grinned impishly at her. "Well, that still gives me until midnight. And if it's dropped in the mail after five it will be too late for the Saturday delivery. So I could drop it off at the post office anytime during the weekend, and he'd still get it Monday."

She looked doubtful, and asked, "Is it something I can do?"

He pinched his lower lip, looking at her speculatively. "You know, as a matter of fact, you can. There's really nothing very involved. Here, let me show you." He got out the Ellsworth Jordon folder. "These are purchases and these represent sales, mostly stocks, but there are some real estate transactions, too. So you list these together—"

"I had some bookkeeping in high school."

"Believe me, that's good enough. That and your good common sense. All you have to do is list these in one column and these in another. You itemize them, of course, but it's pretty much all spelled out. Just follow the form on the earlier reports and do a good typing job."

She was not nearly finished by closing time, but she offered to work on it at home.

"I hate to ask you to," he said.

"You're not asking me. I'm volunteering."

"But won't Herb—"

"Herb is running the Brotherhood service at the temple tonight. And I've got to stay home anyway to baby-sit for his mother."

"Then she—"

"She goes right upstairs after dinner, and by eight o'clock she's fast asleep. Really, I don't mind. It will give me something to do."

"Well, if you're sure you don't mind. I'll make it up to you."

16

Maltzman heard the phone ringing just as he got to the door. He hurriedly fished for his key on the chance it was for him. Sure enough, as he opened the door, he heard his wife say, "Oh, he's coming in right now. Just a minute." She cupped her hand over the mouthpiece and whispered, "It's Mr. Segal."

He took the instrument from her and said, "Mr. Segal? How are you? . . . Fine . . . No, not yet. I tried to contact him a couple of times and was unable to reach him . . . Yeah, I understand . . . I'll get hold of him in the next day or two . . . Oh

sure, I'll let you know as soon as I hear . . . Fine
. . . Fine . . . Bye now."

He replaced the receiver and explained, "About
the house lot on the Point. These big shot finan-
ciers, they want something, and they think you get
it"—he snapped his fingers—"just like that."

"And did you try to contact Ellsworth Jordon?"

"Of course not, but I don't have to tell him that."

"Are you worried that—"

"I'm worried that Ellsworth Jordon might not
want to deal with me and will say that the land is
not for sale. Or he might ask some ridiculous price
that even Ben Segal wouldn't be willing to pay."

"Maybe you could get somebody else, Dalton
Realty maybe, to front for you?"

"And split the commission? Like hell."

"So what are you planning to do?"

"I don't know. I'll have to think about it. I might
see Larry Gore, who handles some of his business.
He's a reasonable guy, and I know he thinks well of
me because he recommended me to Segal. I could
talk to him and lay my cards on the table and
maybe—"

"Maybe you're just imagining things, Henry,"
said his wife. "Maybe you're just working yourself
up like the man in that story who goes to borrow a
lawn mower from his neighbor. Jordon might be
anxious to sell. At least, you ought to ask him."

He pursed his lips as he considered. "You know,
Laura, you got a point. I'll call that sonofabitch
right now and lay it on the line. Hand me the
phone."

"Why don't you wait until tomorrow to call?" she urged.

He stared at her. "Tomorrow? Saturday? Why tomorrow?"

"Well, you know you always feel better, more relaxed after—after—"

"I feel relaxed enough right now. Give me that Goddam phone."

17

When Billy opened the door to admit Lawrence Gore, Jordon called out from the living room, "You're late, Larry." A moment later, when Gore joined him, he pointed to the carriage clock on the mantelpiece.

Gore looked at his wristwatch. "Are you sure, Ellsworth? Mine says just six."

"You bet I'm sure. That clock is absolutely right. I check it every day with the radio time signals. You're five minutes late."

"Well, I'm sorry, Ellsworth." He slid the bracelet off his wrist and, peering at the clock, made a show of resetting his watch.

"All right, all right, let's not waste any more time," said the old man, as though conceding a major point. "Martha's got a date for tonight and wants to leave early, so let's not keep her waiting." And waving his arms, he shooed Gore and Billy into the dining room.

As Gore spread his napkin, he remarked, "Albert Megrim was in this morning. He said you were planning to blackball someone I proposed for the Agathon, Ben Segal."

Jordon chortled. "That's right. And not half an hour ago, Henry Maltzman called me about buying my land on the Point for this same Ben Segal."

"He told you who his principal was? That doesn't sound like Henry Maltzman."

"I told him I wouldn't even discuss it with him unless he did."

"Well, I guess he figures you wouldn't do him out of his commission."

"No commission."

"But—"

"I turned him down." He smiled broadly.

Gore looked mystified. "You know this man, Segal?"

"Nope. Never laid eyes on him."

"Then . . ." Gore took a swallow of water. "This Ben Segal is from Chicago. He's big financier. He's taking over the Rohrbough Corporation and plans to operate it. Now the last time I went over your holdings with you, that land on the Point was one of the properties you said you wanted to sell. Considering the price you're asking, you're not likely to get a buyer in a hurry. I'd say Ben Segal is the best chance you're going to have in a long time."

"That so? Big financier, is he?" He drummed the table.

"That's right. There was an article on him in *Business Week* about a month ago. I took him to the Agathon for lunch, and he liked what he saw and what he had to eat. And asked me to put him up for membership. Just like that. Didn't ask what the dues were or the initiation fee. And it isn't as though he's interested in yachts, or in any of the facilities the club has to offer. It was just that it seemed to him a nice place to dine. A man like that isn't apt to haggle over the price of a piece of land he's set his heart on."

"Well," said Jordon with a sour grin, "I didn't actually close the door. This Maltzman figured I was being cozy, or maybe I didn't like to talk figures over the phone, because he asked if he could come and see me and talk about it. So I told him he could come at half past eight tonight."

"Oh, well, that's all right then." Gore was much relieved.

"I told him," the old man went on, "that I knew he was president of the temple and that since there is a service there at half past eight on Friday nights, according to the bulletin outside, I wanted to see which counted more with him, his commission or his religion." The old man put his head back and laughed obscenely.

Billy looked doubtfully at the old man as though wondering if he were joking. Gore pretended to be amused. "And what did he say to that?" he asked.

"He said if he did come it would be to put a bullet through my head."

"There!" Gore smiled his satisfaction. "You blew it, and now you'll be lucky if you find another buyer who'll pay you half of what you're asking."

"You think so?" Jordon put down his soup spoon and reaching back, took out his wallet from his back pocket. From it he drew a dollar bill and laid it on the table beside his plate. "You want to bet Maltzman won't show at half past eight?"

"Sure."

"Then let's see your money."

"You mean you want me too—" Gore drew a dollar bill from his pocket and placed it on the table.

"That's fine. Now we'll let Billy hold the stakes. It will give him a sense of responsibility."

Martha came in to clear away the soup plates. She waited while the old man hastily tilted his plate, the better to take the last few spoonfuls. "You kind of hurrying us, Martha?" he asked.

"I saw you weren't eating."

"Well, I just stopped to make a financial transaction. All right, I'm done now. Heavy date tonight?"

"Just a date," she said and went out to bring in the main course.

Later, when she came back to clear the table, Jordon asked teasingly, "Who is he, Martha? Who's your date tonight?"

"None of your business," she answered tartly.

The old man roared with laughter. "Now that's a girl with spirit," he exclaimed approvingly. "Cummon, let's go into the living room. We'll have our coffee there, and it will give her a chance to clean up in here."

When Martha served the coffee a few minutes later, she had already changed to her street clothes.

"You going now?" Jordon asked.

"Pretty soon," she replied. "I'm waiting for my date."

"You mean he's going to call you?"

"He's picking me up here. My car is in the garage."

"So he's coming here, is he? What did you say his name was?"

"I didn't say."

"Well now, Martha, let's understand each other," he said pleasantly. "Whom you go out with is your business, but who comes to my house is my business."

His voice had taken on an edge, and because she didn't think it worth fighting about, she shrugged, "It's Stanley Doble. I guess you know him."

"Yes, I know him," he said grimly. "And I won't have it."

"What do you mean you won't have it?"

"I mean, I won't have him in my house."

She smiled thinly. "I guess he don't care any more for you than you do for him. So when he rings the bell——"

"He'll still be trespassing on my land. You want to meet him, you can go down and meet him at the gate, Missy."

"Why, you . . ." She stared at him in disbelief. Then she turned and strode swiftly out of the room. She was back a moment later, in her coat and clutching her handbag. She held a key which she shook under his nose. "Here's your key." She opened her hand and let the key drop in his lap. "I won't need it anymore. I'm not coming back. You can get yourself another girl." She walked to the front door, jerked it open and then slammed it to behind her.

Billy looked from Jordon to Gore as if seeking an attitude to emulate. Ellsworth Jordon, while obviously taken aback, did not seem too upset. Gore had an enigmatic smile on his lips.

"Now you've done it, Ellsworth," he said with quiet satisfaction. "There's a limit to how much you can push people around. Now you're going to have to find yourself another housekeeper."

"That shows how little you know about people, Larry," said Jordon contemptuously. "She'll be back."

Gore was puzzled—and interested. "How do you figure?"

The older man smiled. "Today is the thirty-first, isn't it? Well, I haven't given her her monthly check yet. So maybe she'll wait until Monday or Tuesday to see if she gets it in the mail. Or she may come for it, probably tomorrow. Maybe even tonight after you folks have gone. And there'll be remarks made that will lead to a rip-roaring argument. And after the air has cleared, we'll both admit to having acted a bit hastily."

"You really are a nasty old curmudgeon," said Gore, not without a touch of admiration.

The older man preened himself, and Billy

thought it tactful to remark, "Martha blows up quick, but she gets over it quick, too."

"Well, there you are, Larry," said Jordon. "Now, let's get to important matters. Let's take a look at the quarterly report—"

"Oh, I didn't bring it with me," said Gore easily. "It wasn't finished when I left."

"That report is due today," said Jordon in a dry, flat voice.

"No, Ellsworth. We're supposed to send it out today. That means any time before midnight—"

The old man pounded the arm of his chair. His face grew red. "Goddammit, I talked to you about it on the phone, and then I suggested you come here for dinner. You knew I meant for you to bring it with you."

The doorbell rang.

Instantly Jordon's mood changed. He rubbed his hands in satisfaction. "That will be Martha come back. Go to the door, Billy. But if she has that scallywag Doble with her, tell her I won't see her and I won't talk to her."

Billy opened the door and saw Stanley alone framed in the doorway. He was obviously embarrassed and uneasy. "Martha Peterson?" he asked.

"Gee, she's not here—"

"Is that you, Doble?" Jordon rose from his chair and walked toward the entrance hall. In a loud hectoring voice, he said, "I told you I didn't want you setting foot in this house again. Now get out or I'll call the police."

"I come for Martha Peterson," Stanley said doggedly.

"Well, she's not here. She doesn't work here any-more."

"That's right," said Billy. "She quit when he told her he wouldn't allow you to come here."

"Why . . ." Stanley pushed past Billy, his arms raised, his hands outstretched as though he were going to grab the old man by the neck. Gore, who had followed Jordon into the hall, came between them. He put his hands against Doble's chest. In a low voice, he said, "Don't be a damn fool, Doble. You can get yourself in a mess of trouble. Martha is waiting for you down by the gate."

"I didn't see her."

"You probably didn't notice her as you swung into the drive," Gore said soothingly. "But she's down there waiting. You better go. She might not wait too long."

Stanley permitted himself to be eased toward the door. On the threshold, he stopped and shook his fist. "You're a miserable old sonofabitch, Jordon, and if you're lying, don't think I won't come back."

When he had finally closed the door on Stanley Doble, Gore asked, "What did he ever do to you, Ellsworth, that you're so down on him?"

The old man waved a hand negligently. "Oh, it was over a job of work I hired him for some months back. That front door was sticking, and I engaged him to fix it. He took it off its hinges and planed it down. He rehung it, and it still wasn't right. And he wouldn't fix it without I paid him extra."

"It seems to work all right."

"No, the lock doesn't catch right. She won't close unless you pull her to real hard."

"And for that, you told him—"

"For that and on account of the words we had about it. When I strike a bargain with someone, I expect to keep my part of it, and I expect him to keep his. He said I engaged him just to plane down the door, and my point was that I hired him to fix the door. Now that means it's got to be right."

"Well, all I can say is, it's a lucky thing for you that I was here. He was in an ugly mood, and you could have got yourself a punch in the nose."

"Oh, I could have handled him," Billy said airily.

Both men laughed and Jordon said, "You, Billy? What could you have done? Doble is as strong as an ox. He could toss you over his shoulder with one hand."

"Yeah, but I got me an equalizer." Billy tugged at his belt and with a flourish brought forth a revolver.

Gore shouted, "Put that damn thing down."

"You crazy?" cried Jordon. "Where'd you get it?"

"It's from my cage in the bank," said Billy sheepishly. "Mr. Gore asked me to ride shotgun taking the silver to the museum."

"You young idiot! I don't need any protection." Gore turned to Jordon. "I said it jokingly when I invited him to come along with me tonight. Everybody knows it just means sitting beside the driver."

"Don't you know that in this state if you're caught with a gun you get a year in prison and no one can get you out?" Jordon raged. Contemptu-

ously, he went on, "Every time I think you're beginning to grow up and be a man, you pull some damn
fool stunt like this and I know you're still nothing
but an immature kid. Now you put that gun on the
table there and march straight into your room. And
I'm locking you in."

"Oh stink!" But nevertheless, the young man de-
posited the gun on the table, and sheepishly with
head lowered and not looking at either of the two
men, he went to his room and closed the door behind him.

Ellsworth Jordon calmly turned the key that protruded from the lock and then returned to the recliner. Gore looked at him uncertainly, went to the
door of Billy's room and listened for a moment.
Then he rejoined the older man.

"That was pretty harsh on Billy," said Gore.

"Harsh? I should have taken a stick to him."

"Maybe that would have been better, instead of
sending him to his room like a child, especially in
front of me. After all, you're not his father."

The old man remained silent. The ghost of a
smile appeared on his lips. Gore noticed it and a
wild idea came to him. "Or are you?" he asked. "Is
Billy your son?"

Jordon leaned his head back against the cushion
of the recliner and closed his eyes.

"Is that it? And you wanted him to work in a
bank to get training in handling money."

"You're beginning to annoy me, Larry," the
older man murmured without opening his eyes.
"Beat it. The bowl is in the carton near the door.

Take it and be off. This is my regular time for Transcendental Meditation."

"And Billy? You going to leave him there?"

With his eyes still closed, Jordon smiled and said nothing.

Gore rose and stood looking down uncertainly at the now placid face of his host. Jordon was breathing slowly and regularly, his lips moving barely perceptibly in the recital of his mantra. Finally, Gore picked up the parcel.

18

Lawrence Gore eased his car slowly down the driveway, looking carefully from side to side. Gaining the street, he drove to his own house on the outskirts of town to pick up the cartons of the Peter Archer silver.

By eight o'clock he was on the highway heading for Boston. As he drove, he thought of the events of the evening. He was quite certain now that Billy was Jordon's son. He wondered if Billy knew, if that was the reason for his docility. He tried to think of himself at Billy's age. Would he have tolerated such discipline if he had been visiting with a friend of his parents? Or would he have packed up and gone home? But suppose he didn't have a home? That his parents were dead? Or suppose his parents had explained to him that they were indebted to his host and that he must on no account offend him? He smiled wryly as it occurred to him that he himself tolerated a lot from Ellsworth Jordon. But, of course, that was business.

In the distance he saw the lights of a gas station, and he decided to stop there rather than take a chance that there would be another open at this hour. He pulled in and circled well beyond the pumps. Leaving his car, he walked over to the office, and extending a dollar bill, he asked, "Can I have some change so I can use the pay station?"

"It's out of order. The phone company fixes them, and the next day they're on the blink again. Kids come along at night after we close and plug them up so they can get whatever coins have dropped in the meantime. Or sometimes out of pure cussedness."

"Is there another pay station this side of the road before the tunnel?"

"There's one in the office. You can use that." He led the way into the office, and ringing up No Sale on the register, handed Gore change for his bill.

Gore dialed and whistled tonelessly as he waited. When the answer came, he said, "Molly? This is Lawrence Gore. How are you coming along with the report?"

"Well, I've gone over it again and again, but I

couldn't make the two columns balance. So I typed it up anyway."

"You sure you put all the items I marked A in one column and the L's in the other?"

"Uh-huh. I've checked it and checked it."

"Then I must have marked one of them wrong."

"Maybe I could ask Herb to look it over and—"

"Oh no, you mustn't do that, Molly," he said quickly. "It's bank business and strictly confidential."

"Oh, I just thought—well, of course I won't. Was Mr. Jordon angry about your not bringing it with you?"

"You better believe it. I thought he was going to have a fit. All that got me off the hook was that I pointed out that the day exended to midnight. I thought I could get back early enough to pick it up and drop it off to him, but looking over the instructions from the museum, I see they expect to inventory the stuff in my presence, item by item. That can take some time, and I don't think I'll be able to make it."

She could tell that he was concerned. "I could run it up to him right now," she offered. "Except it doesn't balance."

"Oh, well, he'll spot the mistake in a minute. He'll rib me about it when he sees me, but—No, I can't have you do it. Not where he's—No, you'd be going there alone and—"

"You think I'm afraid of him?"

He smiled at her typical Women's Lib reaction. He glanced at the large wall clock. "Well, if you're sure it's no trouble and you don't mind—"

"Not at all. Glad to help out."

"You're a sweetheart."

"I'm doing it for the bank," she said severely.

"Of course."

19

The ringing of the telephone awakened old Mrs. Mandell. Not that she had been asleep, for she insisted that she never really slept, just kind of dozed. It had interrupted a dream—well, not really a dream, since dreams were a function of sleep. Rather a kind of fantasy that would come to her whenever she dozed off. Although there were variations in detail, the general theme was the same; how things would be if She (which was the way she referred to her daughter-in-law) were gone. Occasionally, the dream was about the nature of her leaving—a fatal accident, a drowning, perhaps, in which Herbert had displayed tremendous courage in his effort to rescue her. He would be grief-stricken, of course, but it would have the effect of drawing him closer to his mother; after a while, he would get over the sense of loss, but still the memory of the tragedy would deter him from marrying again.

Then there followed a series of vignettes of their blissful life together when there were only the two of them. At breakfast—she was sure she'd be able to manage—and he would exclaim over its excellence. "Gee, Ma, this coffee, it's out of this world. And this oatmeal! How do you get it so smooth and creamy?" And when he left for work, he would buss her boyishly and say, "Now you take it easy, sweetheart. Leave the dishes, and I'll do them when I get home." For dinner she would prepare his favorite foods, the rich and spicy dishes he enjoyed so much, and afterward they would spend the evening watching TV or playing endless games of Scrabble, which she adored.

She did not want him to feel that he was obligated to her and would suggest, "Why don't you go out and visit your friends, Herbert? Take out a girl. I don't really mind an evening alone." And he would answer, "Why, Ma, you're my best girl."

Or it might be that She was no longer there because he had divorced her. He had finally realized that She was unworthy of him and that he could not continue to live with her.

Then she might picture him as remarried. His new wife was a shadowy figure, vaguely resembling a buxom Polish maid she had once had, who would give birth almost every year, all boys, and all looking like Herbert. They would crowd around their grandmother, each like one of the pictures of Herbert, at different ages, as he was growing up, pushing and jostling each other to claim her attention.

"Grandma, look at me." Herbert would be beside her and would good-naturedly push them away with, "Go on and play. You're tiring Grandma." Their mother never appeared in any of these scenes. With so large a brood, she was naturally busy, cleaning, cooking, washing dishes . . .

She heard Molly answer the phone but could not hear what She said, of course. She lay in bed debating whether to put on the light and read for a while, or try to go back to sleep, or maybe even get up and go downstairs for a cup of tea. Before she could come to a decision, she heard footsteps on the stairs, slow, careful footsteps, and then the door of her bedroom quietly opened. She pretended to be asleep. The door closed and the footsteps retreated down the stairs. A little later, she heard the sound of an automobile starting up, seemingly right below her window. Mystified, she got out of bed, went to the window and cautiously drew back the curtain just in time to see Molly's coupe ease down the driveway.

Where could She be going? Had something happened to Herbert? Had the call come from the temple? But what could happen to him in the temple?

Mrs. Mandell snicked on her bed lamp and looked at her watch. It was a little after half past eight. Gathering a kimono around her, she went downstairs. The lights in the living room were still on, and she padded about in her mules, looking at the papers on the desk where She had been typing. It occurred to her that She might have gone to mail something. But why now? The next collection would not be made until tomorrow morning. And it couldn't be to buy something, like cigarettes or a magazine at the drugstore. All the stores were closed by this time. Besides, her leaving must have something to do with the phone call She had received. Some friends must have called her and—could it have been a man friend? Was She taking advantage of Herbert's being at the temple to meet a lover?

Mrs. Mandell felt faint at the idea and thought she had better get back to her own room to take a pill, to lie down if necessary. The more she thought about it, the stronger grew the probability of her daughter-in-law's unfaithfulness. Curiously, it had not been one of the scenarios that she had fantasized as a means of ending the marriage, because—because in her mind it would make her son look ridiculous. But now she thought about it because she had to. What should she do? How should she proceed? Of course, if Herbert came home first, that would take care of it. On her return, he would confront her and demand an explanation. But what if She got back first?

She heard a car turn into the quiet street. Her breast filled with a great hope that it might be her son. But a glance at the clock showed that it was a little after nine, too early for him to be coming home from the temple. It must be She returning.

Gripping the handrail, she hurriedly mounted the stairs and got back into bed. A few minutes later the car pulled into the driveway, and shortly after she again heard footsteps on the stairs and then the door of her room being eased open. Again she pretended to be asleep, breathing deeply and stertorously until she heard the door pulled to and footsteps retreating down the stairs.

20

In an effort to increase the attendance, Henry Maltzman had suggested to the temple Brotherhood that they actively sponsor the Friday evening services.

"What do you mean, sponsor?" asked Howard Jonas, the president of the Brotherhood.

"You know, sponsor. Get behind the idea and push. Drum up attendance. Decorate the pulpit. Make arrangements for the collation afterward."

"But that's what the Sisterhood does."

"Yeah, so why shouldn't the Brotherhood take a crack at it for a change? It will spark things up, the competition."

"You mean, at the collation, the men would pour the tea? For the women? 'One lump or two, Mrs. Feldman?' Cummon! That's a woman's job, Henry."

But Maltzman was persuasive, and they finally

agreed to do it one Friday in the month, the other Fridays continuing under the supervision of the women. So this night found Herb Mandell, as chairman of the Brotherhood Committee for the affair, standing at the front door of the temple with Howard Jonas, greeting congregants as they arrived. For this, the first such service, they had sent out cards to all the members. More, they had gone through the Barnard's Crossing phone directory and sent cards of invitation to any whose names suggested they might be Jewish. "So if we make a mistake and send a card to a Gentile and he takes us up on it and comes, what harm will it do? It's like ecumenical."

Mandell took his responsibilities seriously. Whenever there was a lull, he would leave his post at the door to dash down to the vestry to see how the arrangements for the collation were going. Since he was the lead tenor in the Brotherhood barbershop quartet, which was to join the cantor in front of the Ark to lead in the singing of the En Kelohaynu at the end of the service, he was also concerned about a slight hoarseness he had developed that afternoon. So each time he went down to the vestry, he would use the opportunity to dodge into the men's room to examine his throat in the mirror above the washbowl for signs of redness. Then he would shake some salt from a small packet he had brought from home into a paper cup of warm water and gargle for a few seconds.

On the podium two pairs of thronelike chairs, upholstered in rich red velvet, were set on either side of the Ark. The two on the left were reserved for the rabbi and the president of the congregation, while those on the right were customarily occupied by the vice-president and the cantor. At quarter past eight, fifteen minutes before the services were scheduled to begin, only three of the chairs were occupied. Henry Maltzman had not as yet arrived.

"I wonder where he is," Howard Jonas mused. "It doesn't look right that he shouldn't be here."

"He'll probably be along a little later," said Herb Mandell. "He was late last week, too."

"Did he take his seat next to the Ark?"

"Oh no. He slid into a seat in one of the back rows."

"I don't like it," said Jonas. "Frankly, I'm pissed off. It was his idea in the first place, and he rammed it down our throats. So the least he could do is be here and see how it was going. I suppose it's a business matter that came up, and I'd be the first to admit that your business comes first. But where he's president of the congregation, it seems to me that's like a commitment. Not that I'm criticizing, you understand."

"Oh sure." Mandell turned to greet an arrival. "Hello, Mr. Kalb. Glad you could make it. . . . No, take any seat at all."

Jonas nudged him. "Say, Herb, what's your arrangement with Maltzman? You know, about announcing that this is sponsored by the Brotherhood."

"Well, just before we begin the service, he's supposed to say that he is calling on me for a few words. Then I go up and explain that the Brotherhood is sponsoring the service, and I'd like to welcome everybody."

"Then I think you better go up and take that seat beside the rabbi right now, Herb, because if Henry doesn't get here on time, the chances are the rabbi will just start the regular service."

"You think it's all right?"

"Sure. I'll hold the fort here by myself."

Diffidently, Herb Mandell walked down the aisle and mounted the steps to the podium. To the rabbi's questioning look, he responded in a whisper, "Howard thought I ought to come up now seeing as Henry Maltzman might not get here in time."

"Of course," said the rabbi and held out his hand to wish him the traditional *Gut Shabbos*. "And how is your mother, Mr. Mandell?"

"Oh, she's fine. Well, I mean, she's no different."

"She seemed to be in good spirits when I saw her yesterday," said the rabbi.

"Oh, well, that's during the day. It's in the evening when her asthma seems to act up. Then she gets sort of tired and drowsy. I think maybe it's from the pills she takes. She has to go to bed right after dinner. If she sleeps through the night, that's fine. But sometimes she gets up in the middle of the night, and she's like disoriented. She can't catch her breath, and she can't find her medicine. It's kind of frightening."

"Is that so? And yet she always seems pretty good when I come to visit her."

"Well, it's during the day, and she's expecting you, so she gets herself up for it. But we never leave her alone at night. And by the way, Rabbi, don't think we don't appreciate it, your coming to visit her regularly."

The rabbi smiled. "That's all right. I have her on my list of regulars." He nodded toward the clock at the rear of the sanctuary. "You planning to say a few words, Mr. Mandell?"

"Oh sure." With some trepidation, although outwardly resolute, Herb Mandell advanced to the lectern in front of the podium. He waited a moment for the buzz of conversation to stop and then began the little speech he had written and carefully memorized. "As chairman of the committee, I want to welcome you in the name of the temple Brotherhood." He hoped that those who were here for the first time would enjoy the service and draw spiritual strength and comfort from it. Further he hoped that they would make a habit of it and come every Friday night. Quite at ease now, he even ventured a mild joke not in his prepared text, saying he hoped they would not think it was male chauvinism of the Brotherhood sponsoring only one service for every three that were sponsored by the Sisterhood. "It isn't that we think we can do the same in one that they do in three. It's just that we're new at it, and we want to learn from them." No one laughed, but he thought he detected a smile or two. Anyway, they wouldn't be likely to laugh right in the sanctuary, would they?

He ended by announcing, "The cantor will now chant the prayer, How goodly are thy tents, O Jacob."

Sitting there on the podium, in full view of the congregation, he felt the responsibility of demonstrating deep interest in the proceedings, so during the chanting he followed the text in the prayerbook, his finger moving along the line as if to make sure that the cantor did not skip a word. From his vantage point he was able to note such interesting phenomena as that Mr. Liston had a facial tic, that Mrs. Eisner whispered almost continuously to the women on either side of her, and that Mrs. Porush was dozing. But he still managed to preserve his air of great attention. Later, when the rabbi got up to give his sermon, Herb made a point of nodding every now and then in agreement or appreciation.

Just as the rabbi was bringing his sermon to a close Henry Maltzman arrived, looked around guiltily, and then, an uneasy smile on his face, slid into a seat in the rear. From the podium Herb Mandell frowned in disapproval. He decided that he agreed with Howard Jonas that it wasn't right for the president of the congregation to come late to the service. And so late! It was quarter past nine and the service would be over in a few minutes. He found himself watching Maltzman and once their eyes locked. It seemed to him that the president nodded slightly and smiled approvingly? derisively? He could not be sure.

Afterward, in the vestry at the collation, he saw Maltzman several times, moving about among the congregation. Although Maltzman waved to him, he made no effort to approach him to congratulate him, as Mandell thought he might. In fact, it almost seemed as though he were trying to avoid him.

Nevertheless, it had been an exhilarating evening for Herb Mandell. When he got home, his first words were, "I wish you could have been there, Molly. Everything went off just right."

"Oh Herb, I'm so glad for you."

"I'm sorry you had to stay home with Mother. Maybe we should have tried to get that woman Mrs. Slotnick recommended."

"That's silly. You'd have to pay her nurse's rates."

"Yeah. Did Mother give you any trouble?"

"She slept like a baby. And I didn't mind staying home. I had that report to do for the bank."

"How'd you make out?"

"Oh, I finished it," she said, motioning toward the desk.

21

Saturday morning, Gore stopped off at Molly's house before going to Jordon's. When she admitted him, he asked eagerly. "What did he say when you gave it to him?"

"I didn't give it to him," said Molly. "I didn't see him. The house was dark when I got there."

"Why, what time was it?"

"A little after I spoke to you. That was around half past eight."

"He must have gone out. What did you do with the report?"

"I didn't want to leave it in the mail slot. I brought it back with me. That was right, wasn't it?"

"Oh, absolutely. I'll take it up to him now."

She handed him a manila envelope and watched expectantly as he riffled through the typed pages.

"Beautiful," he said. "I really appreciate this, Molly."

"But it doesn't balance."

He ran an expert eye down a column of figures. "Here it is," he announced pointing. "This is an asset, not a liability. You sure I marked it L rather than A?"

She flipped open the file. "This one? You want me to make the correction on my typewriter? I can x it out and—"

"No, don't bother." He made the correction in pencil. "I'll show it to him to explain what held it up."

From Molly's he drove directly to Jordon's house. As he turned in at the gate, he heard an automobile horn, seemingly from the direction of the house. It grew louder as he drove up the driveway, and sure enough, there was a car parked in front of the door. It was Martha, her face contorted with rage as she pushed down on the horn button on the steering wheel.

He got out of his car and approached her. "What's going on? What's the matter? What's the racket for?"

"Oh, it's you, Mr. Gore." Her face relaxed, and she even managed a shamefaced little smile. "There's a month's wages due me. I knocked on the door and rang the bell but there's no answer. The old bugger must have seen it was me and won't answer out of spite. I'd like to put a pin in the bell like we used to do when we were kids on Halloween."

"He's probably gone out."

"No, look at he door. It's not pulled to. He wouldn't leave it like that if he weren't in. You can just push it open."

He walked to the door, as she got out of the car to follow him. He stabbed at the bell button. Sure enough, he could hear it ringing inside.

"See, the bell is all right. You can hear it, can't you?"

He nodded and pushed the button once more. They waited, and she said, "I'll bet he's watching and waiting for me to go away."

He shook his head impatiently and then, with sudden decision, pushed the door open and stepped in. Martha was right behind him. It took a moment for their eyes to adjust from the bright morning sunlight to the dim light of the room, somber with its curtained and draped windows. It was the buzzing of a large bluebottle fly that drew their eyes to the figure of Ellsworth Jordon lying back in his recliner as though asleep. But there was an ugly wound at the base of the forehead, right between the eyes, from which the blood had trickled down both sides of his nose to the corner of his mouth.

Martha screamed. Gore pressed his lips tightly together and managed to repress the urge to retch.

"He's hurt," she moaned. "The poor man is hurt. Why don't you do something?"

"Shut up," he snapped. Without moving, he looked around the room, noting a broken medicine bottle, the fragments of a shattered light bulb, the torn canvas of the oil painting of Jordon's father on the wall.

"We've got to call the police," he said in a hoarse whisper. "I'll wait here while you get in your car and drive down to the corner. There's a pay station there."

"Can't you call from here?" she asked.

"Fingerprints," he replied tersely. "There may be prints on the phone."

As soon as she had gone, he forced himself to approach the figure in the recliner. He touched the icy forehead with his fingertips and then wiped them on his trouserleg. Suddenly he thought of Billy and called out, "Billy? Are you there, Billy?" He giggled in relief as no answer came.

He backed out of the room and left the house, closing the door behind him, but making sure that the lock did not catch. As he went to his car to await the arrival of the police a wild thought occurred to him: that now there was no way of proving who had won the bet he had made the night before.

22

While his men worked in the living room, photographing, measuring, dusting for fingerprints, the state detective, Sergeant McLure, and a police stenographer were in the kitchen—because it had a table to write on—questioning Gore. Lanigan and his lieutenant, Eban Jennings, had taken over the dining room as a command post, where they issued orders and received reports from their subordinates.

They had just finished questioning Martha Peterson, subdued and teary-eyed, and had sent her on home.

"You believe her explanation of the door of the boy's room being locked?" asked Jennings. "You believe this Jordon would lock a young man of eighteen in his room like a teacher would send a kid to stand in the corner?"

Lanigan shrugged noncommittally.

"Even though he knew the kid would hop out the window?"

"It's just crazy enough to be true," said Lanigan.

"Maybe Gore might know something about it. We'll ask him when McLure gets through with him."

"Everything about this case seems kind of crazy, Hugh."

"How do you mean?"

"Well, this Jordon is supposed to have been a millionaire. Right?"

"That's the reputation he had around town. We'll probably find out more about that, too, from Gore. What about it?"

"Well, doesn't this strike you as a funny layout for a millionaire?"

"How do you mean?"

"This dining room now, it's clean enough, but those drapes are pretty faded and these chairs are kind of worn. Same with the other room."

"I suppose that's the result of having a house-keeper instead of a wife," said Lanigan. "A wife is always after her husband to buy new stuff when it gets worn, but a housekeeper will just keep the place clean."

"Yeah. But it's more than that. Here's this big ark of a house three stories high, and yet everything is on the first floor. It don't look as though the rooms on the other two floors are used at all. What was probably the back parlor, he used as his bed-room, right off the living room, mind you. And that little room next to it, that was made into another bedroom for the boy. That looks to me as though he was trying to cut down on his fuel bills."

"Could be," said Lanigan. "The word was that he was always careful with money. On the other hand, it could be that after he had a heart attack, his doctor might not have wanted him to climb the stairs. And naturally, he'd want the young fellow right near him in case anything should happen to him in the middle of the night. I wonder where he is. The bed wasn't slept in."

"Probably off somewhere for the weekend. Stands to reason he wouldn't want to spend it hanging around with an old codger like Jordon. This Martha, now, didn't she used to clerk in the supermarket?"

Lanigan nodded. "That's right. She was on the check-out counter."

Jennings nodded in decided agreement. "That's where I saw her. Nice-looking woman. Yeah, that's the way I like them, something solid that you can get hold of. I could make something of that girl."

Lanigan's look was derisive. "Yeah, you'd like to make a mother of her. That's what you'd like. I wonder Maude puts up with you."

"Now, look here, Hugh—"

"Did you know Celia Johnson? She used to work for Jordon. She gave up a good job to become his housekeeper. She was a bookkeeper with the Water Commission. Five days a week, nine to five. Paid vacations. Blue Cross and Blue Shield. Pension rights. And she gave it up to go to work for him. Gladys knew her. I remember Gladys explaining to me why Celia did it. She was thirty-eight at the time and not getting any younger. Here was a man all alone—"

"And she thought maybe she could make him? Get him to marry her?"

"Sure. Why not?"

"You think that's why Martha Peterson went to work for him?"

"Well, she's not getting any younger either."

"It could be that she just likes housework better than clerking, is all."

"Could be," Lanigan admitted. "But if it's the way I think, it could be the reason she insisted that Stanley pick her up here was that she wanted to make Jordon a little jealous. Spark him up. Show him there's some competition."

Jennings showed some interest. "And that's why she quit her job? Because she saw it wasn't working and there was no sense staying on?"

"Or maybe there was something more between the two than just a job."

Eban Jenning's pale blue eyes showed interest, and his Adam's apple bobbled with excitement. "She could have come back afterward to have it out with him. Or maybe she didn't even go away, but just kind of hung around outside until she was sure the old man was alone and—"

Dr. Mokely, the medical examiner, put his head in the doorway and said, "I've finished here, Hugh."

"Oh, come in, Fred. What've you got?"

"Death instantaneous, of course. What do you expect from a shot right between the eyes?" He set his bag down on the floor and took the chair that Jennings pushed at him with his foot.

"Powder burns?"

"Suicide?" He shook his head. "Not a chance. No powder burns."

"Er—Doc"—Jennings swallowed his Adam's apple—"this Jordon had a bad heart."

The doctor laughed. "Well, he certainly didn't die of a heart attack."

"How do you know?" Jennings persisted. "Five of the six shots were scattered all over the room, so it must have been the last one that got him."

"Why does it have to have been the last one?" asked the doctor.

"Because it hit him square in the forehead," said Lanigan. "So the person shooting could see he'd hit him, and that hitting him there he must have killed him. So would he continue shooting after that? And if he hadn't had a heart attack, wouldn't Jordon have tried to run or hide if someone started shooting him?"

"How would he get a heart attack?" asked the doctor.

"Say he was asleep," suggested Jennings. "Wouldn't the first shot wake him up?"

"I suppose."

"Well, couldn't that bring on a heart attack, waking up and seeing someone firing away at him?"

"All right," the doctor conceded. "So what?"

"Then he could be dead before that last shot that actually hit him," said Jennings triumphantly.

"When you have a heart attack, you don't die instantaneously," said the doctor. "And what difference would it make? It would still be murder, whether he died because he was hit or from fright because somebody was shooting at him."

"Probably no difference," said Lanigan. "But defense lawyers can come up with some funny angles. Can you prove it one way or the other on the autopsy?"

"I doubt it. If there were a longish time interval between the first shot that could have frightened him into a heart attack and the last one that actually struck him, it might be possible to tell—by the amount of bleeding maybe. But by the looks of things, the murderer fired off those shots in rapid succession, like a woman pointing a gun with her eyes closed and firing away until the cylinder was empty. That would mean only seconds between the first shot and the last, and I doubt if anything would show up on postmortem. As to which shot actually got him . . ." He shrugged. "It could be he was lying in that recliner and was awakened by the shots. He leans forward to get up and catches one between the eyes, which throws him back again."

"Can you tell from the angle of entry?" asked Lanigan.

"I doubt it," said the doctor. "The bone would deflect the bullet some, and we don't know if he was lying back or sitting up, and at what angle."

"Well, see what you can do. Now, how about time?"

The doctor smiled. "Oh, I can give you that exactly. It was eight-twenty-nine."

"How can—" Then the chief smiled, too. "Oh, you mean the clock. But suppose one of those bullets hadn't hit the clock?"

The doctor smiled broadly. "Then I'd say half past eight."

"A comedian!" Jennings snorted.

The doctor grinned. "I'll give you a spread after I've done the P.M."

23

"But it's the Sabbath," Miriam protested.

"It's terribly important, Mrs. Small," said Mrs. Mandell. "I couldn't sleep a wink all night. I thought I'd go out of my mind."

"Couldn't it wait until tomorrow?"

"No. No. It must be today."

"Well, he's at the temple right now for morning services and—"

"Oh, I understand. Of course." She even permitted a tinge of sarcasm to enter her voice. "I don't mean for you to run over and get him out of services, but I wanted to make sure he would come over this afternoon. I mean, I wanted to call him in good time before he makes any other appointments."

"The rabbi doesn't make appointments on the Sabbath, Mrs. Mandell. He doesn't transact business on the Sabbath, unless it's an emergency."

"Well, this is an emergency."

"All right, I'll tell him when he gets home." She hung up, annoyed and indignant, wishing that

David had early on established the rule followed by most of his Orthodox colleagues of not answering the phone at all on the Sabbath.

While the commandment to visit and comfort the sick was enjoined on all Jews, the congregation expected its rabbi to perform this function for them, quite content to have him gain the credit for the mitzvah. An altruism on their part that Rabbi Small strongly resented.

Rabbi Small never tried to convince himself that he enjoyed the pastoral visits to the sick. Because of his natural reserve, he felt he was not very good at it. He found it hard to summon up the forced cheerfulness that the occasion seemed to require, to assure patients they were looking well, when in fact they were not. While able to feel sympathy as they talked about their aches and pains, he always grew restive and suffered considerable embarrassment when they then went on to enumerate their related complaints—against the doctor who was not interested in their case, against the nurse who was negligent, against the members of their family who were lacking in consideration.

The most trying item on his calendar was his weekly visit to Mrs. Mandell. Unlike the others whom he visited, who were apt to be in bed, or in pajamas and bathrobe if they were able to sit up, she always came down to the living room, fully dressed, her gray hair combed and brushed and tinted a delicate lavender. She was a tall, fleshy woman with a full, round face that showed no trace of illness. When he would remark on how well she looked, she would smile sadly and shake her head.

"Now," she would say, "but you should have seen me last night when I had an attack. I thought it was all up with me."

But this was not one of his regular visits. It was some sort of emergency, she had said. He was more than a little put out when it looked as though the formula of his regular visits was about to be repeated. "I didn't sleep a wink all last night, Rabbi," she said.

"But that's not unusual for you, you say. Is there some special reason why you had to see me today? Why it couldn't wait until tomorrow?"

"Because tomorrow They would be here. Today They went visiting and won't be back until this evening."

From previous visits, he had learned that in her style book, while her son was always My Herbie, his wife was She, and together, husband and wife, were They.

"So?"

"Well, I must begin, Rabbi, by admitting that when My Herbie decided to get married, I was opposed."

His lips twitched but he said soberly, "Was your opposition to marriage as an institution, or was it to the girl he chose?"

"Well, I thought he ought to wait a while."

"But he's a mature man. He's in his thirties."

"He was thirty-six at the time. He's thirty-eight now. So having waited this long, I felt he ought to wait until the right girl came along. I felt that She was not the right girl for him." Mrs. Mandell shook her head dolefully. "She says She's thirty, although

I think She's more like thirty-two or thirty-three. That's already not so young for a woman. My Herbie is tall and handsome. He could have had any number of girls—"

"But he chose this one," the rabbi insisted.

"Did he, Rabbi? Or did She choose him?"

He smiled. "It comes to the same thing in the end, doesn't it? They're happy, aren't they? That's what matters."

"Oh, I guess She's happy."

"And he isn't?" asked the rabbi, smiling.

"How can he be? She's made a—dishrag out of him. Just because he gets home a little earlier, She has him fix the supper and set the table. Afterward, She has him help in the kitchen with the dishes. She dominates him completely. And She makes love to *him*—right in front of me."

The rabbi opened his eyes wide.

"I mean, She kisses him and fondles him like a kitten. Is that the way for a young married woman to act?"

"It shows she loves him, doesn't it?"

"Does it, Rabbi? Or does it just show She likes men?"

"What are you suggesting, Mrs. Mandell?" the rabbi asked coldly.

But Mrs. Mandell did not feel in the least put out. "Last night, My Herbie had to be at the temple."

"Yes, I know. He was chairman of the committee."

"Now I can't be left alone at night. There's a danger—"

"Yes, yes, you've told me."

"So when They have to go off together, My Herbie arranges for a woman to come and stay with me." She smirked. "A mother-sitter, he calls it." Mrs. Mandell lowered her voice. "Last night She volunteered to stay. She said She had some work to do for the bank." Her mouth twisted in a superior smile. "What kind of work would a bank ask an employee to do after hours, Rabbi? And wouldn't you think a wife would want to watch her husband being honored? But My Herbie is very trusting. And to tell the truth, I thought nothing of it, either. I went up to bed around eight, as usual, and I dozed off. I never sleep."

"I know."

"About half an hour later, just when the service was starting, I imagine, I was awakened by the phone ringing. She spoke for a couple of minutes and then I heard her coming up the stairs to see if I was asleep, so I pretended. She looked in at me and then tiptoed downstairs. Then She left the house, and I heard her car start up. I got out of bed and watched as She drove off. What do you think of that?"

The rabbi was nonplussed. "You mean that where she had agreed to sit . . . What did your son say when he came home and found her gone?"

"Oh, She got back before he did. She came back about half an hour later and came up to look in on me again."

"And again you pretended to be asleep?"

"Naturally. My Herbie doesn't know unless She told him. And you can be sure She didn't tell him."

"Why are you so sure she didn't?"

"Because he'd be furious. You see, there's the danger—"

"Yes, yes, I know," he said hastily.

"So you can understand why I couldn't sleep a wink last night, Rabbi. Why I've been so upset all day. Where did She go? Who did She see?"

"Why did she have to have seen anyone? She may have gone out for a magazine or a pack of cigarettes."

"At half past eight? The stores are closed. And how about the phone call?"

"It could have no relation to her going out. Or it could be some woman friend of hers."

"So She could come over and get a cake recipe, maybe? No, Rabbi, it was a man who called, and She went to meet him. What shall I do, Rabbi? What shall I do?"

The rabbi took a deep breath. "I think you told me you had a sister out west—"

"In Arizona. She has been after me to come out there."

"I think that's what you should do, Mrs. Mandell. The climate would be good for you."

"And leave My Herbie here trusting, believing, while She betrays him?"

"Mrs. Mandell, she is not betraying your son. It's a terrible thing to say about a respectable married woman, especially your own daughter-in-law."

"Oh, you're like everyone else," she said scornfully. "If it doesn't concern you personally, sweep it under the rug and make believe it isn't there." She gave a cunning, calculating look. "But suppose I told you that you are concerned."

"How am I concerned?"

"Because She's plotting to get you out. What do you think of that?" she asked spitefully. "I've heard her on the phone talking to the president, Henry Maltzman, about how they can get rid of you. If I've heard her once, I've heard her half a dozen times. Now, what do you think of her? Now, what do you say?"

"I say you should go out to Arizona to visit your sister," he said resolutely.

24

"Now suppose you tell us just what happened last night," suggested Lanigan genially when Lawrence Gore was seated.

"But I told it all to the sergeant," Gore protested, "and there was a policeman taking it all down in shorthand."

"Well now, that was a statement you were making," said Lanigan. "Sergeant McLure is a state detective and they have their regulations. But we're the local police, and we'd like to hear it, too, not just read what the stenographers types up."

"So you can compare the two statements and badger me if there's a discrepancy?"

Lanigan smiled. "Something like that."

"All right," said Gore wearily. "I was invited there for dinner."

"You go there often?" Jennings asked.

"No. Once before, a few months ago. Almost every Thursday night Jordon would go out to the club, the Agathon, and if I were going, I'd drive him out and back. He didn't like to drive, especially at night. But I'd just drive up to the door and honk the horn and he'd come out. But yesterday I called him to tell him I was taking the Peter Archer silver in to the museum—I expect you've heard about that—and it was his last chance if he wanted his soup tureen to be exhibited. He told me I could pick it up and invited me to dinner."

Gore went on to tell his story without further interruption. Although he went into considerable detail, he did not mention Molly's visit to the Jordon house since he did not have personal knowledge of it, and in any case it was after the murder had occurred. It was only after Gore had finished that they questioned him.

"When you left, the boy was still in his room?" asked Lanigan.

"Jordon hadn't let him out," Gore answered with a shrug. "Since he got out, he must have let himself out—"

"How do you know that?" asked Jennings quickly.

"When I got here this morning, I called out to him. There was no answer. Then I knocked and listened at the door—"

"Did you open it?"

"Of course not," said Gore. "That would have meant disturbing evidence, and—"

Lanigan cut in. "So you figure since he let himself out, he could have got out anytime, maybe even while you were still here talking to the old man."

"He could have," Gore admitted.

"What do you know about him?" Lanigan asked.

Gore spread his hands in a gesture of ignorance. "Not much. Jordon told me he had problems and didn't want him pestered. That's the way he put it. He didn't specify what kind of problems. He'd graduated from a secondary school and had no police record, so I hired him. He seemed to be a decent enough kid, but kept pretty much to himself. I don't know of any friends he had in town. He did his work well, and I liked him. He didn't talk about his family or his background at all. Maybe Jordon told him not to. And I didn't press him. Oh, he did say once that his father had been killed in the war. Since he was too old to have been born during the Vietnam business and not old enough to have been born during the Korean War, I asked him what war. And he said, the Suez Campaign. Well, that was the action in which England and France joined Israel against Egypt. Of course, his father might have been British or French. But he could also have been Israeli, and knowing how Jordon felt about Jews, I didn't pursue the matter."

"Just how did he feel about Jews?" asked Lanigan.

"I'm a banker," said Gore, "and one man's money is the same as another's. So I don't like to talk about religion, and I didn't with Jordon. Once or twice I remonstrated with him when it interfered with business, like when he wouldn't sell some land that the temple people wanted to buy, or once when Henry Maltzman had a customer for a piece of land. All he said then was that he wasn't going to make it any easier for them. I guess he didn't like them." He smiled. "That didn't prevent him from making a pass at my secretary a couple of times, and he knew she was Jewish. She called him a dirty old man."

"That's the one you phoned on your way to Boston?" asked Jennings.

"Uh-huh."

"All right," Lanigan looked up from the notes he had been making. "I guess that about does it. Oh yeah, what about the gun?"

"The gun is one of three that I bought for the bank, one for each teller's cage," said Gore.

"How come?" asked Jennings. "I didn't think banks went in for that kind of thing anymore. I thought they relied on an armed guard nowadays."

"That's right. But we don't have an armed guard. And the tellers have strict instructions not to use them."

"Then what's the point in having them?"

"It gives them a feeling of security. If someone comes in and holds up the bank, they're not supposed to be heroes. But if things should get out of hand, and some wild shooting result . . ."

"Why didn't you take it with you when you left?" asked Lanigan.

"Because I don't have a license to carry a gun."

"How come?" asked Jennings. "A crackshot like you, and a banker?"

Gore smiled. "For just that reason. I might be inclined to use it, and then be sorry for it afterward. So I eliminate the possibility by not taking out a license. I was planning on calling you people Monday morning so that you could send an officer to pick it up and return it to the bank."

"Too bad you didn't think to call last night as soon as you found the young man had taken it. Jordon might be alive today."

25

"Was it anything serious? Was it really an emergency, David?" Miriam asked when the rabbi returned.

He shook his head. "Just the sick fancies of a lonely and embittered woman." He smiled. "Among other things, she accused her daughter-in-law of plotting against me. You know her at all?"

"Molly Mandell? Well, I see her when I take your check to the bank on the first of the month, and I see her at Sisterhood meetings occasionally. She's apt to be rather outspoken there, mostly about women's rights. From little things I've heard she's not one of your more ardent admirers." She hesitated, and then added, "The Mandells are also supposed to be friendly with the Maltzmans."

"What's wrong with that?"

"There's nothing actually wrong with it, I suppose, but it is curious since the Maltzmans are so much older than the Mandells."

"And what's the significance of that?" he asked.

"Well, Henry Maltzman doesn't like you, David. I can see it whenever he comes here. Can't you sense it?"

"Yes, I've noticed it. As you pointed out, his attitude was like that of the officers, especially the line officers, when I was a chaplain in the army. And Henry Maltzman is still very much an officer. There was a grudging admission that maybe we in the Chaplain's Corps might help maintain morale, and hence to that extent we were useful. But otherwise, there was no meeting of minds. I suppose they resented that they couldn't give us orders when they outranked us. I think they felt that way toward the Medical Corps, too. A captain in the Medics once told me that whenever he told an infantry colonel to take his shirt off, he used to wait a minute or two so that the sound of teeth gritting didn't interfere with the sounds he was trying to hear through the stethoscope. Yes, I think Henry Maltzman would prefer a more compliant rabbi to deal with. He may even be trying to do something about it. It certainly wouldn't surprise me."

"And what are you planning to do about it?"

"Nothing," he said simply. "There's nothing I can do."

She was annoyed with him. "You mean, you're giving up? You've had trouble with previous Presidents, and you've fought them—"

"It's different now," he said.

"How is it different?" she challenged.

"Now that they've got an executive committee of fifteen, it only takes eight votes not to renew my contract." He smiled ruefully. "Maybe I outsmarted myself when I turned down the lifetime contract. Although if I had a life contract, they could get me out easily enough by voting something that I couldn't possibly condone. Still, I'll admit it's easier for them now."

"And you wouldn't do anything about it?"

"What can I do about it? Ask the individual members of the board not to fire me? And what would my position be afterward?"

"So what will you do?" she asked, her voice betraying exasperation.

He smiled faintly. "I suppose this time I'll have to leave it in the hands of God and hope for the best."

26

"I hate this kind of case," declared State Detective Sergeant McLure. "It can drag on for months, and we can end up with nothing. Or we might be dead certain we know who did it, and the D.A. will find that we don't have enough to go to court with."

"What's so different about this case?" asked Jennings defensively, as though McLure, from the big city, was casting aspersions on a local product. In any case, the question was rhetorical rather than because he was interested in any answer McLure might give. They were sitting along with Lanigan around the dining room table in the Jordon house. The three of them limp, rather than relaxed, feeling the letdown that followed the tensions and the hectic work of the day.

"Well, if it's a professional job, either we know who had it in for the victim, and then it's a job of breaking down an alibi—because they make damn sure they've got an alibi—or we get someone to talk. You can do pretty good if you've managed to build up a stable of stoolies. On the other hand, if it's amateur, then it's usually a matter of finding out who hated the victim's guts. But in this case, the victim, as near as I can make out, was a pretty nasty specimen. Any one of the people who were here at the house last night might have wanted to give him the business because he quarreled with every one of them. Not to mention the guy who called him on the phone earlier. Or, for that matter, someone whose name hasn't even been mentioned, who could have dropped in on him."

"I suppose that's true enough," said Lanigan, "but—"

"And another thing," McLure went on, "take the matter of the weapon. Usually, it gives you a lead. Or you have the bullet and when you get it matched up with a particular gun, you've practically got your case. But here, the gun was lying on the table in plain sight. So if this Martha came back, or her boyfriend, or this guy that called, or the kid Billy, well, there it was, ready to hand, so to speak."

"Yeah, but on the other hand, there's the pattern of the shooting," said Jennings. "The doc said it was like a woman firing away with her eyes closed until the cylinder was empty. I buy that."

"But it could also be a kid who's crazy about guns, and yet doesn't know anything about them," McLure pointed out. "Or take this Stanley—"

"Not Stanley," said Jennings with conviction. "He goes up to Maine every year and brings back a deer."

"Yeah, but he's something of a boozer, I gather. And if he got tanked up first—"

"What time is it?" Lanigan asked suddenly.

"It's almost six," said Jennings. "Why?"

For answer, Lanigan reached for the phone and dialed a number. Into the receiver he said, "Miriam? It's Hugh Lanigan. Is David there?"

"He's at the temple for the evening service."

"Oh, I figured since it was after sundown it was all right to call."

"Well, it is. But that's when they start the service. It takes about fifteen or twenty minutes. And he'll be walking home, of course. Shall I have him call you when he comes in?"

"Maybe you can tell me. Did you go to the service last night?"

"Yes, of course. I go every Friday night."

Lanigan signaled to Jennings who lifted the extension and simultaneously pulled over a pad of paper. "Was Henry Maltzman there?"

"I believe so. Yes, I'm sure he was. Why?"

"And Stanley Doble? Was he there?"

"I didn't see him, but I wouldn't be likely to since he'd be down in the vestry helping with the preparations for the collation afterward. Why? Is something the matter?"

"Just routine, Miriam. That's all. Thanks."

After making note of the time and the date Jennings ripped the sheet off the pad and filed it in the ever-increasing folder of the case.

"If the medical examiner confirms the time of the killing as half past eight, that eliminates Henry Maltzman," said Lanigan. "As I expected, he was at the temple last night. They start at half past eight." He squared his shoulders and sat up straight, as if to signal that the period of relaxation was over and it was time to get back to work. "Now, let's list what we've got to do. The first thing is to clear away the brush, eliminate the unlikely, so we won't waste any time. Besides Maltzman, Gore seems to have a pretty good alibi. He says he stopped at a gas station to make a phone call around that time. He called from the office, so maybe the gas station attendant remembers. Check with this Mrs. Mandell that he called. She might remember the time. If he's out of it, then we don't have to bother about him either. See?"

"Yeah, but Maltzman, he could have gone there earlier and maybe seen something or heard something," said McLure. "I'd like to question him."

"Okay, then question him. But he's a tough monkey. He was a captain in the Marines—"

"I've had lots of experience with tough monkeys," said McLure, "and when I was in the service I was a buck private, so I kind of like to take on officers."

Lanigan winked at his lieutenant and said, "All right, so let's consider the others. First of all, especially Martha."

Jennings opened the folder and found the notes on their interrogation of her earlier. "She says she left here around seven, and as soon as she got to the street, a bus came along. Got off at Midland Street and walked the two blocks to her house. She decided to stay in and made herself some supper. Stanley came by around seven-thirty. She says she didn't admit him. She watched TV and then went to bed around eleven."

"Seems pretty straightforward," said McLure. "Anything bothering you about it? You think she might have come back afterward? Does she have a car?"

"It was in the garage being worked on. But she could have taken a bus," said Jennings.

"You might be able to check with bus drivers," suggested McLure doubtfully. "Or maybe the neighbors—"

"What's bothering me," said Lanigan, "is the whole setup of Martha as Jordon's housekeeper. She had a job as a checkout clerk at the supermarket. Seems like an easy job. At least you're sitting down rather than on your feet all day. It's forty hours a week, with a paid vacation probably. My guess is it pays about a hundred a week. Now, why would she give that up to become Jordon's housekeeper? He was a hard man with a buck, so I doubt if he paid her more than the supermarket. She'd get here about eight o'clock and she worked until after the supper dishes were done, which would make it some time after seven. Since she did the cooking, she might have had to come in seven days a week, six anyway. Why would she do it? Was she fired from the supermarket job, or did she quit to take the job with Jordon?"

"Some women prefer housekeeping to working in a store," said Jennings.

Lanigan nodded. "Sure. And she got her meals and her time was pretty much her own during the day. On the other hand, Jordon may have led her down the garden path by hinting that the job could lead to her becoming Mrs. Jordon. I don't buy Gore's explanation that Jordon tolerated her slam-banging back at him because he liked independence. To me, it sounds more the way lovers would act. And the whole business with Stanley could have been to spark a little more interest in the old man by making him jealous. And when she handed him her key, that could have been because she realized she didn't have a chance with the old man and the game was over. And after she got home, she could have brooded a bit and then come back to have it out with him, since she knew Billy was going off with Gore and he'd be alone. The old man had a nasty way of talking, and I can imagine him lying back in that chair of his and being amused at the girl realizing she'd been had. Well, the gun was there and—"

"Boy, you're in the wrong part of this business," said McLure. "You should be an assistant D.A. making your pitch to the jury. You realize you don't have a single, solitary fact to back up any of this."

"Well, there's the pattern of the shooting," said Lanigan. "And there's the fact that she came back the first thing in the morning and discovered the body."

"Oh, you take that old saw seriously about the criminal being drawn back to the scene of the crime?" McLure was sarcastic.

"I don't know about any mysterious attraction that the scene of the crime might have for the criminal, but it seems to me that if I had shot a man in the heat of passion the night before and then panicked and run off, I'd want to come back when I was cooler to see if I hadn't dropped something, a handkerchief or whatever, that might incriminate me."

"Well—"

"And remember how we found him, sitting in his recliner. Anybody else who came, my guess is he'd get up and open the door. But when the bell rings and he calls out who is it and finds out it's Martha, he might say, 'Come in, the door is open' and just sit there kind of smiling at her as she jabbered away at him. Anyway, I want you to check her out, Eban. Everything. Start back at the supermarket. Did she see much of Jordon while she was still working there? Was there gossip? Was there someone she confided in? Understand?"

"How about this Stanley guy?" asked McLure. "Now he threatened him, according to Gore."

"We've got to pick him up, of course. And—"

"No, we don't, Hugh," said Jennings. "We've got him down at the stationhouse right now. I called about something else a little while ago and they told me. They found him on Fairbanks Street fast asleep in his car, drunk as a skunk. One of the residents notified the police and they took him in. He's sleeping it off in a cell right now."

"Good. So that leaves only the young fellow, Billy."

"Put out an all points on him?"

"Let's see if we can get it on the early evening news. Make it plain that he's not a suspect, just that we're interested in information that he might give."

Jennings wrote in his notebook and then looked up inquiringly. "Anything else, Hugh?"

"Yeah, go on home and get yourself a decent meal. I'll see you at the stationhouse afterward."

27

Since Rabbi Small did not turn on either the radio or TV on the Sabbath, it was not until he arrived at the temple for the evening service that he heard about the murder. The dozen or so who had gathered for the service were a lot less observant of the Sabbath than the rabbi and hence knew all about it. Most of them were listening to Julius Rottenberg who was a *maven*, that is, an expert in matters criminological by virtue of operating a coffee shop just outside the law courts in the neighboring city of Lynn, and who, therefore, was on intimate terms with the district attorney ("coffee and a cruller and heavy on the cream"), the assistant D.A.'s, all the cops and even the presiding judge ("tea with lemon and a little extra hot water, Julius").

"It's the kid, of course," he was saying when the rabbi entered the chapel where they were waiting to begin the service. Fat and bald and normally with a perpetual, eager smile, Julius now showed a fine high scorn for someone who had suggested that it could be some stranger from his past who had shot Ellsworth Jordon.

"Nah," he said with an impatient sweep of the hand. "The police always say that. It gives them an out. See? But it was the kid that did it. He's crazy about guns. All kids are. What do you expect with all these westerns on the tube, and the gang pictures, too. He pinches the gun out of the bank where he works. To hold up somebody, or even to fire it in the woods? Nah. Just to fondle it. To practice a quick draw, maybe, or twirling it around his finger, like the gunmen do in the westerns. So the old man catches him with it and makes him put it down and sends him to his room. Then everybody leaves—there was some sort of dinner party—and the old man sits down in his easy chair to grab himself forty winks.

"So they're all alone, and the old man is asleep. So the kid leaves his room to get another look at the gun, to hold it and wave it around. And it goes off. So now he's in for it for sure, so he figures he might as well get hanged for a sheep as for a lamb, so he fires away until the gun is empty. And when he's finished, Ellsworth Jordon is dead."

"Yeah, but why didn't Jordon jump up and stop him, Julius?"

Julius nodded with pompous solemnity. "Good question. My theory is that the old man panicked and froze."

A new arrival announced, "Hey, guys, I just heard that the cops arrested Stanley."

"Stanley? Our Stanley? What for?"

"I don't know. All I heard was he was arrested. Did you see him around today?"

"He wasn't here last night either. Look in the vestry and you'll see all the stuff from the collation, the dirty dishes, they're still on the table."

"You think we ought to clean up?"

"That's the House Committee's business."

Throughout the service the rabbi had great difficulty in keeping his mind from wandering. He performed perfunctorily even the Havdala ceremony that divided the Sabbath from the rest of the week. What kept running through his head was that if Jordon was dead, and if Henry Maltzman had been right about him, then the temple might now be able to buy the adjoining land for the religious school.

A little ashamed of his thoughts and his inability to concentrate on the prayers, the rabbi did not stand around and talk with the members of the minyan at the conclusion of the service as he usually did, but excused himself and went right home. He had no sooner entered the house, when the phone rang.

"Rabbi Small," he announced.

From the other end came a hoarse chuckle. "I figured you'd be getting home right about now, Rabbi."

"Stanley?"

"That's right. I'm down at the stationhouse, and they said I could make a phone call."

"You mean you've been arrested? What for? What's the charge?"

"I think maybe I was a little drunk."

"All right. I'll be down and talk with them."

28

The desk sergeant looked at Rabbi Small doubt-fully and said, "Gee, I don't know, Rabbi. You're not a lawyer, are you? I mean, you don't have a law degree, do you?"

"No—"

"Because he's got a right to see his lawyer, of course, but I don't know about anybody else. I guess it would be all right if you were his spiritual advisor, but Stanley not being Jewish, his spiritual advisor would have to be a minister or a priest depending on if he was Catholic or Protestant. See what I mean? I mean just because he works at your temple wouldn't make you his spiritual advisor, and your not being a lawyer . . ." He chewed at his lower lip in vexation. "He said he wanted to make a call, so I figured he was going to call his lawyer, but you say he called you." The sergeant was annoyed, as though Stanley had taken advantage of his trusting nature to deceive him.

"Why don't you ask Chief Lanigan if it's all right?" suggested the rabbi.

"He's pretty busy. Well . . ." He came to a decision and left his desk to walk down the short hall and rap on the door of the chief's office. Lanigan opened the door and saw the rabbi. Without waiting for an explanation from the sergeant, he said, "Hello, Rabbi. What brings you down here? You want to see me? Come on in."

The rabbi nodded to Lieutenant Jennings and took the seat proffered him. "I got a call from Stanley, Stanley Doble—"

"Oh, it was you he called. You want to see him?"

The rabbi laughed shortly. "It's he who evidently wants to see me. I gather he's been arrested. Could you tell me what for?"

The phone rang and Lanigan picked up the receiver.

"All right, put him on." He cupped the receiver and said to Jennings, "Another Billy call."

Jennings said, "That's number seven."

"This is Chief Lanigan," he said into the instrument, and reached for a scratch pad. "What's the name again? . . . How do you spell that? Two *e*'s? . . . Okay, Mr. Beech . . . This motel is where? Where are you calling from? . . . North Adams? . . . Uh-huh . . . Uh-huh . . . All right, and what did he look like? How tall would you say he is? . . . Five foot four? No, the man we're looking for is quite a bit taller. Close to six feet . . . No, I don't think that's anything you can disguise, but thanks for calling. We appreciate it. Bye."

To Jennings he said, "A motel operator from North Adams. A guy just signed in as William Grey, but Mr. Beech thought he hesitated before writing the *e*."

"North Adams is the other end of the state. If the kid doesn't show up pretty soon, we'll be getting calls from Texas and California," said Jennings.

"Even if he does show up," said Lanigan. He brought a large, fleshy hand down across his broad face, as if to wipe out the lines of worry and tiredness. To the rabbi he said, "We've been at it since the first thing this morning. I had a sandwich for lunch and not much more for dinner. Gladys didn't expect me home. And ten cups of coffee in paper cups. The news broadcast was an hour ago, and we've had seven calls from people saying they saw him. You sure it was seven, Eban? Seems like more."

"Yeah, seven. I've been keeping count."

"Plus other calls from people who had all kinds of suggestions and advice. None of it useful. And one from a nut who wouldn't give his name but was sure that we were persecuting an innocent man. We'll get a lot more of those before this is over. All that, in addition to the legitimate calls—from my own people on things and asking for additional instructions, calls from the D.A.—" He smiled broadly. "The hell with it. What can I do for *you*, Rabbi?"

"I came about Stanley. Remember? Am I to infer that his being here is because he's mixed up in this murder in some way?"

"Stanley. Right. Well, Jordon was shot around half past eight. About an hour before that, Stanley had a row with him at his house. He was finally pushed out, but he threatened to come back."

"And that's why you arrested him?"

Lanigan grinned broadly. "Not really. The boys found him sitting in his parked car dead drunk and pulled him in to sleep it off."

"Well, he's slept if off by now, hasn't he?"

"Yes, but there are some questions we'd like to ask him."

"Then how about asking him the questions and letting him go? He's got a job to do."

Lanigan pressed his lips together as he considered. "All right." He spoke into the phone to ask the desk sergeant to have Stanley sent up. "But don't you say anything while I'm questioning him."

"Of course not," said the rabbi.

There was a discreet knock on the door, and the sergeant and a uniformed patrolman marched a woebegone, disheveled Stanley into the room. When the officers had been dismissed, Lanigan said, "Now, Stanley, I want you to tell me everything that happened when you came back to Jordon's house last night."

"What do you mean, came back?" demanded Stanley truculently. "I never came back there. I wouldn't set foot in his lousy house. Does he say I did?"

"All right, then suppose you tell us what you did

when you left Jordon's. You did go to see him, didn't you?"

"I did like hell. I got no business with him. I went to pick up Martha Peterson which I had a date with her. And they said she wasn't there, that she was waiting for me down by the gate. So why didn't I see her when I turned into the driveway? Or if I missed her on account I was looking out to clear the gatepost, wouldn't she have seen me? And wouldn't she have yelled out? But, of course, she could've walked a little away from the gate, so I went back down there. And she warn't there. So then I had to figure out was they lying to me, or did she put them up to it on account she changed her mind and didn't want to see me."

"So what did you do?" asked Jennings.

"I went to get me a couple of beers."

"To help you decide, I suppose," said Jennings sarcastically.

"That's right. And it came to me maybe she'd gone home even before I got there. So I went over to her place, and she was there." He looked triumphantly from one to another of the three men in the room.

"Then what did you do?" asked Lanigan.

"Well, she wouldn't let me in, and she wouldn't go out. We were talking like through the door. She had it on the chain, see. But she as much as told me she'd lost her job on account of me. So I thought maybe I'd go back to Jordon's and have it out with him."

"And what time was that?" asked Lanigan casually.

"Oh, eight, eight-thirty, maybe even a little later. See, I thought I'd have another beer first. Well, I came down by way of Elm Street, and I slowed down to make a left into his driveway, and then I noticed the place was dark. Not that the place is ever really lit up any time I've gone by there. Never enough light to draw mosquitoes. The old skinflint wouldn't spend the money. But this time, it was dark like he'd gone out or gone to bed. And then while I was trying to figure was he maybe in bed, and should I ring or bang on the door so he'd have to get up at least to answer, this car comes tootling along from the other direction and curves into the driveway. So I thought, what the hell, there's no use my going up there where he was having company. So I just went on away from there over to Salem to visit another ladyfriend of mine I got there."

"This friend have a name?" asked Lanigan.

For the first time, Stanley showed reluctance. He glanced at the rabbi uncertainly. Finally, he ventured, "I don't rightly remember her name. We always call her Frenchy, on account of she's what you might call of French extraction."

"This car you saw going into the driveway, what make was it?" asked Lanigan negligently, as though it had no interest for him and he was merely making conversation.

Stanley shook his head. "He was coming toward me and he had his high beams on."

"And this was what time?"

"Like I said, it could've been half past eight, or maybe a little later."

The phone rang, and as soon as Lanigan announced himself, an excited voice came from the other end. "Chief, the young fellow, Green, has just showed. Caught him trying to climb through the window in back."

Both Lanigan and Jennings immediately became alert. Lanigan said, "All right, beat it, will you, Rabbi. I'm going to be busy for a while."

"How about Stanley?"

"Oh, take him with you."

29

The questioning went on for hours. When Lanigan and Jennings arrived at the Jordon house, McLure was already there and had already begun the interrogation, and Billy was sobbing and blubbering. McLure broke off long enough to nod the two men over to a far corner to get them current with the situation.

"He pretends he didn't know about the murder until he got here," he said, "but I'm sure he's the one, and it's only a question of time before I get him to admit it."

"You ever hear of Miranda?" asked Lanigan coldly.

Instantly McLure was wide-eyed innocence. "I haven't accused him, I'm just questioning him as a witness—just for information."

"Then why's he crying?"

"He feels bad about the death of Jordon—he says."

"What was Jordon to him? Did he say?"

"Says he was just a friend of his mother's." McLure's eyes sparkled with eagerness. "And do you know who his mother is? Hester Grimes. She's his mother."

"Who's Hester Grimes?" asked Jennings.

"Oh, you must have seen her on TV. She's a nightclub singer and entertainer. You see her on a lot of these talk shows."

"Where is she?" asked Lanigan. "How do we get in touch with her?"

"She's on tour in Europe. What I got out of him so far is—"

"Never mind. I'll talk to him myself. If he changes his story, you can question him, but otherwise I'd appreciate it if you just sat quiet." Lanigan went over to the boy and sat down beside him. "I'm Chief Lanigan of the police department here, Billy."

"Yeah. I've seen you around."

"I'd like you to tell me what happened," Lanigan went on. "This terrible thing that happened last night, we've got to investigate it. You understand that, don't you?"

Billy nodded.

"Now, Mr. Jordon was killed with the gun that you brought home. Suppose you tell me about that. Did Mr. Gore ask you to take the gun with you?"

"Oh no. He asked me if I'd care to ride shotgun while he took the Peter Archer silver into Boston, but I knew he only meant that I'd be riding beside him. But I thought, what if someone—well, you know, that stuff is pretty valuable, and what could I do? I mean, I'm not one of these big, hefty guys. And Mr. Gore isn't either. So I thought, if we should get stopped—well, I didn't know about the special law here in Massachusetts. I knew you had to have a license, but I figured Mr. Gore must have one, since he's president of the bank and is into handgun shooting and all, and I'd be with him all the time. And, of course, if nothing happened, I'd just put it back and who'd know."

Lanigan did not badger him and he did not try to confuse him, but he was persistent. "Well, how soon after you were locked in did you leave?"

"Oh, right away."

"How right away?"

For the first time, Billy grinned. "Well, when he said he was locking me in, I thought, Oh yeah? and I headed for the window."

"All right. And where'd you go?"

"I went away from there as fast as I could. I went down the back driveway that we don't use anymore, out to Elm Street."

"Why did you go down there? Were you afraid you might be seen if you went down the regular driveway?"

"That's right. I thought Mr. Gore might be coming out, and I didn't want to see him."

"Why not?"

"Well, it was embarrassing. I was good and sore. See, Mr. Jordon had locked me in my room before, and I'd always sneaked out. I didn't mind that. It was like a game we played. See, that was his way of telling me I'd done something wrong. It never bothered me much. I'd just sneak out. And he knew it. It was like a game between the two of us. But he shouldn't have done it in front of Mr. Gore. See, Mr. Gore is my boss, and he's like a friend to me. And here Mr. Jordon was treating me like a little kid. It was awfully embarrassing, so I didn't want to see Mr. Gore. I'd be—well—embarrassed. And I was wondering if I could even go back to the bank."

"So then what did you do?"

"Well, I didn't know what to do, because I sure wasn't going to come back until late, maybe not till midnight. But I don't know anybody in Barnard's Crossing, and there's nothing to do there anyway. So there's a bunch of people waiting for a bus, and just then it came along, so I got on it."

"Anybody you recognized on the bus?" asked Lanigan casually.

Billy shook his head. "No, I didn't see anybody I knew."

"I should think being a teller at the bank you'd recognize a lot of people," suggested Jennings. "And even if you didn't know them, they'd know you and maybe say hello."

Billy shook his head again. "We're in North Barnard's Crossing. Down this end of town everybody banks at the Deposit and Trust."

"What were you planning on doing in Boston?" asked Lanigan.

Billy shrugged his shoulders. "Just hang around and then take a late bus back. But I got to thinking. Mr. Jordon played me a dirty trick, so maybe I could pay him back one. So when I got to Boston, I went to the big bus station and took a bus to New York. See, I figured he'd know if I didn't get back that night, and he'd get worried, and it would serve him right."

"I guess you didn't like him very much," suggested McLure.

Billy looked surprised. "Sure I liked him. Why wouldn't I like him?" His eyes began to tear. "He'd bring me stuff, you know, presents, whenever he came to visit us, from the time I was a little kid. And he invited me to stay with him, didn't he? I remember once, when I'd been here maybe a couple of weeks, I got sick. It was this twenty-four-hour bug. But Mr. Jordon kept coming into my room practically all night to see how I was."

"All right," said Lanigan, "let's get back to your travels. I don't suppose you met anyone you knew on the New York bus?"

Billy shook his head.

"What bus was it, by the way?"

"It was a Greyhound. I took the nine o'clock. They leave every hour. Actually, it was eight-fifty-five."

"What did you do in New York?" asked Jennings.

"Well, it was pretty late when I got in, or rather pretty early in the morning. So I had a bite in the terminal, and then I thought maybe I'd go home. But then I thought the doorman would ask me all kinds of questions. We're kind of friendly, me and the doorman. So then I thought maybe I'd hang around the city, or go to one of those all-night movies in Times Square. See, if I went to my house in the morning, or during the day, it wouldn't be so, you know, funny, and the doorman who is on days I'm not so friendly with, so he wouldn't be apt to ask me any questions. But I figured those all-night movie houses in Times Square, there's apt to be a bunch of drunks in those places. So I didn't know what to do, and just sitting there in the terminal trying to make up my mind, I fell asleep."

"I should think you would have slept on the bus," said Jennings. "I always do."

"I tried but couldn't," said the young man. "I was like upset. Maybe I did doze off and on. But later in the terminal building, I passed right out. When I woke up, it was morning, and I was stiff and felt kind of grubby. So I washed in the men's room and I bought a comb at one of the stores in the terminal"—he fished in his jacket pocket and brought forth a comb—"See, here it is, Souvenir of New York, it says. Then I had some breakfast. And then I took a bus downtown and just walked around."

"Why didn't you go home?" asked Lanigan.

"Well, see, I started worrying about Mr. Jordon. I thought he'd be terribly upset wondering what had happened to me if he found out I hadn't come home to sleep. And what with him having a weak heart and all. So I went back to the terminal and took a bus back to Boston. Then I took a bus back to Barnard's Crossing, and I got off at the Elm Street stop, the same as where I had taken the bus when I left. It was pretty dark by then, so I came up the back way, planning on sneaking into my room. But when I got to the house, I could see something wasn't right. The door of my room was open and I could see into the living room. And then I saw a cop—er—policeman, and I knew something was wrong. I thought maybe Mr. Jordon had called the police when he'd found I wasn't there. And my window was all the way down and locked. So while I was trying to push the latch over, a policeman nabbed me. And then I found out what happened. And I've been thinking that if I hadn't sneaked out, then nothing might have happened."

They continued to question him, but at eleven, Lanigan called a halt. The three men retired to a far corner of the room and discussed the story in low voices. "It seems pretty straightforward," said Lanigan, "but, of course, he may be lying."

"He's had plenty of time to work up a story and get it down pat," said McLure's comment.

"We could question the driver of the Boston bus," Jennings suggested.

"Oh sure," said Lanigan. "We'll get a picture of him, and if the bus driver doesn't remember him, he may know some of the people who take that bus regularly, and they might remember him. Also, the driver of the New York bus, and the ticket clerk."

"It's even more important to check the drivers of

the later buses," said McLure. "I'm betting he took the ten o'clock bus to New York, or even eleven. I've seen it again and again. A guy does something that won't bear thinking about. So he blanks it out of his mind, but he adjusts his story just enough so as to make it impossible. Get it? By saying he took the nine o'clock, it means he couldn't have killed the old man at half past eight. And he keeps the rest of the story the same, so he doesn't have any trouble remembering any lies."

Lanigan looked at him curiously. "You're pretty sure he did it?"

"Cummon. You can see he's a jerky sort of kid that everybody steps on. Take this business of being sent to his room. Is that the way you discipline the average eighteen-year-old? Would any other kid stand for it? Or, for that matter, what kid that age would consent to being shifted off to the country to live with an old man so his ma can be free to go gallivanting around Europe? Okay. His boss feels sorry for him and invites him to go in town with him. That kind of kid is crazy about guns. It gives him a sense of power. Now the old man shames him in front of the boss by sending him to his room. So when Gore leaves and the old man dozes off, he climbs out of the window. But he doesn't go down to get a bus. Oh no, he sneaks around to the front of the house and comes in. And there's the gun on the table. He has this urge just to hold it. My guess is he picks it up and just kind of fondles it, and it goes off. Maybe he shoots out the light, and the place goes dark. Then the kid knows he's in trouble, and he panics and just goes on shooting.

And when he comes out of it, the old man is dead. So he runs—to Boston and then to New York."

"And why does he come back then?" asked Lanigan.

"Like I said, because he's wiped it clean out of his mind. You might have to get a psychiatrist to hypnotize him and bring it back."

"What are you going to do with him tonight, Hugh?" asked Jennings. "He can't sleep here."

"Well, for tonight I figured we'd put him up at the stationhouse in one of the cells. If we get him a place at a hotel, I'm not sure the town would stand for the expense, and he'll be pestered by all kinds of people as soon as the news is out."

"He will anyway when he goes back to work at the bank on Monday," Jennings pointed out.

"Yeah, unless—unless—say, is Tom Hegerty on the island now, Eban?"

"Ever since Labor Day."

"Think he might like a boarder?"

"I know he'd like a helper."

"That's even better. Let's see what we can arrange." He approached the young man and said, "Look, Billy, you can't sleep here because we're still working here. It's pretty late to get you a hotel room, so how would you like to sleep down at the stationhouse?"

"Oh sure. I don't want to put you to any trouble."

"Fine. So that's settled. Now, I'd like you to stay around town for the next few days, but I don't think you ought to go back to the bank just yet."

"Gosh, no. I bet people would be coming up to

my window just to look at me like I was some kind of freak."

"That's what bothers me, too," said Lanigan. "So I got an idea. Do you know Children's Island in the harbor?"

"Where they have the YMCA camp in the summer for the kids? I've never been there."

"Well, Tom Hegerty lives out there, getting the place ready for the winter. How would you like to work there with him as a helper, painting, rough carpentry—"

"Gee, I've never done anything like that."

"You don't have to know anything," Lanigan assured him. "Most of the time you just hand him things or hold them while he works on them or fetch them for him."

"If I can do it, I wouldn't mind. It might be kind of fun living on an island."

"Fine. Then it's settled. I'll arrange it."

He rejoined the other two and nodded to indicate his satisfaction.

"How about Miranda now?" sneered McLure.

Lanigan looked at him in surprise. "What's Miranda got to do with it? All I did was arrange for a job for the young man."

30

When Herb Mandell returned from his after-dinner constitutional to the drugstore for the Sunday papers, he found Henry Maltzman sitting on the sofa in the living room, Molly beside him, their heads close together as they pored over a sheet of paper spread out on the coffee table in front of them. His entrance momentarily startled them, and they sprang apart.

"Oh, hi there, Herb." Maltzman waved to him. "I thought since it's your first board meeting, we'd drive down together, your car or mine, and I could fill you in." He gestured to the paper on the coffee table. "I've been going over the list with Molly. We've got five I'm sure of, three probables and a couple or three possibles."

"I think Mrs. Melnick is another possible," said Molly, "and I think you can list Mrs. Kaufman as a probable."

"It's still not enough to take a chance on," said Maltzman. "I want a straight up-and-down vote without discussion. The only thing to do is to put it over for a week. That'll give us time to contact the probables—"

"I'll talk to Anne Kaufman," Molly volunteered. "I'm sure I can get her to go along."

"Swell. And I'll sound out Joe Krasker and Harvey Gorin. If we get all three, that will give us eight, and we're in like Flynn." He had risen, and taking Herb by the arm, he said, "Now, here's what I want you to do, Herb. . . ."

Maltzman drove—and talked. Herb wanted to make his own position clear on the matter of the rabbi's ouster, but each time he made the attempt, Maltzman said, "Listen, will you." The tone was not peremptory; it was even kindly, but Herb was restive, feeling that he was being treated like a youngster.

Once they had arrived at the temple, however, Maltzman's manner changed. With his arm around Herb's shoulder, he led him up to the other members, who were standing in the basement corridor, and introducing him to those whom he did not know jovially assured them, "Herb is a comer and he'll add some weight to this board."

The group moved down the corridor past the classrooms of the religious school to the directors' room at the end. It was a small room. Like the classrooms, it had beige plaster walls and a low ceiling. Along one side, high up on the wall and hinged on top so that they could be swung inward, was a row of small windows level with the ground outside. Above the windows ran the asbestos-covered pipes for heating the building. It differed from the classrooms only in that, instead of pupils' desks, it had a long oblong mahogany table surrounded by small bridge chairs that took up most of the room, except for a small space at the end near the door, where there stood a blackboard on wooden uprights.

They shuffled to places around the table, while Maltzman remained standing at the end near the blackboard. They had been talking about the murder while awaiting Maltzman's arrival, and they continued after taking their places around the table.

"It must have been the boy," said Harvey Gorin. He ticked off points on his fingers. "He was the last one in the house. He ran off—"

"But he came back."

"They always return to the scene."

"Did he come back, or was he brought back? That's what I'd like to know."

Maltzman rapped on the table. "Let's come to order and get this meeting started. Who killed Ellsworth Jordon is the business of the police—"

Doris Melnick, who had been a high school civics teacher, said reprovingly, "Murder is the concern of every citizen, Henry."

"Oh yeah? Well, count me out of this one. This Jordon was the biggest anti-Semite in town, and whoever did it deserves a medal."

"How do you know, Henry?"

"You knew him, Henry?"

"You ever have dealings with him, Henry?"

"If it's true," said Mrs. Melnick, "I don't think it's wise for you to go around saying so."

"Why not?" demanded Maltzman.

"Because it's apt to cause bad feeling in town for

all of us, and it may suggest to the police that they ought to investigate us."

"Let 'em. We've got nothing to hide. Now let's get this meeting started. If you want to talk about murder, then I'll just walk out because I've got better things to do." He looked around the room. They were restive, but remained silent.

He rapped sharply on the table with his knuckles and announced, "All right, this meeting is now called to order. Before we begin with the regular business, I'd like to say a few words. When I announced last meeting that I was appointing Herb Mandell to fill the vacancy on the board caused by the resignation of Joe Cohen on the basis of the new regulations that permit the president to do so, I did not ask Herb first. I didn't ask him if he wanted to serve on the board. I just told him that I had appointed him and I expected him to serve. Why? I'll tell you. Because Herb Mandell is that sort of guy. You tell Herb there's a job that has to be done and you want him to do it, and Herb's answer is 'Okay.' And that's the kind of guy we need on the board. And that's why I didn't let any grass grow under my feet when Joe Cohen resigned. All right. Now, let's go ahead with the meeting. The secretary will read the minutes."

Herb Mandell listened intently to the reading of the minutes, to the reports of the committee chairmen, to the questions and objections raised on the reports. He would have liked to take part in the discussions, if only to justify the reputation Maltzman had given him, but it was all new to him and dealt with matters about which he knew nothing.

Finally Maltzman announced, "Unless there are any strong objections, I'd like to dispense with any further business and go on to a consideration of the budget. All right? Mike, it's all yours."

Meyer Andelman, chairman of the budget committee, ducked down and retrieved a dispatch case that he had kept on the floor between his feet. "Although we discussed certain items last meeting, and had a look at all the items, I thought it would be a good idea to get it all down in black and white. So I had my girl run off Xeroxes so that you could each have one in front of you as we talk about each item. I'll pass these along so you can follow each and every item as we talk about it. Now, I suggest that we kind of dispense with the rules, and if you got anything to say as we discuss each and every item, why, just talk up and let's have your two cents' worth. Take a minute now to look over these sheets, and then we'll start with item number one and go through each and every item."

It was Herb Mandell's cue. "Mr. Chairman, I'd like to make a suggestion. Since we have this all in black and white, why can't we postpone action on the budget for a week so we can take these home and go over them carefully in the privacy of our own homes?"

Meyer Andelman said, "I'd like to talk to that, Mr. Chairman. It's like this, Herb. This is the first of the month, or the Sunday that's nearest the first. And we always pass the budget on the first of November."

Maltzman cleared his throat. "Well . . ."

"Is it in the bylaws that we have to?" asked Mandell.

"No, it's not in the bylaws," Andelman admitted, "but we always do."

Mandell pressed his advantage. "Then, if it's not in the bylaws, why don't we hold it over so we can do a thorough job now that we have it all down in black and white?"

"But a lot of this we went over last week," said Andelman.

"Well, I wasn't here last week."

"Well, sure, I realize that, Herb, but any item that you can't make up your mind on, you could abstain. Personally, I don't think your vote is going to be all that necessary. I mean, it's my opinion that we're not likely to have any item where the vote is going to be that close where one vote will make a difference. See what I mean?"

"Sure, I understand your point of view, Meyer," said Mandell, "but maybe I can make you see my point of view. It's like a matter of principle with me. See, I'm an accountant. So, it goes against my grain that I should be handed any kind of financial statement and be told to approve it before I've had a chance to look it over and study it. That's my training in me, see? Now, you can say that I can abstain. But as long as I'm an official member of this board, I feel like I've got a kind of responsibility to participate on financial-type matters. Maybe I'm wrong, but that's the way I feel."

"Aw, let's put it over, Mike," someone called out.

"Sure, what's the point of hassling. Herb would

like another week to look it over, so why not? I think maybe I'd like a little more time on it."

"What difference does it make, this week or next?"

Andelman looked around uncertainly. "Well, if that's the pleasure of this body . . ."

Maltzman quickly put it to a vote. "All those in favor of putting off consideration of the budget till next week, say Aye. All opposed, Nay. The Ayes have it."

When the meeting was adjourned shortly afterward, Maltzman signaled Mandell to wait for him. When the others had gone down the corridor out to the parking lot leaving the two alone in the room, Maltzman said, "I just wanted to tell you, Herb, that you did that absolutely perfect. That idea of yours explaining how it was against your principles as an accountant, that was"—he searched his mind for the right word—"that was sheer genius. And you see now why I wanted *you* to do it. If it had been one of the guys who's associated with me, the other side would have smelled a rat. This way, nothing." He winked and punched him playfully on the arm.

31

When the call came in Monday morning, Lanigan's
first inclination had been to send someone, Jennings
or McLure, or even Sergeant Holcombe. But the
weather was fine, a cool early November day, and it
occurred to him that he might himself enjoy a day
in Boston and, more particularly, some time away
from the office, even though it meant going home to
change from his uniform to civilian clothes, which
he considered more appropriate when he went outside his jurisdiction.

When he entered the lobby, the office building
automatically registered in his mind as second-rate.
It was an old building that had been spruced up
with a new self-service elevator and fake plastic
mahogany paneling. The renovation did not extend
to the upper floors, however. The corridors there
were covered with worn linoleum tile of brown and
yellow, which clashed with the bilious lime green of
the walls.

The office of Charles Sawyer, Attorney, was in
keeping with the rest of the building. There was the

same brown-and-yellow tile on the floor and the same lime-green walls. It was a small room with a single window facing another office building. Ranged along one wall were several chairs and a small round oak table on which were a number of old law journals. Seated at a small desk was a pleasant-faced gray-haired woman typing away rapidly. She stopped and looked up inquiringly when Lanigan entered.

"I'm Chief Lanigan of the—"

"Oh yes." And jerking her head toward a door beside her that was ajar, she said, "Go right in. He's not doing anything."

The inner office was somewhat larger, but also with one window. Against one wall there was a glassed-in bookcase with law books, and with files and papers and corporation seals on the lower shelves. A single visitor's chair stood in front of a large green metal desk. Lanigan assumed that when there was more than one client present, either the others had to stand or chairs were brought in from the outer office.

Behind the desk, his fingers laced over his belly, teetering back and forth in his swivel chair, was Charles Sawyer, a smiley man with a round head and small ears flattened against it as though stitched in place. His hair was gray and sparse.

"I'm Chief Lanigan of the Barnard's Crossing Police and—"

"You got anything in the way of identification?"

"Why sure." Lanigan reached for his wallet and flipped it open to show his badge.

The little smile, which Lanigan decided was

merely the way he held his mouth, broadened to show a real smile. "I have to be careful when it's criminal business," he said. "I once had a reporter try to pass himself off as one of the D.A.'s men." He raised his voice and called out, "Emily, when was it that reporter tried to bamboozle me?"

"Two years ago. The Blatz case," came the answer from the other room. Lanigan turned and saw that the door, which he had closed behind him on entering, had opened of itself and was standing ajar again.

"I don't get much criminal business," Sawyer informed him, "but I get some, and I've learned to be careful." He smiled again. "That's what you go to a lawyer for, isn't it? To have someone in your corner who knows how to be careful?"

"I guess so. Were you Ellsworth Jordon's lawyer?"

"Oh, off and on, now and again." He got up and circled his desk and closed the door, pushing it with his shoulder and turning the knob at the same time. This time it remained closed, and he came back to his place behind the desk. "I've complained to the management about that door, but you know how service is these days."

Lanigan smiled sympathetically.

"Not that I mind if Emily hears what we're saying. She knows everything that happens in this office. But someone else might come in while we're talking, another client . . ."

"Of course."

"I was away for the weekend—a little trip—so I didn't hear about Jordon until last night when there was that item about William Green. I try to cooperate with the police as much as I can. Got to, you know, since as a member of the bar I'm an officer of the court. But there didn't seem to be any sense in calling last night after eleven. I figured this morning would be soon enough."

"Oh, that's all right," Lanigan assured him.

"Then that's settled. Now to business." He rubbed his hands briskly. "Ellsworth Jordon came to see me a couple of months ago and asked me to draw up a will for him. Now while Ellsworth was meticulous about money and wouldn't take a dime that didn't belong to him, he also had a strong sense of *meum* and *tuum*. And in this matter the *tuum* was the government, federal and state." His little smile broadened again to show he was amused. "Quite indignant he was about inheritance taxes. He couldn't see why he should have to pay inheritance taxes where he'd already paid income taxes on the money when he earned it. And he wanted me to work out some plan, a trust fund maybe, that would keep the inheritance tax to a minimum, eliminating it altogether if possible. I suggested he might do better with a tax lawyer, but he insisted I do it, even if it involved my engaging the services of a specialist. So I proceeded on that basis. It involved considerable work on my part. There were various suggestions that I made that he took exception to. But finally I got in everything he wanted, or at least had been induced to accept."

"And who was the beneficiary?"

"Why, that's why I called you. It was that same

young man, William Green, Ellsworth's natural son. He was leaving it all to him."

Lanigan nodded slowly. "It explains Jordon inviting him to come and live with him. And yet when I questioned him the other night, he said Jordon was just an old friend of the family."

"The young man may very well think so," Sawyer said. "Jordon was sure he did not know."

"And Billy inherits it all?"

Sawyer shook his head. His smile expanded until it seemed to extend from ear to ear. There was even a gurgle, which Lanigan interpreted as laughter. "No, he gets nothing. Not a dime. My guess is it will all go to the commonwealth."

"But why not? Is there something wrong with the will?" asked Lanigan bewildered.

"There is no will. There is only my draft of the will. I sent it to Jordon a few days ago, and he sent it back with some suggestions for changes penciled in the margin. I got it Friday morning. It was never signed." This time he laughed out loud. "The best laid plans of mice and men, you know."

Lanigan looked at him curiously, wondering why he should take such pleasure in Jordon's plan having been thwarted. "You've known Jordon a long time?" he asked tentatively.

"Oh, yes," said Sawyer archly, "quite a long time."

"You didn't like him?"

Sawyer pursed his lips. "I don't think I disliked him. He rather amused me."

"Amused? Why amused?"

For answer Sawyer gestured at the room. "It

doesn't suggest a prosperous practice, does it? Well, it isn't. I think I'm a good lawyer, Mr. Lanigan, but attracting cases that involve large fees calls for a special talent that I'm afraid I don't have. However, I've always managed to make a living. Nothing spectacular, you understand, but a living. Now, if you're a millionaire like Ellsworth Jordon, why would you come to someone like me to draw up your will, especially when it means coming all the way to Boston from Barnard's Crossing?"

"Maybe he thought if he went to a local lawyer, word might get out about the provisions of the will," Lanigan suggested.

"Most unlikely, Mr. Lanigan, most unlikely, I assure you. Besides, there were other occasions over the years when he made use of my services, usually concerning large, spectacular purchases or sales of land. Never anything small or ordinary like the sale of a single houselot, and never to defend him in a law suit. And I'm sure he's been sued. A man like Ellsworth Jordon is apt to be."

"So what's the answer?"

"The answer, Mr. Lanigan, is Emily—" again a tilt of the head in the direction of the outer office. "Our acquaintance, Ellsworth and I and Emily, goes back to when we were in college. We were all at different schools, but we belonged to a social club called the Collegiates. He was pretty sweet on Emily, took her out a lot, and finally asked her to marry him." The smile broadened. "But she turned him down and married me. I'm quite sure, and Emily agrees, that each time the purpose of his coming here was to let us know how well he was doing. Asking me to draw up his will, of course, was to apprise her of the sum total of his success, and also to inform her that though he had never married, he was not unacquainted with conjugal bliss and was the father of a son."

"You mean he was still in love—with your wife?"

Sawyer shook his head. "I don't think he cared a rap for her. He barely spoke to her on the occasions when he came here. He was just determined to show her what a terrible mistake she had made in turning him down. Do you wonder, Mr. Lanigan, that I'm amused?" He peered at Lanigan through half-lidded eyes. "Interesting, at least, wouldn't you say?"

"Yeah, it's interesting all right. You know anything else about him that's—interesting? Anything that might help me?"

"Well, I might make a suggestion, speaking only as a lawyer, you understand. The fact that the boy had come to live with him suggests that he was still in contact with the boy's mother. And while he did not tell the boy that he was naming him his heir, he might have confided in the mother. It might be worthwhile inquiring where she was Friday night."

"She was in Europe."

"Are you sure?" he asked pointedly.

"Well . . ." A thought occurred to Lanigan, and he smiled. "Where were you—and Emily that Friday night?"

Sawyer began to laugh, a deep gurgling in the throat that sounded as if he were choking. Finally he stopped and wiped his eyes with a handkerchief. "Very good, Mr. Lanigan."

"Well, where were you?"

Sawyer's face showed annoyance. "We were right here, working late on that same blasted will to ready it for Saturday when he said he'd be in." He smiled again and purred, "No doubt the night watchman noted the time of our departure on his register."

32

It was Herb who opened the door to the sergeant. They had finished Sunday dinner. His mother had gone upstairs to her room for a nap, and while Molly was in the kitchen finishing the dishes—the division of labor between them called for him to wash and for her to wipe and put away—he had been in the living room reading the Sunday paper.

"Sergeant Holcombe," his visitor announced and showed his badge pinned in his wallet.

"What can I do for you, Sergeant?"

"Can I come in?"

Herb stood aside for him and motioned him to a chair.

"You're Mr. Mandell? You're up at the high school, aren't you?"

"That's right."

"You got my kid sister in bookkeeping."

From the kitchen, Molly called out, "What is it, Herb?"

"Just some school business," he called back.

The sergeant was embarrassed. "Oh, I didn't come to see you about my sister, Mr. Mandell. I wouldn't come to your house and on a Sunday. I'd go to the school. Chances are, I wouldn't go at all. I mean, it would be my dad who'd come to see you. It was Mrs. Mandell I came to see."

"What about?"

"Oh, it's just routine, Mr. Mandell. Could I see her for a minute. Could you ask her—"

But it was unnecessary, for Molly had finished with the dishes and had come into the living room. She looked questioningly at the sergeant.

"It's just a matter of routine," he apologized. "I've got some questions—"

"Of course, Sergeant." She seated herself beside Herb on the sofa and waited as the sergeant flipped pages of a notebook to a clean page.

"It's about this business Friday night. Mr. Gore said he stopped at a gas station on the road to Boston and phoned you—"

"You mean they suspect Mr. Gore?" she asked indignantly.

"Oh no. It's just that the chief wants everything neat and tidy. This is a pretty important case, and everything has to be just so. I guess what he's after mostly right now is pinning down the exact time when—well, when it happened. Now Mr. Gore don't remember what time it was when he stopped at the gas station, but he remembers calling you. And the attendant at the gas station don't remember what time it was but he remembers Mr. Gore making the call, mostly because the outside pay station was out of order and he used the one in the office. So I thought maybe you might remember." He looked at her hopefully, pencil poised over his notebook. "He did call you, didn't he?"

"Oh yes, he called all right," she said, "and I remember what time it was, too. It was half past eight."

The sergeant wrote happily in his notebook and then looked up. "You're very sure of the time, Miss. How can you be so sure?"

"Because I looked at my watch, of course."

"And how did you happen to do that? Did he ask what time it was?"

"Oh no. I was working on a report for the bank. The reason for Mr. Gore's call was to see how I was getting on. I was practically finished, and I looked at my watch to see about how soon I would be done."

The sergeant shook his head in wonder. "For the bank, you say. I guess this talk about bankers' hours is just a lot of talk."

She smiled. "I very frequently take work home, and I know Mr. Gore does almost every night. Most people at the bank do, that is, the executives."

He digested this with a slow nodding of the head.

"So he called and asked you how you were getting on and you looked at your watch and said you were almost finished."

"That's right."

"And it was half past eight by your watch?"

"M-hmm."

He smiled as he rose to go. "And did you? Did you get it done?"

She smiled back at him. "I did, Sergeant."

The sergeant read over what he had written. "Anything else you can tell me, Mrs. Mandell?"

"Like what?"

"Oh, anything that might have bearing on this business."

She hesitated and then shook her head slowly.

A thought occurred to him. "The chief may want me to type this out and then have you sign it," he said.

"Then I'll sign it, of course."

As Mandell showed him to the door, the sergeant said, "My sister, the one who's taking your course, she likes it."

"Glad to hear it," said Mandell. "What did you say her name was?"

"Same as mine. Holcombe. Doris Holcombe."

"Oh yes. Tall, blond girl. She's a good student."

"I'll tell her you said so, Mr. Mandell."

"You do that, Sergeant."

33

The voice on the telephone was excited and impatient. "Rabbi Small? I'd like to see you about something. It's terribly important. Do you have office hours?"

"If it's terribly important, my office hours are twenty-four hours a day. Whom am I talking to?"

"You don't know me. My name is Segal. It's about—well, I'd rather not say over the phone. If you'd let me know when I can come—"

"I'm free for the evening, Mr. Segal. You can come over anytime. Right now, if you like."

"I'm on my way, Rabbi."

Twenty minutes later as they shook hands, Rabbi Small said, "I've heard about you, Mr. Segal."

"Oh? You take a flyer in the stock market?" And as the rabbi smiled in obvious negation, "Oh, I know. The real estate man, Mr. Maltzman, spoke to you. He said he was going to. He hasn't got back to me yet. Is it all right?"

"I'm sure we'd all like to have you join our

temple, Mr. Segal. There's no special ceremony necessary."

"But the Bar Mitzvah—"

"You were Bar Mitzvah when you reached the age of thirteen, whether you had a ceremony or didn't. It just means that by our law you are of age." He went on to explain the significance of the ceremony and how it had developed to its present proportion. Segal listened, but with no great interest.

"Good," he said when the rabbi finished. "You know after I agreed to do it, I got to thinking about it. I was prepared to go through with it, but it occurred to me that it might be kind of embarrassing. I'm certainly glad I don't have to."

"Is that what you wanted to see me about, Mr. Segal?"

"Oh no, nothing to do with your temple. It's about this William Green who's involved in the murder. Have you been following it at all?"

"I read the local papers, and I listen to the news broadcasts."

"You see, Rabbi, I'm living in the hotel for the time being, and I take my meals there, too. You can't help overhearing conversation, and that's all they're talking about. The general consensus seems to be that this William Green did it. I gather that he's new in town and that he was just visiting with the man who was murdered. And there seems to be some suggestion that the young man is somewhat strange, that he has no friends and keeps to himself. I heard one man say that the proof he was guilty was that the police were keeping him under wraps.

I guess there was some truth to that, because in one newspaper story, it said they were unable to contact him, and in the news broadcast this evening, it said he was unavailable for questioning by the reporter. Then he went on to say he was the son of Hester Grimes, well-known nightclub and TV entertainer. That brought me up sharp, Rabbi, because I know Hester Grimes."

"And you mean he isn't her son?"

"Oh, I don't know about that. I mean, I don't know her that well. What I'm trying to say . . . Look here, I get asked to serve on lots of committees for civic campaigns and charity drives. It isn't that I'm more charitable or civic-minded than the next fellow, but while the rationale is that I'm supposed to have proven administrative and executive ability, the main reason is that it's presumed I'll make a large contribution to the cause and induce my wealthy friends to do the same. Well, last year I was involved in a charity bazaar where we got a lot of show people to come—to do a benefit. And when they come, the members of the committee are expected to entertain them, take them to dinner, have them to the house, the works, because they're not geting paid, you see. Although some of them do. Anyway, I drew this Hester Grimes. I arranged to have her picked up at the airport and brought to our hotel. Then we had dinner, and after her stint at the bazaar, we had her come back to our place. She is a delightful, charming woman, and we sat around and talked, and she told us quite a bit about herself. Grimes is her stage name, Rabbi. Her real name is Green."

"Then that accounts for—"

"Her original name is Esther Green. She's a Jewish girl, Rabbi."

The rabbi pursed his lips and considered. He was silent for quite some time as Segal waited expectantly. Then he said quietly, "What is it you would like me to do, Mr. Segal?"

"Well, Rabbi, here's this young man, just a kid, eighteen or nineteen years old, who is new in town, has no friends, and his mother is somewhere in Europe and probably doesn't know anything about this. Now I'm new here and I don't know this town, but I know how administrators work. They don't go looking for trouble, and when it comes, they try to get rid of it as soon as possible, the easiest way. I know if he's charged, he'll be represented by a lawyer, maybe one that the court appoints, but . . . look, I don't care how fair and decent the policemen or the town fathers are, I know that a young immature boy will be treated like a grown man, and a friendless stranger won't get the same kind of treatment that a resident of the town with family and friends would get. I thought you, as rabbi of the community, and since it's a Jewish boy, you could claim some standing. I mean, even if I got him a lawyer, he couldn't just enter the case and say he's representing William Green where he hadn't asked for him. You see?"

"All right. All right, Mr. Segal. I'll arrange to see William Green and let him know, well, that he's not alone."

34

Henry Maltzman drummed his fingers impatiently on the desktop. "If you want to sell your house, Joe, you'll fix it up. Have it painted—"

"Painted?" Krasker was aghast. "That will cost me a thousand, fifteen hundred bucks, maybe more."

"So what? I'll get you another five thousand for it."

"Will you give me that in writing?"

"Yeah. That'll be the day. Look, Joe, get this through your head. Houses aren't bought; they're sold. And if you want to sell them, they've got to be attractive. I took a party out to see your place last week, and he pulls out a jackknife and starts jabbing it into the doorframe where the paint is all bubbled and chipped. I asked him what he was doing, and he said he wanted to see if the wood was rotted. Get the point? When a place is run down, the customer always thinks it's worse than it is. Now, it doesn't have to cost you all that much to spruce it up. It doesn't have to be an A number one job, like if you were doing it for yourself. I got a couple of Greek boys that will slap some paint on it for cheap, and it will look real good."

Krasker finally let himself be convinced. "All right, let them come down and give me an estimate."

Maltzman leaned back in his chair and smiled his satisfaction. "I'll talk to them personally and tell them I want them to give you the best price they can. I throw a lot of work their way, and they're good boys. Now, how about Sunday? I'm depending on you to come through for me."

Krasker squirmed uncomfortably in his seat and focused his eyes on the desktop. It was not easy to disagree with Henry Maltzman. "I don't know, Henry," he said. "I've been thinking about it a lot. It seems a terrible thing to fire a rabbi, especially where he hasn't done anything."

"That's why, because he hasn't done anything," Maltzman answered quickly. "I've proposed I don't know how many ideas that would build up the temple, increase the membership, and instead of going along, or even remaining neutral, he's actually bucked me, said he wouldn't permit it, or that it was against religion or something. And practically every other president has had the same experience with him. Besides, we're not firing him. We're just voting not to re-hire him."

"What's the difference?"

"Cummon, Joe! I checked into this, you know. When he first came, he was given a one-year contract, like a trial. Then he was given a five-year contract. Then a few years back, he was offered a life contract, and he turned it down. He wanted it only for one year, to be renewed each year. Now what does that mean? It means he wants to be free to leave. So each time his contract expires, it's like a new deal, like when a lease expires. I'm not suggesting we send him a letter saying he has to leave, or that we're getting another rabbi. I just want for the secretary to send him a letter saying, 'Dear Rabbi, the board voted eight to seven or ten to five or whatever it is against renewing your contract.' Now that doesn't mean he's fired. It means he's like a tenant at will. He would stay on for years maybe. It's just that he won't have a contract."

"Would we pay him?"

"Oh sure. If he does the work, we've got to. We'd pay him the way we pay Stanley, the janitor. *He* doesn't have a contract."

Krasker nodded. "All right, so he's a tenant at will. But like you said, he could stay on for years. How does that help you? You want him out. And I don't mind admitting, I'd rather have somebody else. But how does it help, if he's still here even though he doesn't have a contract?"

"It wouldn't—much," Maltzman admitted. "Although I think it would help some. Stands to reason, if the guy has no contract, he can be fired anytime. Okay, so say something happens where he interferes with what we on the board want to do. We can always say, 'If you don't like it, Rabbi, pick up your marbles and go somewhere else.' But it's my hunch it won't happen that way. I'm banking that as soon as he gets the letter from the secretary, he'll sit down and write a letter of resignation.

That's the way I figure it." He smiled. "And we'll send him a letter right back, accepting his resignation."

"Well . . ."

"I'm counting on you, Joe."

"Well, what happens if we take a vote and the rabbi wins?"

Maltzman shrugged his shoulders. "Nothing. We're back at square one. The secretary writes him a letter telling him that the board voted to renew his contract, and—"

"No," Krasker shook his head impatiently. "It's bound to get back to the rabbi who voted against him. And that could be embarrassing if you have to come to him about your kid's Bar Mitzvah, or daughter's wedding."

"Sure, I've thought of that. So we'll vote by secret ballot. The votes go to the secretary to count. If the rabbi wins, he just announces it. If the rabbi loses, if there's a little fuss, he announces the score. He doesn't name names because you don't sign your ballot."

"Well, how does it look?"

"It looks close, Joe. Damn close. I don't mind admitting, I'm counting on you. I went over it yesterday with Bill Shaefer. You do his accounting, don't you?"

"Oh, yeah, I've had his account for years."

"Well, I went over each and every name, and with yours we have eight, which is just enough. Bill was sure you'd go along, but I said I wanted to hear it from you myself, personal. How about it, Joe? Can I count on you?"

The reference to Bill Shaefer, one of the bigger accounts, was not lost on Krasker. "Oh sure, Henry. It's just that I wanted to know all the ins and outs. Know what I mean?"

"Oh, sure. I don't blame you." He reached for a file on his desk.

But Krasker was reluctant to leave. "What you said at the meeting Sunday, about this guy Jordon, was it true? About him being an anti-Semite?"

"It's true all right."

"Because I've got this account, a doctor, and we were talking about the murder, and he was saying what a nice guy Jordon was, and how he always made a big contribution to the Hospital Fund."

"So what? He also probably liked dogs, and was kind to children. Hitler liked dogs, too, and music. But he didn't like us. One thing has nothing to do with the other."

"Well, I just thought you'd like to know."

35

Anne Kaufman was a silversmith with a shop in town. It was just a hole-in-the-wall sort of place with a workroom in back, where she sat on a high stool at her bench making the rings, pendants, earrings, and cuff links that she sold in the tiny store. When the doorbell jangled, she would dismount from her stool and come out front to wait on trade.

In spite of the difference in their ages—her children were already in high school—Anne and Molly Mandell were close friends. Molly had used her good offices at the bank to help her get the loan that had enabled her to set up the shop in the first place, and she was grateful. And since they were both downtown in the business district most of the day, they saw each other frequently, which was why Molly had offered to speak to her about Maltzman's plan.

When Anne called to ask if she had made plans for lunch, it seemed like a good opportunity.

"No, Anne. I thought I'd get a sandwich at Creighton's. What did you have in mind?"

"I thought maybe you could get a sandwich at the deli and bring it here, and I'd make some coffee on the hot plate."

"Sounds good to me. See you around noon."

When she arrived a few minutes after twelve, Mrs. Kaufman locked the door and hung up the Back at One O'clock sign in the window. She offered her visitor the old wicker arm chair in which she occasionally relaxed, while she herself perched on her work stool. She poured coffee, and then as Molly unwrapped her sandwich, she said. "Did you know this Ellsworth Jordon? The paper said he was a director in the bank."

"Oh, I knew him all right," Molly said grimly. "He'd come in almost every day. Not because he was a director, but because he had nothing else to do. The other directors, you don't see them from one month to the next."

"Was he—you know—anti-Semitic?"

"He was a dirty old man. That's what he was." She smiled sourly. "I don't know if he was anti-Semitic or not. All I know is that he kept making passes at me and he knew I was Jewish."

"He did? What kind of—"

"Oh, you know, the usual accidental-on-purpose pat on the fanny."

"And didn't you ever tell your boss?"

"I mentioned it once, but he was so upset, I thought I'd handle it myself."

"What did you do?"

"Oh, the next time he did it, I was prepared for him. Instead of kind of jumping the way you naturally would, I didn't move, but I gave him a sharp jab with my elbow."

"And what did he do?"

She laughed. "*He* jumped—and had a coughing fit." She munched on her sandwich, and then asked, "Why are you so interested in Jordon?"

"Well—" Mrs. Kaufman glanced up at the angled mirror on the wall which gave her a view of the front door. "This morning I was sitting right here, working like always. The door opened and I looked up and saw it was these two old biddies who keep coming in and never buying anything. So I didn't hurry to come out. I could hear them talking, though, and one of them said that everybody knew it was the Jews that did it because he was 'so down on them.' That was the expression she used. That he had tried to arrange a secret agreement not to sell them property on the Point and that's why they did it. Then I coughed, or cleared my throat, and I suppose they realized that if they could hear me, I might be able to hear them because I saw in the mirror one of them put her finger to her lips and nod toward the shop here."

"Hm, that's interesting. So what did you do?"

"I didn't do anything," said Mrs. Kaufman. "After a while, I came out. One of them asked if she could see a certain piece I had in the showcase, and I told her it was already sold and the customer was coming in tomorrow to pick it up. Maybe they sensed they weren't welcome. Anyway, they didn't ask to see anything else. They left. And then I called you."

"You bothered?" asked Molly.

"A little," Anne admitted.

"You can't get upset over everything that people say," Molly said, trying to reassure her.

"But if they're saying it, maybe others are, too."

"So what can we do?"

"I think we ought to do something," Anne insisted. "Maybe the rabbi could—"

"Rabbi Small? You think you'll get him off his duff to take action on anything?"

"Well . . ."

"Listen, Anne, don't expect Rabbi Small to do a damn thing about anything. He actually said so when Henry Maltzman came to see him about equality for women in the service. According to him, one change produces other changes, and some of them could be bad, so he wasn't going to take any chances. Now I ask you."

"Well, that has to do with religion, but this is a matter of—of—"

"Of law? Of politics? All right. Last week, the selectmen voted to reconsider their approval of traffic lights near the temple. Come to think of it, that was some of Ellsworth Jordon's dirty work. Well, did Rabbi Small do anything about it? Did he so much as write a letter to the press protesting the action of the selectmen?"

"You don't know. He may have done something, or—"

Molly's eyes danced with amusement. "Oh, you think maybe it was Rabbi Small who killed Jordon?"

"Molly! What a thing to say! I mean, he might have spoken to the selectmen, or is planning to."

Molly shook her head. "If it's action you're looking for, don't expect it from Rabbi Small. We've got to make up our mind to that. He's good at telling us all the things we can't do, and what the Talmud says about it, but when it comes to taking positive action, forget it."

"Then what can we do?"

"Get another rabbi," said Molly promptly.

"How? And how can you be sure the next one will be any better?"

"We won't take one unless he has a proven track record. As to how . . ." Molly then proceeded to explain Maltzman's plan.

They discussed it at length. Anne raised objections, pointed out problems and difficulties. But when Molly left and returned to her office, she was able to phone Maltzman that her friend had agreed.

36

"He's on Children's Island," said Chief Lanigan. "What's your business with him?"

"What's he doing on the island?" asked Rabbi Small.

"Living there. Working there. The first night he came back, he slept in one of the cells right here at the stationhouse. But I couldn't have him stay on where he hasn't been charged. And I couldn't have him go back to Jordon's house, even if he had wanted to. We've got the house sealed up. He didn't want to go back to working in the bank just yet. Thought he might be pestered by people asking him a lot of questions. Then I thought of the Hegertys. They live on the island until about Thanksgiving, fixing up, painting, putting up shutters on the cabins against the winter. They can use any help they can get. So I put it up to them, and the boy seemed willing, even interested, so it was arranged."

"What's his status? He's not under arrest—"

"No, he hasn't been charged. The D.A. doesn't

think we have any real evidence against him. On the other hand, we do want him around for a while. This seems an ideal arrangement."

"Does he have a lawyer? Has his mother been notified?"

"What's he need a lawyer for? He hasn't been charged, I tell you. As for his mother, he doesn't want her to know. Thinks she might come running home, if she did. Well, he's eighteen, so he's of age, so . . ."

"How can I get to see him?" asked the rabbi.

Lanigan smiled. He tilted back in his chair and interlaced his fingers over his belly. "Well, if you had a boat, I suppose you could row out there. Or you could hire somebody to take you out there in a launch. Or I could have the police harbor boat take you out there. But I doubt if I would since I don't rightly see that you have any concern in the matter."

Rabbi Small related the gist of his conversation with Ben Segal. "So, since his mother is Jewish, the boy is Jewish, and as the only rabbi in town—"

"Doesn't it depend on the father?"

"With us, it's the mother," said the rabbi.

"Do you know the father?"

The rabbi shook his head.

Lanigan smiled. "Suppose I told you it was Ellsworth Jordon?"

If he expected to shock the rabbi with the revelation, he was disappointed. "It explains how he happened to be living there, doesn't it? It doesn't surprise me too much."

"It might explain Jordon's anti-Semitism," mused

Lanigan. "I mean, if he were very much in love with this Hester Grimes, or Esther Green, and she turned him down."

"On the other hand," the rabbi suggested, "she might have turned him down because he was anti-Semitic."

"Also possible," Lanigan admitted. "You might be interested to know that Jordon was planning on making Billy his heir."

"The young man told you this?"

"No, I got that from Jordon's lawyer. According to Billy, Jordon was just an old friend of the family. Either he doesn't know Jordon was his father or he isn't saying." He eyed the rabbi speculatively. "If you see him, will you tell him?"

The rabbi's face was bland as he asked, "Are you hinting that you'd like me to?"

Lanigan showed vast unconcern. "It might be interesting."

The rabbi smiled and shook his head. "That's for his mother to do if she wants to. If she's kept his paternity secret all these years, she presumably had reason, and it's not for me to come blundering in. No, I just want to talk to him."

"Why?"

"Because it's my job," the rabbi answered promptly. "He's alone, without family or friends, and he's in trouble. I—"

"What makes you think he's in trouble? He hasn't been charged."

"Because you said there wasn't any real evidence against him. But that suggests that he is a suspect.

And while you don't have evidence now, you are probably looking for it, and—"

"We're looking for all kinds of evidence," objected Lanigan. "No matter which way it points."

"Sure, and if you find any that points his way, the district attorney will charge him, and since it's a murder, he'll go to jail while his court-appointed lawyer, an overworked public defender, gets a series of postponements in an effort to find time to prepare his defense. And in the meantime, the boy will be in jail. All I'm asking for is the chance to see him and talk to him and get to know him. Even more, to get him to know me, so that if anything untoward happens, he can call on me and, through me, on the Jewish community here. Anything wrong with that? Now, how do I go about hiring a launch?"

"Oh hell, I'll have the police launch take you out."

37

"I don't think I've ever met a Rabbi before," said Billy. Then with some concern, "Did you come out so that you could pray for me?"

They were sitting on the porch of one of the camp cabins. He sat on the top step, his back against the newel-post, dressed in stained coveralls several sizes too big for him, while the rabbi sat on the railing, the collar of his topcoat turned up against the breeze coming from the water.

"I hadn't planned to," said Rabbi Small, looking off toward the tiny dock against which the police harbor boat that had brought him bumped gently with every wave. The policeman who operated the craft, in a heavy turtleneck sweater, instead of his uniform blouse, lay on his back on the dock, his cap over his face, basking in the rays of the afternoon sun. He rolled over and waved to the rabbi, who waved back. He turned to face the young man again. "Of course, if you'd like me to—"

"Oh no. I mean, I don't care if you do or not." Then lest he appear ungracious, he said, "I mean that if you came out here to pray for me, it would mean that I was in trouble, wouldn't it? Am I?"

"I don't know," said the rabbi. "I came because I heard you were a Jew, and I'm the rabbi here."

"Oh, but I'm not that kind of Jew."

"No? What kind are you?"

"Well, I'm one because my mother is. You know, it's what you're born. My mother's agent, Sol Katz, he's always talking about 'We Jews,' so I asked my mother and she explained that there were two kinds—like Sol, who believed in the Jewish religion, and like us who didn't believe in it but were Jews because we happened to be born Jews. But we were really just Americans. That's right, isn't it?"

"It's one way of looking at it," the rabbi admitted. "Is that what Mr. Jordon thought, too?"

"Oh, we never talked about anything like that."

"No? What did you talk about?"

The young man laughed. "Money, mostly. He was always talking about stocks and bonds and how you figure out if they're good stocks to buy, you know, by the financial statement. And land, and houses, and how you go about buying what's going to increase in value. His idea was that money was important because if you had enough of it, you could be independent. And if you were independent, you could say anything that came into your mind. And if you could say anything, you could think anything—"

"Surely, it was the other way around, wasn't it?"

"No," Billy insisted. "That's the way he put it. If you felt you could say anything, then you could think any way you wanted to. But if you didn't feel you could say whatever came into your head, then you tended not to think of things."

"I see. And did you like him?"

"Sure I liked him. And I think he liked me. Course, he didn't ever say so, because——well, because that kind of thing he wouldn't say to your face." He canted his head to one side as he considered. "He was a funny kind of guy. Sometimes he'd seem awfully mean, but you couldn't tell. Like, he'd say nasty things to Martha sometimes, and she'd flare back at him. And he'd just laugh. Afterward, he would explain that he did it to let her know she was like part of the family, and not just a servant. You understand?"

"I think so."

"Some things he was very particular about," the young man went on, "like time, for instance, because he said each person had just so much of it and no more. He had this clock on the mantelpiece in the living room, and he'd check it by the radio time signals every day. And if you were late to dinner, say, even if it was only a couple of minutes, he'd glare at you and point at it without saying a word. But you could see he was angry.

"And money. Down to the last penny. Like Martha did the shopping. He'd give her money, and then at the end of the week, she'd give him the tapes from the supermarket, or the other stores, and whatever money was left. And if she was short, even if it was only like three cents, he'd tell her and make her give it to him. And once, when it was the other way, and he didn't happen to have any change on him, she said it was all right, and that made him angry. He said, 'It's not all right,' and went off to his bedroom and fished in his bureau drawer and got the necessary few coins."

"What did he call you?" asked the rabbi.

"He called me Billy mostly. But sometimes when he was a little annoyed with me, he'd call me Sir."

"And when he was greatly annoyed with you?" asked the rabbi, smiling.

"Then he didn't call me anything," said the young man promptly. "He just didn't talk to me. Of course, when he got real wrathy, he'd send me to my room. And if it blew his mind, like—like the other night, he'd lock me in."

"And how did you feel about that?"

"Well, the first time it happened, it was because I hadn't written to my mother, and he'd promised her I would. He got all red and worked up and I was afraid he might have a heart attack. He had heart trouble, you know. So I just went into my room. But I was real kind of upset, being treated like a little kid like that. So I thought, what the hell—oh, I'm sorry."

"That's all right," the rabbi said. "Everybody uses the expression these days."

"Well, anyway, I thought, why should I stay here? So I just raised the window and split. See, I promised Mr. Gore I'd help him with his silver stuff, and I didn't want to disappoint him. And I came back the same way, but if he heard me, he didn't let on. Then before he went to bed, I heard him turning the key in the lock. So that meant he knew I'd been out. And the next morning it was as though nothing happened. And that's the way it was every time after that." He began to laugh. "Once he kept me locked up for three days, and I went to the bank every day through the window. He even came into the bank one day, and of course he saw me, but he acted as though I wasn't there." He laughed again, joyously. "That was real funny. I'd get home from the bank, and there was my dinner in my room. See, it was like a game between us. I figured out, he couldn't hit me, or withhold my allowance, or anything like that. And I guess he was afraid to yell at me, maybe on account of his heart, or maybe because it might lead to a real fight where we'd say things that—well, that we'd be sorry for."

"Then why did you run off to New York if it were just a sort of game?" asked the rabbi, curious.

The young man sobered. "That was different. That was in front of Mr. Gore. He knew about my going out the window because I told him. It was like a joke. But to do it right in front of him like that. I thought I'd never be able to face him again. You understand?"

"I think so. Tell me, have you informed your mother about—about what happened?"

The young man shook his head.

"Don't you think you ought to, considering that he was an old friend of hers?"

"What for? She might feel she had to come back to take care of me. Well, I'm all right. And she's going great over there, so why should she cancel?"

The rabbi nodded. He jumped off his perch on the railing and said, "I've got to be going now, but if you come into town, I'd like you to come and see me."

"Sure, why not? Any special reason?"

"No-o, but if you should need any help . . ."

"What kind of help?"

The rabbi smiled. "Any kind at all."

38

Wednesday evenings, the Board of Selectmen met, and the rabbi had made a note of it on his calendar. Shortly after dinner, he called Lanigan at the stationhouse to ask if he were planning to attend.

"I'm expected to be present at the selectmen's meetings, and I usually go unless something special has come up. You're concerned about the traffic light business? How about dropping over here so we can plan our strategy?"

"I'll be right over."

"How does it look?" the rabbi asked eagerly as soon as he was seated in the chief's office some fifteen minutes later.

"I had a brainstorm right after you called," Lanigan said. "Those fellows on the board are pretty considerate of each other. I've seen it happen any number of times. One of them asks for reconsideration of some motion, and the others go along as a matter of courtesy. Then, if he withdraws his request for reconsideration, they go along with that, too. So I called Albert Megrim. My idea was that maybe we could convince him to withdraw the request he made last week."

"And?"

"He wasn't in. I spoke to his wife. She says he doesn't come home for dinner Wednesdays. He goes to the Agathon and eats there and then goes on to the meeting. So I thought we'd go and see him at the Agathon."

"You mean both of us?"

Lanigan looked at him quizzically. "Does it bother you going there? Because it's the same for me as it is for you. They don't have Catholics any more than they have Jews."

"Well, we're going there on business."

"That's the way I feel about it," said Lanigan. "I've been invited there to dinner on occasion, and I've always made some excuse. But as you say, this is business."

As they drove, Lanigan explained the reason for his strategy. "Chances are, if we let matters take their natural course, we'd probably come out ahead anyway. But you can never tell. The other night, Sturgis was sounding off at the Republican Club about how important it was for the town to hold down expenditures. He might vote against it just because it costs money, and he might feel he has to be consistent. And Cunningham, who is on a pension, is always worrying about the tax rate. Then Megrim might vote against it just to be consistent with his having asked for reconsideration. And there you have a majority, and we'd be sunk."

"And this way?"

"This way, well, if we can persuade Megrim to withdraw his motion to reconsider, and if the rest go along and permit him to, then we're back to the original vote to install the traffic lights."

At the club, the steward informed them that Megrim was in the bar. "Down the corridor as far as you can go, and it's the door to the left."

Only Albert Megrim and Dr. Springhurst were present when they entered the room, and the select-man rose when he saw them. "I've been expecting you, Hugh," he said. In response to Lanigan's in-quiring look, he explained, "I called home a little while ago, and Alice told me you'd called and were coming out. Rabbi Small? I've seen you around, but I don't think we've ever met. Do you know Dr. Springhurst?"

"I know Rabbi Small," said the elderly minister.

"We met at the Ministers' Conference," said the rabbi.

"We came about the traffic light business, Al," said Lanigan when they were seated.

"I figured as much when you brought the rabbi with you," said Megrim. "Let's see, I guess it comes up tonight. What do you want?"

"Well, after you voted for it a couple of weeks back, you asked for reconsideration last week," said Lanigan. "I figured it was because Ellsworth Jor-don asked you to."

"That's right. He was an abutter, and he hadn't been notified."

"Yeah, but he's not concerned anymore," said Lanigan brutally.

"You want me to vote against it, when I was the one that asked for reconsideration?"

"Why not? You asked for reconsideration after you voted for it. But I don't see why you have to vote at all. Why can't you just withdraw your motion to reconsider?"

"Because the board already voted to reconsider," Megrim said.

"So what? They voted it because you asked them to, as a courtesy to a member of the board. If you said you'd like to withdraw your motion to reconsider, would any of them object?"

"Well, maybe not."

"What's it all about?" asked Dr. Springhurst.

Megrim explained, and Lanigan added, "My interest is that it would save me posting a man there every day."

"And what was Jordon's objection?" asked the doctor.

"As an abutter, he's supposed to be notified," Megrim said, "and he didn't receive notification. He was pretty indignant about it. Claimed the board was high-handed. So I asked for reconsideration. I don't even know if he objected to the traffic lights down at the temple. He was just sore that he hadn't been informed."

"Oh, I think he probably did," said Dr. Springhurst. "I think his objection was that the temple would be helped by the arrangement."

"What makes you think so?" asked the rabbi.

"I'm quite convinced of it," said Dr. Springhurst.

"Ellsworth Jordon was a lonely old man without friends or family. He'd come here to the bar about once a week or so. Why here? Because in a bar, you can sit around and talk with anyone informally. You'd never see him in the dining room, or anywhere else in the club. Just here. In a bar you can talk freely and say the most outrageous things and be indulged. If it's quite bad, people tend to assume you're in your cups and they tolerate it." He smiled wanly. "Maybe that's why I come here, too. Anyway, I remember a little while ago, he was here when we were talking about admitting to membership this Ben Segal who has taken over the Rohrbough Corporation. Ellsworth said he would blackball him because he was a Jew, although it was fairly obvious that those around the table at the time were favorably disposed to admitting him. It's true we don't have any of your people on our rolls, Rabbi, but then I don't believe there have ever been any applications from them. The curious thing is that the one who sponsored Segal was Larry Gore, who is kin to Jordon, I understand."

"Was Gore here when he said it?" Lanigan asked.

"Oh no." Dr. Springhurst shook his head. "Occasionally, Gore would bring him and then call for him here to take him home. Ellsworth didn't like to drive at night. But Gore never stayed. He would immediately go down to the pistol range and spend time there. He's quite rabid on shooting, I understand. Club champion, I believe."

"That's right. Larry doesn't drink," said Megrim.

"I remember that night when Jordon sounded off on Segal and your people in general. Sounded a little crazy to me, to tell the truth. Said he hated them because all Jews had become Christians, or some such nonsense. And I'd heard him at other times, too. He'd make little digs, sly remarks. All right, I'll go along. I'll ask the boys to let me withdraw my motion." A thought crossed his mind, and he looked curiously at Rabbi Small. "I suppose from your point of view Jordon's death was punishment from on high for his attitude toward your kind."

"Oh no," said the rabbi quickly. "I'd hate to think so."

Megrim opened his eyes wide. "You would?"

"Naturally," said the rabbi. "Because the corollary would be that either any wicked person who was alive and prosperous was not really wicked or that God was unaware of his actions."

Dr. Springhurst chuckled. "Ah, then you believe as we do that the wicked are punished after death."

"No-o, we don't believe that either," said the rabbi. "That would mean depriving men of free will. We feel that virtue is its own reward, and evil carries with it its own punishment."

"But if he's healthy and prosperous and happy," Lanigan objected.

"But he is diminished. He's less than he was by virtue of his sin. It's like a speck of dust on a fine mechanism. It doesn't stop it, but it prevents it from functioning with the accuracy that was its original potential. And every additional sin or wickedness decreases the potential of the machine still more."

"And a good deed is like a spot of oil on the mechanism?" Dr. Springhurst suggested.

"Something like that."

Megrim glanced at his watch and rose. "We better get going if I want to get to the meeting on time."

"Just a minute, Albert," said Dr. Springhurst. "I'd like to ask the rabbi what he meant when he said that punishment and reward after death deprived man of free will?"

The rabbi, who with Lanigan had also risen, paused and said, "Well, I suppose it depends on what you mean by free will."

"Why freedom of choice, of course. The right to choose—"

"Between bread and toast?" the rabbi challenged. "Between turning right or left at a crossing? The lower animals have that kind of free will. For man, free will means the freedom to choose to do something he knows is wrong, wicked, evil, for some immediate material advantage. But that calls for a fair chance of not being discovered and punished. Would anyone steal if he were surrounded by policemen and certain of arrest and punishment? And on the other hand, what virtue is there in a good deed if the reward is certain? Since God is presumably all-seeing and all-knowing, no transgression goes undetected, and no good deed fails to be noted. So what kind of free will is that? How does it differ from the free will of the laboratory rat that is rewarded by food if he goes down one path of a maze and is given an electric shock if he goes down another?"

"Then what happens after death according to your people?"

The rabbi smiled. "We don't pretend to know."

Dr. Springhurst looked bemused. "That's a very interesting point of view." He rose and held out his hand to Rabbi Small. "Tell me, do you take a drink occasionally? Or is it against your principles, or your religion?"

"No, I drink on occasion. In fact, it is enjoined us every Sabbath and most of our holidays."

"Then would you do me the honor of coming down here some evening and having a drink with me?"

"I'd be happy to, Doctor."

39

Although Rabbi Small preferred working at home, on Thursdays he made use of the rabbi's study in the temple, because on that day the cleaning woman came to help Miriam ready the house for the approaching Sabbath, and the whine of the vacuum cleaner and the odor of furniture waxes and polishes made concentration all but impossible.

He had no sooner entered, doffed his topcoat and seated himself behind the desk, when there was a knock at the door, and before he could answer, it opened and Morton Brooks, the principal of the religious school, entered. He was a flamboyant youngish man of roughly the rabbi's age, that is, in his early forties. Because he had once been a bookkeeper in a Yiddish theater in New York, and had occasionally been given a walk-on part to save the cost of another actor's salary, he considered himself essentially of the theater and was presumably merely marking time while waiting for a call from an agent to return to it. He was dressed very modishly in a leisure suit with flared trousers and a fancy shirt, open at the throat. His neck was encircled by a colorful kerchief, negligently knotted at the side.

"Why do you knock, when you don't wait until you're invited in?" asked the rabbi petulantly.

"Why? I saw you from the end of the corridor, so I knew you were alone."

"Then why do you bother to knock?"

Brooks perched unceremoniously on the corner of the desk, crossed his legs and said, "Oh, just to give you a chance to get dignified and stuffy."

The rabbi smiled and tilted back in his chair. "All right, I'm as dignified and stuffy as I'm likely to get. Anything special?"

"I came to ask you about the decision of the selectmen on the traffic lights. They met last night, didn't they?"

"I'm sure they did."

"Then you didn't go? Look, David, that was important. You should have been there."

"Oh, I did better than that," said the rabbi with quiet satisfaction. "Before the meeting I went to see Albert Megrim, the man who asked for reconsideration, and he agreed to withdraw his motion."

"You did?" He looked at the rabbi with a new appreciation. "How'd you happen to do that?"

"Oh, it was Chief Lanigan's idea. The police are as interested in getting those lights as we are. We decided it would be best if I didn't go to the meeting so that Megrim's request would be regarded as a straight parliamentary procedure."

The phone rang. It was Henry Maltzman. "I called your house, Rabbi, and you weren't home." The tone was accusing.

"No, I'm here."

"I just wanted to let you know that the board of selectmen agreed to go ahead with the traffic lights."

"Oh, that's good news."

"I expected to see you at the meeting, Rabbi. It's your job."

"Well, I—"

"However, it worked out all right. I spoke to Megrim just before the meeting started, and he agreed to withdraw his motion."

"Well, that's fine."

"Just wanted to let you know."

When the rabbi hung up, Brooks, who had been able to hear both sides of the conversation, said, "Why didn't you tell him, David?"

"To vie with him for the credit?"

"To let him know you were on the job, and that you pulled it off. He accused you of neglecting your work."

The rabbi shrugged.

Brooks shook his head pityingly. "David, David, you just don't understand. In a job like yours, or like mine, you've got to be covered every minute. You can't let them get a single thing on you. Remember, they are the enemy."

"Who are 'they'?"

"The president, the board of directors, yes, the congregation, the parents. Remember, we are public figures, which means the public is always looking for something to criticize in us. And that means we've got to fight back." He got off the desk and began to stride up and down the room, and as he continued, it was in the tone of a professor lecturing to a class. "There are two reasons why it's important. One is to set the record straight. And the other, and perhaps more important, is to let them know you can't be kicked around. It makes them think twice before they tangle with you. Now, this Maltzman, he doesn't like you, David."

"How do you know he doesn't like me?"

"I can see it. I can see it when he talks to you. Your vibes don't harmonize."

"Vibes?"

"Vibrations. You know, everyone gives off vibrations like a—like a tuning fork. And when two people get together and their vibes don't match or harmonize, there's a discord."

"I see. And my vibrations don't match his?"

"To tell the truth, David, yours don't match most

people's. You're not everybody's cup of tea. You're not an easy man to like. *I* can because of my training."

"Really? What training is that?"

Brooks showed astonishment. "Why my training in the theater, of course. An actor takes on the personality of the character he is playing. Right? So this gives him practice in understanding people. And remember, David, to understand is to forgive, even to like."

"I'll try to remember."

The sarcasm was lost on Brooks. "All right. So we can take it for granted that Maltzman would like to get rid of you. And for a man like Maltzman, to want is to act. So what else is new, you say. It comes with the territory. But this time, David, it's different." He stopped his pacing in front of the desk and looked down sympathetically at the rabbi. "You know what's kept you here all these years, David? I'll tell you. Inertia. Just plain inertia. The presidents and their good friends on the board may have wanted to get rid of you on occasion, but the congregation wouldn't go along. Why? Inertia. It was too much trouble. It meant argument and fighting and taking sides. But the situation is different now. I've heard women say that the only way they'll ever get equality in the service is to get another rabbi first. See, it's the congregation, or at least the women in the congregation, that wants you out now. So, I ask you, what are you going to do?"

"I'm getting out of here," said the rabbi, pushing back his chair.

"You are?" Brooks was aghast.

"That's right. I'm taking the afternoon off. It's too nice to be indoors."

"Oh, for a minute there, I thought . . . Gosh, I'd go with you, but I've got to coach a couple of Bar Mitzvahs."

40

It was not annoyance with Morton Brooks that led Rabbi Small to leave his study so abruptly. Secretly, he rather enjoyed his cheekiness, his theatrical pomposity. While Brooks' little lecture on temple politics may have triggered the reaction, the reason for walking out was that he was fed up—with the temple, with Maltzman, with his own position as rabbi. He wanted to get away, if it were only for an hour or two, from the reach of the telephone, to where he would not be likely to meet a member of his congregation with a question or a complaint.

He got into his car and set out on the road to Boston with the vague idea that in the city he would achieve the anonymity that, for the moment at least, he craved. But as he drove along the main road, with its heavy traffic, it occurred to him that once he reached the city, he would have to drive around looking for a place to park, and that by the time he found one, it would be time to head for home. So instead, he turned off and took the road to Revere, the nearby resort town with its long stretch of beach faced by an equally long stretch of amusement booths, most of which would be closed at this time of year. There he could perch on the seawall, or sit in the public pavilion facing the ocean, and watch the waves roll in. There, if anyone approached him, it would be to ask for the time, or a match, or to make some observation on the weather.

There were very few people about, and as he had surmised, most of the amusements had closed down, their bravely decorated fronts made tawdry by the unpainted wooden shutters that were intended to protect them during the winter. Here and there, however, one was open, the proprietor leaning over his counter, looking hopefully up and down the street on the chance of interesting one of the few passersby, calling out when one went by, "Step right up. Everyone a winner. No losers. Step right up."

A few of the ice cream and hot dog stands were open, and in the distance the rabbi saw a store that looked as though it might serve coffee. He hoped he could get it in a paper cup and take it to the pavilion to sip at while he did nothing. He heard his name called, and stopped and looked around. The only one in sight was a tall young man in a T-shirt and blue jeans leaning across the counter of the shooting gallery he had just passed. He retraced his steps.

"Gee, I wasn't sure it was you, Rabbi. I mean, seeing you here."

Then he recognized him. "Sumner, isn't it?"

"Uh-huh. Sumner Leftwich. I was in your post-confirmation class a couple of years back. You come down here often?"

"No, not often. You work here all the time? I thought you were at school."

"I am. Mass State. I just work here off and on. It belongs to my girl's father. I help him out once in a while. With business as slow as it is, I can study here just as good as at home or in the library. And I get a few bucks for it." He looked at the rabbi shyly. "Care to test your skill, Rabbi? Ten shots for a quarter."

"I've never shot a rifle."

"Nothing to it, Rabbi. You just aim and squeeze the trigger. You don't pull it, you kind of squeeze it."

The rabbi looked up and down the street and decided the young man had not had many customers that day. He fished a quarter out of his pocket and watched with interest as the young man slid a tube of cartridges into the chamber of the rifle.

The rabbi put the rifle to his shoulder and peered through the sights at the row of clay pipes, the moving line of ducks, the rabbits hopping one after another, the giant pendulum swinging slowly back and forth. Then he vaguely remembered that there was a recoil when a gun went off, and he removed his glasses and carefully put them in his breast pocket. This time when he sighted, he saw only white blobs and splotches. But what of it, there were plenty of things to hit.

He pulled at the trigger again and again until a click told him that he had exhausted his ammunition. He laid the gun down on the counter and put on his glasses.

"Perfect score," said the young man, grinning broadly at him.

"Really?"

"That's right. Ten shots and ten misses. The sights must be off. Here try this one. On the house."

"No, really—"

"Go on, Rabbi."

The rabbi shrugged, and once again took off his glasses and put the rifle at his shoulder. When he put it down on the counter again, the young man shook his head to signify that he had done no better this time.

"I guess it's you, Rabbi, not the rifles."

"I'm afraid I'll never be a marksman," said the rabbi. "I was heading for that shop to get a cup of coffee. Can I get you one?"

"Yeah, I could go for a cup of coffee. Cream and just a little sugar. If you tell him it's for me, he knows how I like it."

When the rabbi returned with the coffee cups, Sumner said, "Say, Rabbi, what do you think about having a special class, or a kind of club, for the kids who are now in college?"

"We tried that one year, and so few came that we gave it up."

"Yeah, well I had an idea . . ."

Finally after a decent interval, he was able to break away. He decided to go back to Barnard's Crossing, reflecting that perhaps it was ordained he should not leave his job.

41

Outside of Boston, McLure, as a State Detective, had always had things pretty much his own way. In the smaller cities and towns where murder was rare, the police had little experience and welcomed his expertise. When he was assigned to the Jordon case, he had expected no differently, that the Barnard's Crossing police would cooperate—it was his word—with him rather than, as it turned out, he with them. He was annoyed that Chief Lanigan should give him assignments and evaluate his findings in much the way he did with his subordinates. Nor did McLure get much satisfaction when he hinted to the district attorney that this was not the way he was accustomed to work.

"I know, Sergeant. I know exactly how you feel," the district attorney said soothingly. "But Barnard's

Crossing is a funny kind of town. It was established back in colonial days by a bunch who left Salem because they weren't having the local authorities tell them what they could do and what they couldn't. They practically had no government at all for a number of years. And because they're kind of off the beaten path, they still don't like outsiders coming in and interfering. You're a foreigner there. Did you know that? If you lived there all your life but were born someplace else, you'd still be called a foreigner. Now, this is a local crime, and Hugh Lanigan, who is a Crosser for all that his folks were Irish Catholic, knows the scene better than any outsider could. He knows how to deal with these people."

Typical was his assignment to question Henry Maltzman. "How about if I bring him down here and we really put the boots to him?" he suggested to Lanigan. "After all, he's the guy who said he'd put a bullet through his head."

"Oh no, you can't handle Henry that way," said Lanigan. "He's a funny guy. You've got to handle him with kid gloves. Besides, we know he was at the temple when the murder took place. The rabbi's wife said so, and that's good enough for me. I don't expect we'll get much from Henry, but since he did make the threat, we've got to check it out as part of the routine."

Because it was routine, McLure did not give it high priority, and it was the Thursday after the murder before he finally called on Maltzman at his place of business. He identified himself and Maltzman led him into his private office.

Once he was seated, McLure took out pencil and notebook and asked abruptly, "Now, what time was it you went to see Jordon that Friday?"

Maltzman grinned. "Where did you get the idea I ever went to see him?"

"You phoned him, didn't you?"

Maltzman shrugged. "I make a lot of calls. That's what the real estate business is all about. Sometimes I'm on the phone for a couple of hours and I think the receiver is growing out of my ear."

"We know that you called him," said McLure.

"So maybe I called him," said Maltzman with a shrug.

"And you said you'd put a bullet through his head."

Maltzman's grin broadened. "Who says so?"

"We have information to that effect" McLure said doggedly.

Maltzman cocked a speculative eye at the ceiling. "You know, I don't see how you can," he said. "It doesn't add up. You say I called him on the phone and threatened to put a bullet through his head. Now, unless he has a phone with an extension and had someone listening in, you just can't have that information."

"We have it from Jordan himself," said McClure angrily. "He told people who came to see him that you had just called—"

"He's a liar. Or he was. You're telling me that Jordon told someone that I called him. And they told you. That's hearsay, and from someone who is not here to verify it. And how would he have known it was me who called? Cummon, Sergeant."

"All right, Mr. Maltzman, let's try it a different way. Suppose you tell me where you were last Friday night."

"I didn't go to Jordon's house. That's for sure."

"Not good enough, Mr. Maltzman. Where did you go?"

"That's none of your business."

"This is a murder case, Mr. Maltzman. We can make you tell."

"Can you? Maybe in a court of law after I've been sworn. But certainly not here in my office just by flashing a badge at me."

"Suppose I take you down to the stationhouse."

"You got a warrant, Sergeant?"

It dawned on McLure that Lanigan had been right, and that maybe Maltzman had to be handled with kid gloves. Abruptly, he changed his tactics. "Look, Mr. Maltzman, a murder has been committed, and it is your duty as a citizen to help the police any way you can to expose the perpetrator."

"Now, I go along with you there, Sergeant. I'm a strict law and order man myself. You ask me anything that has any bearing on this, and I'll answer to the best of my ability."

"Fine, Mr. Maltzman. I'm glad you see it in the proper light now. What we'd like to know is where you were that Friday evening."

Maltzman slowly shook his head.

"What's the matter? Don't you remember?"

"I'm just not going to answer that question."

"Why not? You said you'd answer any question I asked you."

"Only if it has bearing on this case."

"You let us be the judge of that, Mr. Maltzman," said McLure confidently.

"Come on, Sergeant, let's not play games. Suppose I told you I was at a basketball game. How would that help you solve your problem?"

"Were you?"

"No, I wasn't." Maltzman rose to indicate that he had nothing more to say.

McLure protested, "Now look here, Mr. Maltzman—"

"If the only help you expect to get out of me is to find out where I was that night, there's no point in our continuing."

"Why, what else can you tell me? You got any other information?"

"I certainly have, Sergeant. I can tell you the kind of man Ellsworth Jordon was. He was a nasty, mean, cantankerous, penny-pinching, anti-Semitic sonofabitch, and if you're planning on questioning all who might have wanted him dead at one time or another, or might have said they'd put a bullet through him, you've got your work cut out for you, because you'd have to question about half the town and just about everybody who ever had dealings with him. And now, if you'll excuse me, I've got work to do."

42

In spite of his chagrin, McLure, as a good policeman, reported to Lanigan the next day on the results of his conversation with Henry Maltzman. If he expected the chief to be indignant, he was disappointed. Quite the contrary, both Lanigan and Jennings derived considerable amusement from the recital. They even seemed to take a kind of satisfaction in their fellow townsman standing up to and outwitting him, the outsider.

"He actually told you it was none of your business?" Lanigan chuckled. "Well, that's Henry Maltzman for you. You probably got his dander up in the way you approached him. Well, don't worry about it. I'll drop in on him one of these days and get a statement from him, just to tidy up our records."

"Just to tidy up your records, huh?" McLure was nettled. "You don't see him as a possible suspect?"

"No, I don't," said Lanigan judiciously. "I'm wondering why you do."

"Because he's a Jew."

Lanigan's voice had an edge as he asked, "And what's that got to do with it?"

"It's got everything to do with it. I've been checking up on Jordon, and doing a lot of listening. He didn't like Jews, and he showed it. And it wasn't by just making an occasional remark. He owned a lot of property in town, and he wouldn't sell to them. I've even heard talk about a Gentlemen's Agreement. Now, that's against the law. And keep in mind that Maltzman is in the real estate business. I know lots of Jews. For the most part, they're good, law-abiding people. When they go bad, it's usually a white-collar crime. But there's a new breed among them, like these Israelis, who don't hesitate to hit back. That's how Maltzman struck me. A Jewish captain in the Marines, he'd be one of them. If he went to see Jordon and there was a row, he wouldn't just walk out meekly. He'd hit back."

Lanigan nodded. "I won't say it's unthinkable. What's more, Henry has a temper. As a Marine, I'm sure he learned how to handle a gun. But the pattern of the shooting doesn't fit him. And he has an alibi. We know he was at the temple when the murder was committed."

McLure lumbered to his feet. "I wish I had a dollar for every airtight alibi I've cracked. If you don't mind, I'm going to keep checking on Brother Maltzman."

When McLure left them, Jennings said, "You know, Hugh, there's something that bothers me about Maltzman at the temple that night. Let's see the file, will you? Yeah, here it is. When we asked the rabbi's wife if Maltzman had been at the temple, she said, 'I believe so. Yes, I'm sure he was.' "

"Yeah?"

"Well, when she said she believed so, doesn't that mean she wasn't sure?"

"Oh, I don't know. That's just a manner of speaking."

"But that was something she should have been sure about. Hugh. You ever been to one of their services?"

"No, I can't say that I have."

Jennings smirked his satisfaction. "That's because you Catholics wouldn't join this Visit a Church program we had a couple of years ago. Your Father Regan was all for people coming to visit his church, but he wouldn't encourage his people to go and visit other churches. You see, Hugh, you Catholics tend to be kind of narrow-minded about certain things, whereas we Methodists—"

"Get the point, Eban, get to the point."

Jennings turned pale blue eyes on his chief and said, in tones that were both hurt and forgiving, "That's what I was doing, Hugh. You see, they have this kind of platform, and in the middle of it, they have this Ark where they keep their holy writings. Now on either side of this here Ark, they got these fancy chairs, two on a side. The rabbi and the president of the congregation sit on one side, and the vice-president and the cantor sit on the other side, except when he's singing, the cantor, I mean, which is most of the time, and then he stands up front—"

"Get on with it, Eban."

"Right, Hugh. So what I'm saying is that Maltzman is the president, so he'd be sitting right next to Rabbi Small if he was there, and the rabbi's wife wouldn't have any doubt about it, because he'd be up there on the platform in plain sight."

"So maybe that night he didn't sit up there, but sat down with the rest of the congregation."

"That's what I think, Hugh. Like if I ask you if Father Regan was in church Sunday, you'd say, 'Of course he was.' But if I ask you was Mrs. Murphy in church Sunday, you might say, you think so, and then maybe you'd remember and you'd say, 'Yeah, I'm sure she was.' "

"Who is Mrs. Murphy?"

"Oh, you know. I just took her like an example."

"All right, what's your point?"

"My point is—well, why wouldn't Henry Maltzman be sitting in his regular place? Maybe that night he was kind of nervous and uncomfortable and didn't want to be sitting up there, right in front of everyone."

"More likely, I'd say, he may have come in late, after things got started and—yea-ah, maybe he came in late." Lanigan drummed the table with his fingers. "If he came in late, he wouldn't want to walk all the way down to the front and then go up to the platform—"

"Especially, if he was kind of nervous and uncomfortable."

"All right. We didn't ask Miriam what time he

got there, so she didn't say, not knowing why we were asking in the first place. Okay, Eban, there must have been at least a hundred people there that night, so someone must have noticed when Henry arrived."

"We have a man on duty directing traffic into the parking lot Friday nights. Maybe he noticed."

"Right. Check around, and when you find out, then I'll go to see Henry."

43

"That's the start of the run," said Sergeant Holcombe, "so there's no chance of the driver being mistaken. He says that only two people got on, and neither was Martha Peterson. He knows the two well because they take the eight o'clock to Lynn every night."

Chief Lanigan interlaced his fingers behind his desk and stretched back in his chair. "She could have taken a cab."

"I checked both the local cab companies," said the sergeant. "And the ones in the nearby towns. I went as far as Lynn. Beyond that, Revere or Chelsea, they wouldn't be able to make it in time."

"Unless they happened to have a car in the area and two-way radio," observed Jennings.

"Yeah, but I didn't think she'd be likely to have called them in the first place," said the sergeant. "Would you like me to check them?"

"No, don't bother," said Lanigan. "If she thought of going back, she would have planned on taking the bus. And if she realized it was too late for the eight o'clock, she would have waited for the half past. And if for some reason she felt she wanted to get there right then and there, she would have called one of the local cabs."

"Maybe she didn't want anyone to know," suggested Jennings. "Then she might have called a cab from another town."

"Why wouldn't she want anyone to know?" demanded Lanigan. "She wasn't going out there to kill him. She didn't know about a gun lying on the table. She would have gone there just to demand her pay, or to argue with him a little. Or to let him argue with her so they could make up and she could get her job back. All right, Sergeant, what about the time before eight? Could she have gone out earlier, and maybe got a ride—"

"No, Sir. That's pretty tight. That neighbor of hers who is something of a snoop, I guess, heard her come in and was pretty sure she didn't go out. Besides, she heard her arguing with Stanley through the door around eight—"

"How'd she know it was around eight?" asked Jennings.

"The TV program was just changing," he said.

"Everything gets timed by the TV programs these days," said Jennings.

"All right, Sergeant," said Lanigan. "Anything more on Stanley Doble?"

"No, sir. I'm still working on the Salem end."

"Okay, keep on with it," said Lanigan in dismissal. To Jennings, he said, "I guess that lets Martha out. Too bad."

"Why? Did you want to pin it on her? What have you got against Martha Peterson?"

"Nothing. It's just the pattern of the shooting seems to fit a woman, a woman with her eyes shut firing away. That's the way the medical examiner saw it, and that's the way I see it. But Martha is the only woman we know about, and now she appears to be out of it."

"That car that Stanley says he saw turn into the driveway," suggested Jennings, "that could have been driven by a woman."

"Possible, but I think that Stanley dreamed it. Or he might be a lot smarter than we give him credit for. Remember, he offered that as the reason he didn't go up to see Jordon."

"Yeah, but I can't see Stanley shooting Jordon."

"Why not?"

"Because of that same pattern of the shooting," said Jennings. "He goes hunting every season and he always comes back with something."

"Yeah, but he was drunk that night."

"So what? You think on a hunting trip he's likely to be sober?"

"Hm. It doesn't leave us much, does it?"

"There's Billy."

"Yeah, we keep coming back to Billy," said Lanigan moodily.

"You don't like the idea of it being Billy? Do you?"

"Do you?"

"Well, if he did it—"

"Yeah, but what if he didn't? We don't have a single particle of evidence against him any more than we have against the others. But what happens when I lay it all out in front of Clegg. He sees right away that he has the best case against Billy—his bringing the gun in the first place, Jordon shaming him in front of his boss, his running off. But more than that, the boy is alone here and has no friends which makes him an easy mark."

"But Clegg is a pretty decent guy and—"

"He's the district attorney, which means he's first of all a pol. And that means he's interested in publicity. So here's a suspect whose ma is a TV personality. Have you any idea what Clegg could do with that? And do you know what it could do to Billy, and his mother?"

"Okay. So all that's left is Maltzman."

"Did you check on him?"

"When could I check?" Jennings was aggrieved. "You've had me here with you all the time. But I did leave word that Patrolman MacIsaac was to stop by as soon as he came on duty. He was on duty at the temple that night. Maybe he—"

"You put MacIsaac on duty at the temple?"

Jennings grinned. "Well, it seemed kind of fitting." He glanced at his watch. "He should be here about now." He pressed the button on the intercom and spoke to the desk sergeant. "Has MacIsaac come in yet?"

"Just coming in the door now, Lieutenant," came the metallic squawk in reply.

"Fine. Send him in."

MacIsaac was a tall young man with a bony, freckled face and red hair. He was relatively new on the force and still in awe of the chief. He stood at attention in front of the desk.

"You were on duty at the temple a week ago Friday night?" asked Lanigan.

"Yes, sir, every Friday night. The cruiser drops me off a little after eight and picks me up around nine."

"Nine? The service starts at half past eight, doesn't it?"

"Yes, Sir, but folks keep coming in after that for a little while. Some of them, just as I'm leaving. They have some refreshments after the service, I understand, and I guess some of the folks come for that, and to stand around and visit. That's what Stanley Doble says. He comes out to talk to me sometimes. Now, take that Friday night, the cruiser didn't come by until a quarter past and somebody came in right about then. It was the president himself, Mr. Maltzman."

"How do you know it was Mr. Maltzman?" asked Jennings. "You know him?"

"Oh, sure. We bought our house from him. He stopped his car when he saw me, and we talked for a minute. He asked me if there was a crowd. And I said I thought there was."

"You sure it was a quarter past nine?"

"Well, after nine I began wondering what was keeping the cruiser. And then Mr. Maltzman came along, and like I said, I talked to him, and then I noticed the cruiser had come along and was parked at the curb waiting for me. I asked Sergeant Lindquist, who was on the wheel, how come he was so late. That was just after Mr. Maltzman went on to park, you understand. And the sergeant looked at his watch and said it was only a quarter past."

"So what time did Maltzman get there? This is important."

"Well, I'd say between ten past and quarter past."

When he had gone, Lanigan said, "I think I ought to have a little talk with Henry Maltzman. And I want it down here at the stationhouse. Now I really want to know where he was."

"What if he won't come and tells you it's none of your business like he told McLure?"

"I'll make sure he comes. I'm getting a warrant from Judge Turner and I'm going to have you bring him in."

"A warrant charging him with murder?"

"That's right."

"You think he did it?"

"No, I don't. But he's going to talk, or he'll stay here—"

"You think he knows something that could help us?" persisted Jennings.

"I doubt it."

"Look here, Hugh," said Jennings earnestly, "you're kind of frustrated about this case and

you're letting it get the better of your judgment. If
you don't really think he knows anything that will
help us and—"

"I've got a conference with the district attorney
first thing Monday morning. I'm going to have to
tell him that I don't have a shred of evidence
against any one person. We'll go over every one
involved in the case, and when we come to
Maltzman, am I going to say I don't know where he
was at the time of the shooting because he said it
was none of my business? This from the guy who
threatened to kill him? In the very way we found
him killed?"

"Yeah, I see your point. I just wonder how the
Jews in town will react, especially your friend,
Rabbi Small."

Lanigan nodded. "Maybe I ought to tell him
about it first."

44

Before the change in the bylaws, there had been
three vice-presidents. The intention was that the
first vice-president would succeed when the

president's term expired, the other two would then move up and only a new third vice-president would be elected by the congregation at large. Envisioned, had been a kind of self-perpetuating board about whose composition the general membership would have little to say. It never worked. They continued to elect three vice-presidents, but the positions were purely honorary.

Under the new order, there was only one vice-president, and his sole function was to chair the meeting in the absence of the president. Barry Fisher had not wanted to run for vice-president but had agreed to only because Henry Maltzman had asked him. He had been a friend of Maltzman's and devoted to him ever since they had been in high school together. Now, in middle age, they were even closer, in part because his insurance agency nicely complemented Maltzman's real estate business, and they were in a position to do each other favors. While it was regrettable that "the girls," their wives, didn't hit it off together, it did not seriously interfere with their friendship. They saw each other several nights a week to go to the hockey or baseball games in Boston or to work out at the local Y. They lunched together or conferred on the phone almost daily.

It was Saturday afternoon and they had just finished a game of squash, which Barry Fisher, who was thin and wiry, had won quite easily. He was good at racket games, his long legs easily covering the court and his long arms reaching seemingly impossible shots. As usual, he explained apologetically, "I guess I was lucky."

To which Maltzman gave his usual magnani-
mous answer, "No, Barry, you're good." And then
added complainingly, "Jesus, you don't even sweat."

"Maybe I got nothing to sweat."

They showered and toweled down and then went
to the locker room to dress. Seeing they were alone,
Barry Fisher asked, "How does it look for tomorrow?"

"In the bag," said Maltzman. "We've got eight
votes, solid."

"So that's eight to six. I'd say that was pretty
close."

"A margin of two votes. What do you want?"

"Yeah, Hank, but if one of ours decided to go
the other way, that would make it a tie, seven to
seven."

"So then it would be up to me to cast the tie-
breaking vote. But those eight votes, believe me,
they're solid."

"No chance of picking up any of the six? How
about Jessica Berger or Linda Svolitch?"

Maltzman shook his head. "Allen Glick sounded
out Jessica. No go. She was on some committee
with the rabbi's wife and thinks the world of her.
Now, I ask you, is she going to vote against
renewing the rabbi's contract?"

"And Linda?"

"You mentioned her because she's Women's Lib.
Right? Well, I figured her as a possible, too, in spite
of their being like kind of Orthodox. So I talked to
Mike Svolitch. Well, according to him, the sun rises
and sets on Rabbi Small. Lucky I didn't come out
and ask him point-blank, because I'm sure he

would have gone running to the rabbi." He chuckled. "The way I put it to him, I said I'd heard a rumor that some of the board including Linda were planning to vote against renewing the rabbi's contract and whether there was any truth to it."

"Playing Mickey the Dunce," said Fisher admiringly.

"Right. So when he told me how he and Linda felt about the rabbi, I backed off and said something like, some wise guys got nothing better to do than pass around rumors. No, those six votes are as solid as my eight."

"I still think it's awfully close, Hank. Say, I got an idea. How about I make a motion, where it's a secret ballot and all, that the president be allowed to cast a vote just like anybody else. After all, the president of the United States does it. I mean, he votes in elections. Some of them go back to their hometown to do it. It shows them on TV all the time."

"Nothing doing, Barry," said Maltzman peremptorily.

"But why not? Then it would be nine to six and—"

"I'll tell you why not. Because then you make it an issue. You make it like important, and somebody is going to smell a rat. Then there'd be a discussion, and people would say things, and other people would react. I can see some of the diehards maybe even walking out so we don't have a quorum. No, I want it like a straight matter of business, just like any other piece of business, like the vote on the light bill, or on the insurance. The only reason for having it a secret ballot is so the members can be free to vote any way they want to. But that's all. Get it?"

"But what if there's a holler afterward? What if they ask for reconsideration?"

"How're they going to do that? The only one who can ask for reconsideration is someone who voted with the majority. That's parliamentary law. Okay, so let's say they get into a sweat and go around lining up people to call for a referendum. But before they can get something like that off the ground, we've already sent out a letter to the rabbi telling him we voted not to renew. And if I know the rabbi, we'll get a letter of resignation from him in the next mail. And I'll shoot a letter right back, expressing regrets and all that crap, but accepting his resignation."

45

They had finished Sunday dinner, and Mrs. Mandell, in the absence of Molly, had put away the dishes as Herb relaxed in the living room over the Sunday paper. She appeared in the doorway, remarking, "It wasn't that way with your Pa and me, especially on a Sunday."

"Huh?" Herb looked up from his newspaper. "What did you say about Pa?"

"I said your Pa wouldn't think of going out without me any more than I'd think of going out without him on a social occasion. Some of our friends, the men used to go out once a week, regular, to a lodge meeting or bowling. At least, that's what they said. But not your Pa. If I couldn't go, or even if I just didn't want to go, he wouldn't go. And it was the same with me. A bridge or a Sisterhood luncheon, all right, I'd go alone so long as he was at the office. But in the evening or on a Sunday, when he was home, never. That's what I was brought up to think marriage was supposed to be, two people being together. But I guess things are different these days."

"Aw, cummon, Ma, knock it off. They're having a special showing of the Peter Archer silver at the museum, which her boss organized the whole thing. And which she helped with a lot. So if he invited all the employees of the bank, she naturally got to go. Like if the principal of the high school should run some kind of party for the faculty, I'd have to go, wouldn't I?"

She sniffed her disagreement and disapproval. "You think he would have fired her if She told him She couldn't go, or cut her salary? He seems like a very fine gentleman, her boss. And it seems to me, he would have thought a lot more of her if She had said, 'I'm sorry, Mr. Gore, but I never go anywhere socially without my husband, and he can't come on account he's got a very important meeting of the board of directors of the temple, which he is a member of.' "

"Oh, sure," he scoffed, "and I suppose a couple of Fridays ago when I was in charge of the Brotherhood service at the temple, I should have said I couldn't make it because Molly had to stay home."

"That was different. That wasn't social. That was religion."

"The Friday evening services are more social than religious. The point is she stayed—"

"Maybe She had reasons for staying behind while you went off."

"What do you mean by that?"

All week long she had wanted to tell him, but there had been no real opportunity. She had rehearsed her story over and over and had planned, when the occasion came, to speak quietly and calmly as if in sorrow and only out of duty, but now that the chance had suddenly presented itself, her eyes glittered and she spat out the words spitefully, "I mean She didn't stay very long after you left. She thought I was asleep. She thought I didn't hear her, but I did. I heard the car start and I got out of bed and watched through the window and saw her drive off."

"You dreamed it."

"Oh no, I didn't." And now she did speak quietly. She even managed a little smile. "I wasn't sleeping. I may have dozed off the way I do sometimes just sitting in my chair here. But I wasn't sleeping. I heard her talking on the phone. Then I heard footsteps on the stairs, and I could tell She was tiptoeing up. So I made believe I was asleep. Sure enough, She pushed the door back a little and looked in. Then She tiptoed downstairs again. Well, I can tell you I was wide awake then. And pretty soon I heard the back door open and close. Then I heard the car starting up and I got out of bed and peeked through the curtains down at the driveway and I saw her leave. It was just about the time you were starting the service at the temple, and She didn't get back until after nine. She came upstairs to have another look at me when She came back, and I made believe I was asleep again."

For no reason at all, it flashed across his mind that Henry Maltzman had come to the service late that night, a little after nine. "I still think you dreamed it," he said.

"Do you? Well, why don't you ask her? See what She says."

They had finished Sunday dinner, and Laura Maltzman had gone off to visit her mother at the convalescent home as her husband prepared to leave for the board meeting at the temple. He had just shrugged into his jacket when the doorbell rang. It was Lieutenant Jennings.

"I've come about the Jordon business, Mr. Maltzman. I'd like you to come with me to the stationhouse to answer a few questions that Chief Lanigan wants to ask you, and maybe make a statement."

"What if I'm not interested in the Jordon business?"

"You can tell that to the chief down at the stationhouse."

His eyes dancing with amusement, Maltzman asked, "You got a warrant, Lieutenant?"

"Yes."

Taken aback, Maltzman stammered, "You—you have?"

"Right here."

As Jennings reached into his breast pocket, Maltzman said hastily, "All right. I believe you. Look here, you want me to come down to the stationhouse to make a statement and answer a few questions. All right. But I've got an important meeting over at the temple in a few minutes. I'll come down right after it's over."

His Adam's apple bobbing nervously, Jennings shook his head. "No sir, my orders are to bring you down right now."

"Look here, you can't just barge in here and interfere with my plans and—"

"Oh yes I can, so long as I got a warrant."

"I'll talk to Lanigan. What's the number?"

"Won't do you no good. He's not there yet. His orders were for me to have you there when he gets there. So let's not have any trouble, Mr. Maltzman."

Maltzman bit his lips as he considered. Finally he said, "All right. I'll just leave a note for my wife telling her where I'm going." He went into the kitchen, and when the policeman followed, he said, "Don't worry, I'm not going through the back door." He thumbtacked the note to the bulletin board and reached for the phone on the shelf beneath it. "I've got to make a phone call."

"You calling your lawyer?" asked Jennings politely.

Maltzman bared his teeth in a tight little smile. "Not yet." He dialed Barry Fisher's number. "Barry? Hank. Look, something important has come up, and I won't be able to get to the meeting today . . . I know, I know. You go right ahead with the meeting and proceed just the way we planned . . . Look, Barry, we have eight solid votes. So with you in the chair, we'll have seven votes. Seven to six is just as good as eight to six . . . Right . . . Right . . . Bye now."

He turned to the lieutenant and said, "Okay, let's go."

They had finished Sunday dinner, and Miriam had shooed the children upstairs to watch television so that they would not disturb Daddy who was trying to read. When the doorbell rang and she saw that it was Chief Lanigan, she said with a mischievous smile, "Just happen to be in the neighborhood, Chief? It's Chief Lanigan, David."

"No, Miriam," Lanigan said soberly, "this time I came on purpose." And he told the reason for his visit.

"Do you honestly think Maltzman shot him?" asked the rabbi.

Lanigan squirmed uncomfortably. "It's not for me to say whether he did or he didn't. That's for a judge and jury. I'm just conducting the investigation."

"Then do you honestly suspect him?"

"What's that mean? Do I think he's a born killer? Of course not. But which of the people involved is? All I know is that he threatened Jordon that same day. Said he'd put a bullet through his head. And that's how Jordon was killed. That's enough right there for us to act. But I didn't push it because I thought he was at the temple at the time that the murder was committed. Then I found that he wasn't. That made his stock as a suspect jump sky-high. And when we ask him to account for his movements that evening, he tells us it's none of our business. Well, I've got to see Clegg tomorrow, and if I tell him I didn't press Maltzman for an explanation because he said it was none of our business, he'll think I'm not up to my job, and *he'll* go ahead and charge him."

"So you're arresting him to get him to talk?"

"That's right." He glanced at his wristwatch. "Right about now, I'd say."

"And if he doesn't talk?"

"Then I'll put him in a cell for the night," said Lanigan promptly. "And the next morning, I'll confer with Clegg, and it's my guess that he'll haul him up before the nearest judge and charge him. And then make an announcement to the press. And since it's murder, there'll be no bail and he'll stay in jail. I'm sorry, David, but that's the way it's going to be."

The rabbi nodded.

"I'm sorry."

"Thanks for telling me."

46

If Mrs. Mandell had hoped that her son would confront his wife when she got home, she was disappointed. When Molly returned, she called out, "H'lo, Mother. Manage with dinner all right?" gave her husband a wifely peck, and flounced up the stairs to the bedroom, saying, "I've got to change, I promised one of the girls I'd help her with her bridge."

She came down a few minutes later, having changed from the dress that she had worn to Boston to the comfortable slacks and sweater she thought more suitable to Barnard's Crossing.

"Who is it?" Herb asked, as she headed for the door.

"Oh, no one you know," she said vaguely. "One of the girls in the office."

No sooner had the door closed behind her than he got up, stretched lazily and announced, "Well, I better get going, too. You'll be all right, Ma?"

"I'll be all right. But what's your hurry? You've got plenty of time yet."

He had a good half hour in fact, but just then he did not want to spend it with his mother, defending Molly against her insinuations.

"Yeah, but there's like a caucus before the meeting that they asked me to come to. Some of the men want to talk over something important we're going to take up."

He drove to the public beach and parked. The food stand had remained open because the weather had held fine, and people continued to come, to walk along the edge of the water or to sit and watch the surf. He bought a cup of coffee and took it back to the car.

There were several cars parked, one with a couple in a close embrace, which unaccountably annoyed him. He sipped at his coffee and puffed on a cigarette and rationalized Molly's behavior. He admitted that his mother had probably not been dreaming and had indeed seen what she said she had. But what of it? The phone call she had heard must have been the one that Gore had made. And then she had gone out for a half an hour or so. Well, she had been working hard all evening on the report and wanted a bit of fresh air. Of course, she shouldn't have left Ma all alone, but she did first go up to see if she was all right. And Molly had insisted right along that Ma wasn't as helpless at night as she claimed. And, of course, she wasn't. He knew that his mother had a tendency to exaggerate and dramatize her condition—for sympathy, and maybe because she was lonely. But still . . .

He set the car in motion and started for the meeting. He decided not to mention the matter to

Molly. There was tension enough between the two women, maybe normal between a girl and her mother-in-law living in the same house. But if Molly got the idea that his mother was spying on her and, what is more, tattling to him, then it could start an unholy row. And who knows where that could lead?

The board members were shuffling into seats around the table when Herb arrived. He nodded to those who caught his eye and slid shyly into the nearest chair. Barry Fisher got up and closed the door of the room. Then taking the place at the head of the table, he announced, "Henry called me to say something important had come up and that he wouldn't be able to make it today. So let's come to order and get on with the meeting. If I remember right, we agreed to devote this meeting to the budget and nothing else, so I think we can dispense with the reading of the minutes and committee reports. Let's see, you wanted time to study the budget, Herb. That's why we postponed consideration until today. Right. Well, have you had a chance to go over it?"

"Uh-huh."

"Okay, then let's get started. The first section is housekeeping expenses. You want to say anything about the figures, Mike?"

"I thought we were going to take it item by item, Mr. Chairman."

"That's right."

"So why don't we take the first item, the first line item, I mean?"

"Okay."

"Well, the first item is heat. You notice we increased that item over what we allotted last year. Now, I could have just added our supplementary allocations for heat last year to the original budget figure and let it go at that. But I thought we ought to increase that figure by about ten percent on account of we got to figure on a possible price increase in oil."

"On the other hand, Mike, last winter was exceptionally cold. It's not likely we're going to get another winter like last year."

"Well, I heard a guy on TV claim that the climate might be getting colder. According to him, there's a good chance that we're getting into another Ice Age. Something to do with the ozone layer."

"Aw, that's just science fiction. We can't have another winter like last year. The country couldn't stand it."

"So you think Congress will pass a law against it, Bill?"

They wrangled about it, gnawing at it like a dog with a bone, and then finally accepted the original figure. They proceeded to do the same with the next item, and the next. On the whole, the women members tended to be more businesslike and more inclined to stick to the point, but they were also given to whispering together and sometimes lost the thread of the argument and demanded to have it restated.

"Okay, the next item is salaries. You want to say something on that, Doris?"

"Yes, I do," said Doris Melnick, who was chairman of the school committee. "When Mike asked me for the figures on individual teacher's salaries, I told him I couldn't give it to him and that I'd have to give him just the lump sum for the whole faculty. I'd like to explain the reason for that. We on the school committee negotiate each teacher's salary with the individual teacher, separately and confidentially. That's been our policy from the beginning, and it has worked well. No teacher knows what any other teacher is getting, unless he tells him. That way, negotiating each one separately, I mean, we can give the better teacher a little extra if it should be necessary, and you don't get jealousy and disgruntlement—"

"Dis who?" It was Jack Pollock, who had a reputation as a clown and felt he had to live up to it.

Mrs. Melnick, who had been a schoolteacher and knew how to cope with naughty boys, fixed him with a stare and said, "Disgruntlement, Mr. Pollock. Is the word unfamiliar to you?"

"Oh no. Let's not have any disgruntlement. I'm a strong gruntlement man myself."

They argued about it, of course, because they argued about every point that was raised, but in the end Mrs. Melnick had her way and they voted on the total figure.

Since the cantor's salary was fixed by contract, it would seem that there was no room for discussion on that item. Nevertheless, the question was raised as to whether the cantor ought not turn in the honoraria he got for his services at funerals and weddings, and more particularly for preparing boys for the chanting portion of the Bar Mitzvah ceremony, since these were normal duties of the job. It was a point that was raised every year, and with the same arguments on both sides.

"Say he's got a dopey kid that he has to spend a lot of extra time teaching him his Bar Mitzvah, and the kid's old man is appreciative and wants to give him an extra few bucks for his trouble—"

"If I were a cantor, frankly I'd resent it. After all, what's an honorarium? It's just a tip, ain't it?"

"Yeah, but what's a tip? It's a token of appreciation. Right? You get a good waiter, you give him a good tip. You get a bum waiter, and either you don't give him anything, or you give him just exactly the minimum. At least that's the way I do."

"In lots of restaurants they pool their tips."

"What I'd like to know is how you plan to work it. You going to announce that honoraria are forbidden to the cantor? Or are you going to let him collect them and then turn them in to the treasury? And how are you going to be sure he turns in everything he gets? Are you going to ask the donor to report how much he gives?"

In the end, they left matters as they were, just as they had done every year previously. Stanley Doble's salary involved little discussion. But there was some talk, largely anecdotal, about the man himself.

"Remember when he came in stinko one Friday night?"

"How about his not coming in at all, like a week ago Friday night when the Brotherhood sponsored the service?"

"I'd rather have him stay away altogether than come in drunk."

The suggestion, by one of the women, that maybe they ought to look around for a replacement, one more reliable, was immediately overridden by the chairman himself. "Forget it. We could get plenty of janitors who'd be more reliable, but where are we going to get one who can do what Stanley does? Anything goes wrong, and this building is now getting to the point where things do go wrong pretty regular, Stanley can usually fix it, whether it's with the plumbing or the wiring or with the heating system. He's a pretty good carpenter, and he spends most of the summer painting, repointing the brickwork, and just getting everything ship-shape for the winter. Of course, sometimes he goofs off and gets drunk, and you can't always depend on him. But look at it this way. If he were one hundred percent reliable and always sober, he wouldn't be working for us as a janitor. So I see it as a trade-off, and as long as it doesn't get worse, I think we've got the best of the bargain. Now, if there's no further discussion on Stanley, I suggest that we go on to the last item, the rabbi."

This was Herb Mandell's cue. He raised his hand and, when recognized, said, "It seems to me, Mr. Chairman, that this item is a little different from the others."

"Oh yeah? How is it different?"

"Well, in the others we were concerned primarily with the question of salary. Now, in the case of the rabbi, it's not so much salary, since he has like an ongoing contract subject to annual renewal. I mean, the salary is fixed except for a cost-of-living increase, so we can't discuss that. The real question is on renewal."

"You got a point there, Herb," said Cy Morgenstern. "So what do you suggest?"

"Well, it seems to me that on this one we ought to vote by secret ballot. I mean, if somebody wants to vote against the rabbi, he ought to feel free to do so without being worried that it would get back to the rabbi and he'd maybe get sore at him."

The chairman stroked his chin reflectively. "That seems reasonable enough," he said. "All right, we'll do it that way." To the secretary, he said, "Gladys, why don't you pass out some paper. We'll vote Aye and Nay. If you want to vote for renewal of the rabbi's contract, you vote Aye. If you're opposed, you vote Nay. Everybody got it?"

The secretary tore several pages out of her notebook and then proceeded to fold and tear these in quarters, which she passed down the table.

"Can you spare it?" asked Pollock, ever the comedian.

"It's big enough for a three-letter word," said Mrs. Melnick, always the schoolteacher. Then with twitching lips, "Do you know how to spell it?"

"Keep me after school if I can't?" He leered at her.

A few marked their ballots openly and boldly, but most cupped one hand over the paper while they scribbled furtively with the other. The former folded their ballots once and negligently tossed them onto the table to be passed on. The more cautious folded them at least twice and personally handed the resultant little cushions of paper to the secretary, in some cases even leaving their seats to do so.

As he waited for his neighbor to finish so that he could borrow his pencil, Herb began to have doubts. He had nothing against the rabbi. He was doing it because Molly and Maltzman wanted him to. Molly and Maltzman. Molly sneaking out when she was supposed to be with his mother and Maltzman coming to the service late. Molly and Maltzman, their heads together as they pored over their lists. Molly off to help a girl with her bridge party—"Oh, no one you know"—and Maltzman calling to say he couldn't come to the meeting. His neighbor passed him a pencil. Herb hesitated a moment and then wrote Aye.

The secretary had waited until all ballots were in. Now she proceeded to unfold them and separate them into two piles. She counted first one and then the other. Then she announced, "Thirteen votes in all. Seven vote Aye, six Nay. The Ayes have it."

47

"What are we going to do now?" Miriam asked tragically after Lanigan left.

The rabbi shook his head. "I don't know that there's anything we can do. It's up to Maltzman, and if he—"

"Oh, I don't care anything about Maltzman. I was thinking of the congregation and the community, and how the town will react."

"You mean how the town will react to the congregation? Believe me, Miriam, there'll be no reaction at all. People don't think that way anymore. They no longer feel that the actions of an individual are a reflection on the group he comes from. If there is an announcement in the press, there may be some editorializing on the fact that he's a prominent member of the community, and by that I mean Barnard's Crossing rather than the Jewish community. They'll mention that he's president of the temple, along with mention that he's president of the chamber of commerce and a big shot in the veterans' organization. The point they'll be making is that he's a community leader. That's all."

"Well, even for his own sake, don't you think you ought to try to help him?"

"What can I do?"

"I don't know what's got into you lately, David," she flared at him. "You don't seem to care anymore. When it looks as though the board might not renew your contract, instead of making a fight for it, you say you'll leave it to God to take care of. And now, when the president of the congregation is arrested for murder, you say 'What can I do?' Do you think he actually did it?"

"No, I don't."

"Because he's not the type?"

"Every type is capable of murder, or anything else," he replied gravely. "Who can know the depths of another person? No, I don't think he's guilty for the very reason that Lanigan arrested him, because he won't talk. It seems to me, if he had actually done it, he would have tried to arrange for an alibi, or offered some plausible explanation, even if it were only that he had taken a nap and overslept. But to tell the police that it is none of their business, that suggests that he has an alibi, an ironclad alibi, that he can produce if it becomes absolutely necessary."

"You think he's shielding someone?"

"Possibly. But I don't think so. Maybe if he had come late to the Friday service that one time, then it could have been because he happened to see something, perhaps some good friend of his whom he had seen going into or coming out of Jordon's house at about the time the murder was committed. But Maltzman came to the service late the Friday before that, and since then. Come to think of it, he hasn't sat beside me for the last three or four Fridays. No, there's something he's involved in that takes place every week at the same time. And he won't tell what it is because he's ashamed of it, or finds it embarrassing."

"You think he may be seeing a woman?" asked Miriam eagerly.

"Possibly, considering his reputation. But I doubt it. Because each time I've seen Laura Maltzman in her regular seat in the front row, and she was there from the beginning of the service. Then afterward she joined him for the collation, and everything seemed to be normal between them."

"But if she didn't know—"

"That could happen once. He might pretend an important business engagement and tell her to go on ahead and he'd meet her afterward. But not Friday after Friday. Anything he's doing, I'm sure she knows about."

"I suppose—yes, she'd have to. Then maybe he's taking some kind of course."

"Then there would be no reason for not telling the police. No, it's something that takes place every Friday night at the same time, that she knows about and seems to approve of, and yet is embarrassing to the point that .. ." He snapped his fingers. "You hit it right on the head, Miriam."

"I did?"

"He *is* taking a course—a course of treatment— from a psychiatrist."

"Oh, David, I think that's it. Henry Maltzman strikes me as just the kind of man who would be ashamed to have it known that he was getting psychiatric treatment. He'd be afraid that people would think he was crazy. But that gives us something to go on. If you talked to him and hinted—"

"He wouldn't talk to me," said the rabbi flatly. "Even if I could get to him, he'd shut up as soon as he sensed what I was hinting at. But, you know, it might be worthwhile talking to Laura."

"Why Laura?"

"Because I could tell her point-blank what I thought. If I'm right, then there's a good chance that I could induce her to give me the name of the doctor. Then—look here, I'm going over to see her right now."

For a few minutes after her husband left, Miriam was buoyed up by his certainty. Then doubts began to set in. Laura Maltzman might be just as obdurate as Henry. She might have the same view of psychiatric treatment. Or even if not, she might feel it was disloyal to reveal what her husband was so anxious to keep secret. Perhaps there was another way, and a plan began to form in her mind. She reached for the phone and called the local hospital.

"You have lists of local doctors, haven't you?" she asked the switchboard operator, trying to keep her voice from trembling. "Can you—"

"Hold on. I'll connect you."

She took several deep breaths, and to the person who answered this time, she was able to say crisply, "I would like a list of the local psychiatrists whom you recommend."

"Who is this calling, please?"

"Mrs. Small."

"Mrs. David Small? The rabbi's wife?"

"That's right. Can you help me?"

"I'm Mrs. Clausen, Mrs. Small. The rabbi checks in with me when he comes on his regular visits. He's all right, isn't he?"

"Oh yes. This involves a case he's working on. He asked me—"

"I understand. Well, there aren't too many. You're thinking of those who practice in the area, I suppose. Because there are a number who live here, but their offices are in Boston. Let's see—"

"Do you happen to know which of them will see patients in the evening?"

"Well, if it's an emergency—"

"No, I mean who will schedule patients for regular treatment."

"Well, that limits it even more, doesn't it? Let's see, Dr. Boles used to, but I know for a fact that he doesn't anymore. He's quite old. Abner Gordon doesn't as a rule, but he just might if the rabbi spoke to him, especially if he were interested in the case. I mean if it involved something he was doing a paper on."

She finally came up with a list of four names, two of which Miriam discarded because they were obviously Jewish. She reasoned that Maltzman might feel that if the doctor were Jewish, there was a greater chance of someone in the Jewish community finding out. Of the remaining two, one was a woman. For a couple of minutes Miriam agonized over the choice and then decided that Maltzman would be more inclined to tell his personal troubles to a woman than to a man.

"Dr. Sayre? I wonder if I could have an appointment—"

A firm contralto voice asked, "Whom am I talking to, please?"

"My name is—Myra, Myra Little."

"Miss or Mrs.?"

"It's Ms."

"Very well. And what is it you want to see me about?"

"It's—I don't like to say over the phone—I wouldn't want—I mean if someone were listening—"

"Who referred you to me, Ms. Little?"

"Well, it wasn't a doctor. It was one of your patients, Henry Maltzman."

"Oh yes." It was merely polite agreement, which might mean nothing, but it gave Miriam the courage to continue.

"He said you sometimes took patients in the evening, which is the only time I could come."

"I do take *some* patients in the evening."

"Well, could I have an appointment for Friday evening, around half past seven?"

"Friday evening? Let me see. Why that's Mr. Maltzman's time."

"Are you sure, Doctor. Because he said—"

"Quite sure. He—"

But Miriam had hung up, leaving the doctor looking puzzled at her telephone which had inexplicably gone dead.

When the rabbi returned shortly after, he showed

his disappointment. "I should have called first," he said. "There was no one home when I got there."

"It doesn't matter, David," she said. "It doesn't matter." She was excited at her success and yet fearful of his disapproval.

The rabbi listened in silence as she told him what she had done and repeated her conversation with Dr. Sayre.

He shook his head in wonder and then smiled. "As I remarked earlier, who can know the depths of another person?"

"Are you angry? Was it wicked of me?"

"The Talmud forbids pricing a merchant's wares if you have no intention of buying. It raises his hopes of making a sale and then causes him needless distress when you disappoint him. I suppose the same would apply to a doctor." He threw his head back and laughed joyously. "But it was awfully clever of you. And now, I'd better see Lanigan." He hesitated. "You don't have any other bright ideas you might try while I'm gone, do you, Miriam?"

"Oh, David!"

"Now, Chief, I've given you my personal assurance that I was nowhere near the Jordon house that night, or during the day for that matter. And I'm willing to say that under oath. I know damn well you don't suspect me of having anything to do with it, and I consider it a serious infringement on my rights."

Lanigan listened with growing impatience. Finally, he exploded. "Goddammit, this isn't a parking offense. This is murder and—"

The voice of the desk sergeant came over the intercom. "Rabbi Small is here, Chief, and he'd like to see you."

"Tell him I'm busy now. Maybe later."

"Yes, Sir, but he says it's terribly important and he has to see you right now."

"Well, all right." To Henry Maltzman, he said, "I've been treating you with kid gloves, but when I get back, Henry, you'll talk, or I'll have Lieutenant Jennings put you in a cell and you won't get another chance to talk until tomorrow morning. Keep an eye on him, Eban."

His greeting to the rabbi when he came out was, "This had better be good, David."

"It is good, Chief," said the rabbi earnestly and told him of Miriam's exploit.

Lanigan chuckled. "While you were out of the house, eh? She's a corker. When you get home, ask her if she'd like a part-time job with the force. All right. We'll probably check with this Dr. Sayre, but for now it's good enough." And, as the rabbi turned to leave, "Oh, and give Miriam my love."

Back in his office, Lanigan looked sourly at Maltzman and said, "Okay, you can go now. The lieutenant will check you out."

"Did Rabbi Small come here about me? Is that why you're letting me go?"

"Go on. Beat it before I change my mind."

48

Returning from the board meeting, Herb was surprised to find Molly at home. "Your bridge didn't last very long," he remarked.

"Oh, I wasn't planning to stay. I just went to help with the decorations. It was a shower and bridge for a new bride."

"Mother?"

She pointed ceilingward. "Resting." Then she said eagerly, "How did the meeting go? As planned?"

"No, the rabbi got his contract renewed. It was close, but the rabbi won."

"But, but how? Henry was sure he had eight votes."

He smiled sourly. "I guess he had to twist an arm or two to get the eight. But then he outsmarted himself with his idea of a secret ballot." He was enjoying himself as he spelled it out for her. "You see, when you vote in secret, how is Big Brother Henry to know how you voted?"

"I don't understand." She seemed bewildered, unable to take it in. "I just don't understand."

"Oh, that's all right," he said breezily. "There are lots of things *I* don't understand." The coincidence of Maltzman's absence from the board meeting while she was presumably out playing bridge had made him change his mind. He now had to confront her. "For instance, I don't understand why you went out the night I was running the Brotherhood service and you were supposed to be staying with Mother." He saw that he had startled her and that she had the grace to blush.

"Stanley told you? I *thought* it was his jalopy I saw as I turned into the driveway."

"What driveway?"

"Ellsworth Jordon's, of course. I went to deliver that report I'd been working on."

"Gore asked you to?"

"No, I offered."

"Why?"

"Because I could tell that Larry was worried about not getting it in on time. The bank could lose the account. Jordon could be very nasty about things like that."

"And you delivered it?"

She shook her head. "The house was dark when I got there. I thought he must have gone to bed early, or gone out, so I came away." She hesitated, "I've thought about it ever since, that maybe . . . Do you think he might have been—you know—dead at the time?"

"He might have been," he admitted cautiously.

"But since you didn't see him and didn't know it, there was nothing you could do. So why not just forget about it?"

"But when that policeman came to ask about Mr. Gore's phone call, I should have told him that I went to the Jordon house that night."

"Gosh, yes. You certainly should have. It might be an important clue. Why didn't you?"

"Because you were right here with me," she said with a touch of acerbity. "I didn't want to say I had gone out when I'd promised I was going to stay in. I thought of seeing the detective later and telling him, but I kept putting it off and then never got around to it. But if they should find out I concealed information—"

"How would they find out?"

"Well, Stanley mentioned it to you, didn't he? What if he should mention it to the police?"

Learning that it was Jordon rather than Maltzman she had gone to see had lifted a great weight from his mind. He was now thoroughly ashamed of his doubts of her loyalty. He felt a great tenderness for her. He could see that she was worried and a little frightened, and he longed to allay her fears. On the other hand, having led her to believe that it was Stanley who had told him, it would be foolish now to admit that he had learned it from his mother.

"Oh, I don't think Stanley is apt to go to the police. Why should he?" He went on to explain at some length that people did not normally go running to the police, even when they had important information, simply because they didn't want to get involved; that people like Stanley who got drunk occasionally and were apt to get arrested for it were even less likely to help the police; that they had an innate antipathy toward them; that she had nothing to fear.

But he saw that she was not convinced. Finally he said, "I'll tell you what, I'll go to the rabbi and ask him what we ought to do."

"What's he got to do with it? Why go to him?"

"Because he is very friendly with Chief Lanigan. They see each other socially, I understand. I could explain to him just exactly how it happened. After all, he knows us and he knows my mother. Maybe he'd be willing to talk to Lanigan, and we wouldn't have to. Or at least he'd smooth the way for us."

"No, we can't go to the rabbi for help."

"Why not?"

"Because we wouldn't feel right about it. Here, I—we have been working to get him out. We can't just turn around and ask him to help us."

He grinned. "Don't let that worry you. Because I voted for him, and I guess it was my vote that settled it."

"*You* voted for him?"

Too late he realized he had talked himself into a trap and that his best course was to make a clean breast of it.

"I was jealous," he said candidly. "That night when you went out, Henry Maltzman came to the service at the temple late, after nine. And then last Sunday when I went out for the paper, he was here and you seemed to be—you know—awfully friendly. And then today you went out to this bridge thing, and when I got to the meeting, I found that Henry had called to say he wasn't going to make the scene. So I put two and two together and—"

"You were jealous of Henry Maltzman? You thought I might be playing around with Henry Maltzman? I would have thought you'd know me better than to think I'd be attracted to a professional macho type like Henry Maltzman."

"Forgive me," he begged. "I love you so much, Molly, that sometimes I just can't think straight."

She relented. He was such a boy. She came over and, putting her arms around him, murmured, "Silly Herbie."

He brightened. "But it all worked out for the best, didn't it? Because now I've got the right to ask the rabbi for a favor."

49

"You see, Rabbi, she's so loyal. When she sensed that Gore was upset that he wouldn't be able to get that report in the old man's hands on time, she offered to bring it over. I guess she thought Gore might lose the account. Jordan was that type of man." He laughed. "The funny part of the whole thing is that the report didn't even balance."

"Then what was the point of bringing it since it was incomplete?"

"That was my view, Rabbi. But Gore felt that what was important was to get it in on time."

"And she couldn't tell the detective that she had gone there because you were present during the interrogation?"

"That's right. She was planning to see him afterward and tell him, but you know how it is, she kept putting it off."

"Does she know that it was your mother who told you that she left the house?"

"Uh-uh. She thought it was Stanley, because I'd

just come from the temple, from the board meeting, you know—"

"Why Stanley?"

"Well, she thought she'd seen his car just as she was turning into Jordon's driveway, and she assumed he saw her. And I let her think so. I mean, I didn't contradict her."

"I see. Now what do you want me to do?"

"Well, I thought where you and Chief Lanigan are supposed to be so friendly, I thought maybe you could explain it to him, just how it happened." He looked eagerly at the rabbi.

"No, Mr. Mandell. You must see that it wouldn't do. Chief Lanigan would still have to question your wife. That's his job. And the net effect of my trying to smooth the ground first would only make him suspicious."

"So what should we do?"

"My advice, Mr. Mandell, is that you and your wife go and see Chief Lanigan as soon as possible, this afternoon, or right now, if you can, and tell him the whole story just as you've told it to me. He may be annoyed with you for waiting this long, but the longer you wait, the worse it will be. And if he finds out on his own, it could be very serious for you."

Later when Miriam noticed that the rabbi appeared to be unusually abstracted, she asked, "Are you bothered about the Mandells, David? Do you think Lanigan will give them a rough time?"

"Oh, I'm sure he will, if only to impress on them the seriousness of withholding evidence from the police in a capital case. But a lot of it will be put on, because he knows that people do it all the time. He's told me on more than one occasion that it's one of the facts of life as far as the police are concerned. What bothers me is that Mrs. Mandell's story tends to show that Stanley was near the Jordon house at the crucial time, and Lanigan might decide to follow that line and pull him in."

"But he's innocent—"

"Then he'll get off eventually, I suppose. But in the meantime they'd give him a hard time. They might reason that if she was able to identify his car, he should have been able to identify hers, and that in not telling them he was concealing information."

"But Mr. Mandell didn't find out from Stanley. It was his mother who told him that Molly had gone out."

"True. But Mr. Mandell won't dare say so, because his wife will be there and he doesn't want her to know. It seems terribly unfair to Stanley somehow."

A couple of hours later, however, the rabbi received a telephone call that proved his fears were groundless, or at least misplaced. It was from Herb Mandell. He was angry, perhaps a little frightened. It showed in the sarcasm of his tone. "I want to thank you for your advice, Rabbi. We did exactly as you suggested. Lanigan questioned Molly for over an hour. He had the poor girl crying before he was through. But that's not all. He told her he didn't want her leaving town. Thanks to your advice, she's now a suspect and will be followed everywhere she goes by cops."

"Oh, surely not—"

"No? Well a few minutes ago I looked out the window, and there's a car parked in our street, diagonally across from our house, and there are a couple of cops sitting in it. And I'll bet you everything you like there's one parked on Francis Street, too, so they can see if anyone comes out the back door."

"I'm sure you must be mistaken, Mr. Mandell. Chief Lanigan may want her to be available to give evidence. If you like, I'll get in touch with him and find out, if I can, just what the situation is."

"I'd like."

50

After releasing Maltzman, Lanigan had suggested to Jennings that he go on home and relax a little.

"Good idea, Hugh. The missus has been complaining about eating alone the last couple weeks. How about you? Why don't you go home, too?"

"I will a little later. I want to get everything organized for my meeting with Clegg first. I'll see you in the morning."

Not many hours later, however, while he was

dozing on the divan in the midst of the litter of the Sunday paper, Jennings was awakened by a call from Lanigan. There were new developments. Could he come down?

He could tell that his chief was excited. "I'll be right over, Hugh."

Although he arrived in less than ten minutes, Lanigan growled at him, "What kept you?" And as Jennings, his Adam's apple bobbing, was on the point of being indignant, "Never mind. For the first time, we've got a break. We *can* place someone at the scene just about the time the murder happened. We don't have to prove it. She admits it."

"She?"

"Right." He told of the Mandells coming to see him. "From the beginning, I've felt the pattern of the shooting was the basic clue in this case. Doc Mokely put his finger on it when he said it was like a woman shutting her eyes and firing away until the gun was empty. And that's exactly the way it looked to me. That's why I was so anxious to trace Martha's movements. When we had to cross her off, I thought the boy might fill the bill, but I wasn't happy with the idea. So along comes another woman—"

"But she said the place was dark, and Stanley said it was dark."

"Jordon used only the first floor, and that's practically hidden by the trees. From the street he wouldn't be able to tell if there was a light on in the living room or not. As for Mrs. Mandell, what else is she going to say?"

"Yeah, Hugh, but what's her motive? Why would she want to kill Jordon?"

"I don't know. Why would she want to volunteer to deliver this report when it involved leaving her mother—"

"Mother-in-law."

"All right, so it was her husband's mother. She wouldn't go and watch her husband be a big shot over at the temple, because the old lady was not supposed to be left alone at night. Yet she volunteers to sneak out and deliver this report to Jordon. Well, I don't know what there was between her and Jordon, but I got just the suspicion of a hint in going over the folder. When we questioned Gore, he said that Jordon had made a pass at his secretary. Now, that's what Mrs. Mandell is—his secretary. And what's it mean that he made a pass? It could be just a dirty old man giving a nice-looking young woman a pat on the behind. Or it could be that Gore spotted some hanky-panky between the two, and Mrs. Mandell covered it by saying Jordon made a pass at her."

Jennings screwed up his mouth and shook his head.

"I know it isn't much. I said it was just a hint. So what I want you to do is check around with the folks at the bank, every single one of them. Subtle like, you understand. And see what you can come up with. Rumors, gossip, anything I can use as a starting point for a real interrogation of the lady."

"Sure, Hugh, but a lady who works in a bank, it's hard to see her as a killer."

"If it isn't a professional killing, Eban, then it's

always somebody like Mrs. Mandell, an ordinary person like the corner grocer, or a schoolteacher, or even a cop. Sure, sometimes they turn themselves in right afterward. But it isn't remorse, usually. It's because they're sure they're going to be discovered. But sometimes they're smart, and the crime goes unsolved. Right?"

"Guess so."

"And another thing I want you to do, Eban. I want the Mandell house watched."

"You think she might make a run for it?"

"I doubt it. But when I go to see Clegg tomorrow and he says he'd like to talk to her, I don't want to find that she decided to visit an aunt in Canada. Just post someone near the house. It doesn't make any difference if she spots him. It would be even better if she does. There's nothing like knowing you're being watched to get you nerved up and edgy. So arrange for it now, and then go on home. You can't start on the bank assignment until tomorrow anyway."

"You going home, too?"

"No, I think I'll go up to the Jordon place for another look around."

... his ...

... meant ...

... and as a ...

... annual ... ...

"All right," he said ... ...

"Just because ... that night ...

51

When the Rabbi called the stationhouse, he was told that the chief was not there.

"Can you tell me where he is?"

The desk sergeant was evasive. "Gosh, Rabbi, I don't rightly know."

He called Lanigan's house and Mrs. Lanigan said, "No, Rabbi, he's not here. Is it important?"

"It's terribly important."

"Then I'll tell you where I think you can find him. He called to say he was going to have another look around at the Jordon house."

Lanigan was not too pleased when he opened the door and saw who his visitor was. "Oh, it's you," was the way he greeted him. But then he added, "Well, come on in. I owe you something for your help with Maltzman, I suppose."

The rabbi looked about curiously as he entered the living room. He pointed to the recliner. "That's where the body was found?"

"Uh-huh."

He pointed to the clock on the floor. "And the clock?"

"That's where we found it. Nothing has been moved except the body, of course. Originally, the clock was on the mantelpiece there. When it was hit by a bullet, naturally it skidded off onto the floor." He pointed about the room. "Another bullet hit that painting right in the mouth. And one hit the light, and another the finial on the lamp, and one hit the pill bottle over there on the floor. That was on the table there originally, according to Martha Peterson, the housekeeper. But if you want to talk, come in the dining room. I've been using it as my office."

Lanigan sat down at the table and, gathering the papers he had spread out before him, put them back into their folder. The rabbi sat down on the other side. Elbows on the table, his chin resting on his hands, Lanigan faced his visitor and said, "I suppose you're here about Mrs. Mandell."

"That's right. Is she suspect?"

Lanigan pursed his lips and then said, "No comment."

"Because if she is," the rabbi went on, "it puts me in a most awkward position. You see, she came to you on my advice. On my urging, in fact."

Lanigan considered. The rabbi was his friend, and as a fair-minded man, he could see some justice in his request for information. And what harm would it do? He could be relied on to keep confidential matters confidential.

"All right," he said. "She's suspect."

"Just because she was here that night?"

"That, and because she's a she." He smiled. "Come on back in the other room, and let me show you." He led the way and stopped about fifteen feet from the recliner. "Jordon was lying back in that armchair, dozing or asleep. Ballistics figures the person with the gun was standing right about here where I'm standing. Now, suppose he fires and misses. A twenty-two doesn't make much noise, but in a room like this, it would be enough to wake anyone, no matter how sound asleep he was. So Jordon wakes up. Is he going to just lie there with someone pointing a gun at him and shooting? Of course not. He'd try to get up, make a run for it, hide, anything but just lie there waiting for the next shot. Right?"

"Go on."

"So we figure it was the first shot that got him. But it was right in the head, in plain sight. The killer knew immediately that he'd hit him and that he was almost certainly dead. If he had any doubts and wanted to make sure, he would have come closer and fired another shot into him. But no, he stands right here and goes on shooting until the cylinder is empty. Why would he do that? One shot might go unnoticed, but half a dozen might very well be heard and noticed. It doesn't make sense. So we come up with a scenario, as they call it these days, of a woman grabbing up the gun, and shutting her eyes and firing away until there's a click and no more bullets. Then she opens her eyes and sees that she has killed him. Of course, there's a possibility that the first shot didn't hit him, but that it gave him a heart attack and he either died of that

or was unable to move. But it doesn't change anything, and the medical examiner said it was most
unlikely. Well, the only woman in the case, the only
one we knew about, was Martha Peterson, the
housekeeper. And we concentrated on her. But we
backtracked her and came up with clear evidence
that she couldn't have been here at the time. So
then we thought of Billy Green——"

"As someone who might shut his eyes tight while
firing a gun?"

"Something like that. Or he might shoot the old
man and then figure he might as well fire off the remaining bullets. We even considered Stanley Doble
on the grounds that he might have been so drunk
that night that he didn't really know what he was
doing. But we weren't comfortable with either of
those."

"And then I sent you Mrs. Mandell."

"Right."

"But couldn't it be that after Jordon was killed
with the first shot, the murderer went on firing for a
good reason?" said the rabbi doggedly. "He might
have shot out the lamp, for instance, because he
didn't want to be seen."

Lanigan grinned. "It would have been a lot
easier to just snap the switch, wouldn't it? Of
course, you could dream up reasons for shooting all
the items he hit. He shot the portrait because he
hated the original. He shot the pill bottle because
he's one of these nature food nuts and is opposed to
medicines. He——"

"He could have shot the clock to establish an

alibi," the rabbi observed. "He could have set it ahead and then shot it to stop it."

Lanigan's grin broadened. "Sure, except that no one connected with the case offered an alibi, not Stanley, not Billy, not Martha Peterson, not Gore—"

"He had an alibi," the rabbi pointed out.

"Not one that he offered. All he said when we questioned him was that he stopped on the road to Boston to make a phone call and that it was sometime after eight. Now, he could have, because in the office of the gas station where he made his call, there was a big clock on the wall advertising some kind of motor oil. The easiest thing in the world would be to say to the station attendant, 'Hey, is that clock right?' But he didn't. The point is he didn't offer any kind of alibi. We had to dig it out."

"Maybe that's the best kind."

"What kind is that?"

"The kind where the police dig it out for you."

The phone rang, and with a muttered damn, Lanigan went to answer it. He picked up the receiver and, after listening for a moment, said. "Yes, he is. Just a minute." He called out, "For you, David. It's Miriam."

The rabbi took the phone and Miriam said, "Oh, David, do you know how long you'll be? Because the Reuben Levys called. They're in town, in Cambridge, for a wedding. They didn't want to call yesterday because of the Sabbath. But they'd like to see us if we can make it. I said I'd call them back."

"The Reuben Levys?"

"You know, from the seminary."

"Oh, of course. The Voice."

"That's right."

"The Voice is in town? Well, what do you know. Yeah, I'd like to see him, but—Look, why don't you call him back and ask if you can call him a little later."

"You mean, I should call him now and—all right, I understand."

It was an abstracted Rabbi Small who returned to the living room. Lanigan smiled sympathetically. "An old friend call you up?"

But the rabbi did not answer. He stopped and stood straight and tense with his arms rigid at his sides, the fists clenched. His head was thrown back and he was staring at the ceiling.

"What's the matter?" asked Lanigan in alarm. "Anything wrong?"

The rabbi relaxed and said sheepishly, "No, I just thought of something. Tell me, have you ever fired a gun with your eyes shut?"

Lanigan blinked at the unexpectedness of the question. "No," he said cautiously, "can't say that I ever did."

"Well, I did," said the rabbi, and told about his experience at the shooting gallery in Revere. "I can see pretty well with my glasses, but when I take them off, I might just as well shut my eyes as far as anything more than a couple of feet away is concerned."

"Then why did you take them off?"

"Well, I'd heard that there's a recoil from a rifle, and I was afraid I might break them."

"From a twenty-two in an amusement park shooting gallery?"

The rabbi blushed. "They seemed to be in the way when I put the gun to my shoulders. I probably wasn't holding it right. The young man at the gallery seemed amused, too. But I wasn't trying to hit anything anyway, just giving him a little business on a dull day."

"And how did you do?"

The rabbi smiled. "I got a perfect score."

"You did?"

"Uh-huh. Ten shots, ten misses. The attendant thought the sights might be off and gave me another rifle, and I did equally well with the second. Do you get the point?"

"I get the point that you're a terrible shot."

"No, no, it's more than that. Here was a narrow space, maybe fifteen feet wide at the most, full of all sorts of things—rows of clay pipes, ducks moving along in one direction while rabbits hopped along in the other, a large circle on a pendulum swinging back and forth. You'd swear that any bullet fired in the general direction of the rear wall would have to hit something. And I missed every time. I thought about it afterward, wondering how I could have achieved that incredible score. And then I realized that the empty space was many, many times greater than the space taken up by the targets. My point is that if Molly Mandell or Martha Peterson had shut her eyes and fired off six shots in the general direction of that recliner, you would have found the bullets buried in the wall or the ceiling. To hit all those small objects—"

"The painting isn't small."

"But the shot struck right in the mouth. And the finial on the lamp, and the pill bottle and, of course, the victim right between the eyes—that was very good shooting, I'd say—the work of a marksman."

Lanigan looked at the rabbi suspiciously. "Are you trying to hornswoggle me with some of that Talmud hocus-pocus—what d'ye call it—pilpil?"

"Pilpul? No. But I'm suggesting another Talmud technique or method. You see, they were intent, those old scholars, on deriving the true meaning of God's commandments. So they tested their interpretations by considering all kinds of examples and all possible alternatives, no matter how remote or farfetched. Because, only if it applied to an extreme case, could they know that their interpretation was correct. It came to me in a flash when Miriam called to tell me about Reuben Levy—"

"Who's he?"

"A classmate at the seminary. Come to think of it, I told you about him once. Instead of using a good story to amplify a sermon, he did it the other way around and built the sermon on the story. You suggested it was like the man who got a reputation as a crackshot by shooting first and then drawing a target around the bullet hole."

"Oh, yes, I remember—"

"And it came to me that you could work it the other way around just as well. Suppose you had half a dozen targets and you hit each one in the bull's-eye, dead center, and then erased all the targets except one. Then someone looking at all those scattered shots, not even touching the outer circle of the one remaining target, would be certain that it was bad shooting and that the shot in the bull's-eye was a pure fluke. And I remembered what they said at the Agathon when we went over there, that Gore was a crackshot and club champion. So I suggest another scenario. A man, a crackshot, having dispatched his victim with a single shot right between the eyes, standing there, cool, confident, a little self-satisfied smile on his face, emptying the gun by firing at one tiny target after another."

"Are you suggesting that he took the chance of firing all those shots just so as to cover the accuracy of the first shot? It doesn't make sense. He could have—"

"Not to cover the first short. To cover the second."

"The second?"

"The clock. He had to set up an alibi. So after shooting Jordon, he advanced the clock to half past eight and then stepped back and shot it in order to stop it and establish the time of the murder. But if he had left it at that, just the two shots, the police would have suspected immediately. So he covered it up by firing off the rest of the bullets. Then all he had to do was to establish that sometime close to half past eight he was far away from here."

"But dammit, he didn't establish an alibi. I told you—"

"Oh yes, he did," said the rabbi quickly. "He set out for Boston and on the way stopped to make a phone call from the office of a gas station. If there's an attendant there, especially if it's sometime near closing time, there's a good chance that he'll remember the time. And the person you call may remember. If it's a housewife, she knows the time she serves dinner and what time they finish eating and how long it takes to wash the dishes, especially if she's going out to do an errand. Unless the alibi calls for split-second timing, there's a good chance that between the two, the gas station attendant and the housewife, the police will be able to triangulate a point in time that will be reasonably and sufficiently accurate. But you can't call just anyone, not while you're on the road to Boston. You can't call any old acquaintance and say you were thinking of them. Not while you're driving along the highway. It has to be in connection with something important, some matter of business. So he called Mrs. Mandell."

Although Lanigan was impressed, he was not yet ready to yield. He even managed a supercilious look of unconcern. "And his motive, David? You're not suggesting he did it just to prove to himself what a good shot he was."

The rabbi smiled. "No, nothing so psychologically exotic. My guess is he did it for money."

"You thinking of that report not balancing?"

"That struck me as significant, but—"

"Forget it," said Lanigan flatly. "We had an accountant go over Jordon's account. It was in apple pie order."

"That wasn't what I had in mind," said the rabbi. "I was thinking of the remark that was made at the Agathon that night by Dr. Springhurst, that Jordon was without friends or family. And later, the seemingly contradictory remark that Gore was kin to Jordon. I assume that what he meant was that Jordon had no close or immediate family, but that Gore was a second or third cousin. But if there were no other relatives, and Jordon died intestate, then naturally Gore would inherit. Now, suppose that Jordon had confided to Gore that Billy was his son and that he was planning to make a will in his favor. . . ."

"I see what you mean," Lanigan admitted, "and it's possible. Of course, you realize there's not a particle of proof for any of this."

"Fingerprints?" suggested the rabbi hopefully.

"Of Gore's? Plenty of them, but it's only what you'd expect. He spent the evening here."

"I meant, on the clock perhaps. Billy told me that Jordon set great store by that clock and didn't allow anyone else to wind it. So if Gore's prints are on it, that would be some kind of proof, wouldn't it?" The rabbi squatted down and squinted at the clock lying on the floor.

Lanigan had gone back to the dining room for his folder, and now he returned, rifling through it. Let's see, here are blowups of various prints, and—oh, here it is—a summary of the fingerprint expert's findings. 'Carriage clock, on floor, no prints.' I guess it was wiped clean."

"But isn't that in itself suspicious? There should be prints, if only Jordon's from when he last wound it."

"Not if Martha wiped it in the course of her normal cleaning and dusting."

"Then hers should be on it," said the rabbi.

"Unless she used those cleaning mitts some women use. There's a pair in the kitchen." He joined the rabbi and squatted down on his heels beside him.

"How do you wind it?" asked the rabbi.

"Oh, the back is hinged." He picked it up by the folding brass handle on top and brought it over to the table. It was about five or six inches high, and the case consisted of rectangular plates of beveled glass, two of which had been smashed by the bullet, set in a brass frame. "It's called a carriage clock, and they usually come in padded leather cases. An old-fashioned travel clock is what it is. You carried it by this handle, and when you got to your inn or hotel, it could be set on the mantelpiece. When you had to wind it, you took it out of its leather case and opened the back. See that square stem in the hole there? That's where you wind it. You need a key."

"Two keys," observed the rabbi. "The stem in the center hole must be for resetting the hands. It's smaller than the other. Where would he have kept the keys, do you suppose?"

"Well, we have a clock in the living room that you wind. We keep the key on the mantelpiece behind it." He strode over to the mantelpiece, pointed and called out, "One key, Rabbi, but it's a double key. One end is for winding the spring and the other for setting the hands. The one we have at home, you wind in front and you set the hands by just moving them."

"Martha wouldn't have bothered to wipe that,"

said the rabbi, "especially if it were kept behind the clock."

"Certainly not if she were wearing cleaning mitts." He went back to his folder. "The summary doesn't mention it. I doubt if our man checked it for prints. I'm going to call him."

52

As they sat in the dining room awaiting the arrival of the fingerprint expert, Lanigan ruminated about the case. "I dismissed Gore as a suspect even before we dug out his alibi for him. I figured he was the one person who couldn't have done it, because he was the one person who knew there was someone else in the house. He was the only one who saw Billy sent to his room and locked in. Somehow he must have found out that he had left."

The rabbi nodded. "When I met with Billy on the island, he said Gore knew that he did it regularly when the old man sent him to his room. He had told him and they had laughed about it. Still, my guess is that Gore didn't just gamble on it. He may have heard the window go up—"

"Yeah, it's wooden sash and the door is thin. If Gore was standing just outside the door, he'd hear it all right," Lanigan agreed.

They talked of Gore and the kind of man he was. "He's well thought of in town," said Lanigan. "Public-spirited fellow, like getting up this silver collection, for instance. He's divorced and I heard it said at the time that maybe it was because he was so public spirited. You know, being active in all kinds of causes and not being home too much. I don't know the kind of money he makes as president of the bank, but he lives moderately. We may find when we start checking that he's been gambling. If he's tight for money, Jordon's couple of million would help out."

"You don't have to be short of money to try to acquire a couple of million," observed the rabbi.

"That's for sure."

"And if he were certain the money was coming to him, after a while he might get to thinking it was actually his and Jordon only a sort of temporary custodian."

The doorbell rang. It was the fingerprint expert. Lanigan led him over to the mantelpiece and pointed at the key. "When you were working here, Joe, did you check that key?"

"I didn't even see it, Chief." He felt that he had to defend himself. "Look, we don't go over everything. We'd be here for a week. Just the likely things and places. I wouldn't go dusting the ceiling, for instance, or the floor or—"

"All right, all right, Joe. Nobody is criticizing you. I want you to do that key now."

They watched as he dusted with his powders and then looked with his magnifying glass. "Yup, there's a nice print there. Tip of the thumb, I'd say. And I'm pretty sure it's the right thumb."

"Okay, Joe, here are blowups of the different prints you took here. I want you to go over those and see if this matches one of them."

"Oh, I know this one, Chief. That's Ellsworth Jordon's."

"Oh!" The sigh of disappointment came from both Lanigan and the rabbi. Lanigan shook his head in annoyance and frustration, but the rabbi said, "How about the other side?" He pointed at the key. "That print is toward the large socket that you use for winding the clock. Maybe there's one on the other side pointing toward the small socket that you use to set the hands."

"It's an idea," said Joe. From his bag he got a small screwdriver, and inserting the tang into the socket, he flipped the key over. Once again he dusted with his powders and a moment later announced, "Yeah, and this one's different."

"Are you sure?" asked Lanigan eagerly.

"Aw, Chief!" Joe was reproachful. "I couldn't make a mistake on this one. There's a little line scar right across it. This one is Lawrence Gore's."

"What made you think of Gore?" asked Lanigan. "Had you thought of him before you got the call from Miriam?"

The rabbi nodded. "From the time I heard about the quarterly report that Molly Mandell tried to de-

liver. By way of excusing her folly, her husband
pointed out that it didn't even balance."

"Yeah, he told me that, too. And you mentioned
it. Was it your idea that Gore was pilfering the till?
Because he wasn't, you know. We checked it out."

"No, that didn't occur to me. What struck me as
strange was that, knowing that the accounts didn't
balance, Gore was still willing to have Molly deliver it to Jordon. On the one hand Gore was terribly anxious lest the report came in a day late, and
on the other he was seemingly unconcerned that it
did not balance. It didn't make sense. Normally, he
would have said there was no point in delivering it
until he'd had a chance to correct it, that it would
infuriate the old man even more than if it came in
late."

"Yeah," Lanigan admitted. "Come to think of
it—"

"So it occurred to me that Gore might not have
objected to Molly's delivering it, knowing it was
safe because Jordon was dead."

53

Rabbi Reuben Levy had put on weight since Rabbi Small had last seen him. He remembered him as tall and almost painfully thin, but in the intervening years, he had filled out and was even beginning to show a paunch.

When Rabbi Small remarked on it, Rabbi Levy said ruefully, "I know, I know. But we've got over a thousand families in our congregation and hardly a day goes by when there isn't a Bar Mitzvah or an engagement party or a wedding. And we're invited to all of them. It makes it hard to keep your weight down."

His fine baritone voice was even richer and more resonant now. And he had the presence and self-assurance to go with it. They were seated in the cocktail lounge of the elegant—and expensive—Hotel Lafayette in Cambridge, and Rabbi Small and Miriam were impressed by his ability to summon a waiter by a mere lift of the head and a jut of the chin.

Mrs. Levy, as the wife of an eminently successful

rabbi, also had poise and certainty. She was not actually patronizing or condescending, but she did manifest the sophistication of the big city.

The two rabbis talked of their former classmates, and Rabbi Levy, by reason of being from the New York area, hence in the center of things, knew what most of them were now doing, the congregations they were serving and what problems they were having with them.

"And how are you managing with your congregation, David?" he asked.

"Oh, I have my problems, too," Rabbi Small replied.

"You're on a life contract, aren't you?"

Miriam spoke up, "He was offered one some years ago, and he refused it. He'd rather be on a year-to-year basis."

Rabbi Levy's eyes opened wide. "But why, David?"

Rabbi Small shrugged. "I prefer it, I feel freer."

"But isn't there a hassle every year when your contract has to be renewed?"

"Occasionally," Rabbi Small admitted.

"There's one right now," said Miriam, "for the coming year. And David refuses to do a thing about it."

"Now that's a mistake, David," said Levy portentously. "We must never forget that while the rabbi serves the congregation, he serves them by leading them like the conductor of a great symphony orchestra. And just as the conductor controls the orchestra by having the first-desk men absolutely loyal to him, the rabbi has to have a hard

core"—he made a fist to suggest the hard core—
"of faithful friends among the leaders of the congregation, who will push his policies, further his plans
and, yes, rally to his cause when he gets into trouble."

It crossed Rabbi Small's mind that Levy was
quoting from a sermon, or perhaps from an address
he had given to a group of rabbinical students. Or,
he reflected, maybe his mind just works that way.

"I'll have to remember that, Reuben," he said.

It was after midnight when the party broke up,
and the Smalls made their way to their car for the
long drive home to Barnard's Crossing. Rabbi
Small fumbled with the lock and then handed the
keys to his wife and said, "I think you had better
drive, Miriam. I think I may have had a little more
than I intended to."

"Are you all right, dear?" she asked anxiously.

"Oh, quite all right, but I expect I'll have a
headache in the morning."

He did have a headache the next morning and
woke up too late to attend the morning services. In
fact, when Lanigan came by just before noon, he
was still in bathrobe and slippers. Though quite
recovered, he looked wan.

Lanigan surveyed him critically. "You got a
touch of the grippe, or did you have a big night last
night?"

"I'm afraid I celebrated my reunion with my old
classmate a bit more than the occasion warranted.
God, how do you Gentiles do it?"

"The first time?" asked Lanigan sympathetically.

"Well, no, not really. On Passover we are required to drink four cups of wine, and a couple of times it's got to me. And then on Simchas Torah, that's when we finish the reading of the Scroll and start all over again, there's a tendency to express our joy and happiness with strong drink, sometimes too enthusiastically. Oh yes, and on the Feast of Purim, excess is practically ordained."

"Isn't it terrible?" said Miriam.

Lanigan chuckled. "They say tomato juice is good for it. I dropped in to tell you how things are going. I felt you had a right to know. We took Gore into custody last night, and it made the news broadcast this morning. Did you hear it?"

The rabbi shook his head. "I slept until ten."

"I've no doubt," said Lanigan with a grin. "Well, all it said was that Lawrence Gore has been taken into custody in connection with the Jordon murder. We expect to have further information on the noon broadcast."

"How did he react when—"

"I led our little party myself. I didn't want any mistakes, you know, like forgetting to read him his rights. Then I told him what we had on him. And do you know what he said? He said, 'That was pretty good shooting, wasn't it?' What do you think of that?"

"Well, I suppose there are all kinds of things people are proud of."

"He was quite open with us, seeing we had him dead to rights. He did get upset once though, over something Jennings said about Billy. He insisted that he'd never intended to make it appear that the boy had done it. Said it several times."

The rabbi nodded. "I imagine it bothered him. He must have been aware that it was likely. Did he say that he would have come forward and confessed if Billy had been charged?"

"I didn't ask."

"And Billy?"

"I went out to the island to see him this morning."

"To tell him he was free to leave?"

"Aw cummon, David, we never charged him. He was free to leave any time he wanted to."

"If he could swim the distance or hire a rowboat?"

Lanigan looked sheepish. "I'll admit there were impediments, you might say—"

"And how did he take the news about Gore?"

"Well, now, that's interesting. He said he wasn't surprised. He thought it must have been Gore who did it. Because when he went out the window, Gore was the only person there with the old man. And also because he was killed by a perfect shot right between the eyes. So I told him about the other shots and Gore's alibi. And all he said was, 'Oh, well,' as if none of it made any difference. What do you think of that?"

The rabbi smiled. "I suppose it shows that it takes age and experience and the wisdom of maturity to be fooled. What's he going to do now? Go back to New York?"

"No. He likes it on the island and wants to stay until Thanksgiving when the job will be about finished. His mother is due back about then, and he thought he'd wait until she got back to the States.

By the way, he asked to he remembered to you. He's coming in with the Hegertys for the weekend and wondered if you'd be willing to see him."

"I'd like to very much. He's coming in Friday? Saturday?"

"Friday afternoon, Tom Hegerty said."

"Maybe he'd like to come to Friday night dinner," suggested Miriam.

"I'm sure he'd enjoy that," said Lanigan. "I'll tell him."

"It was Ben Segal who put me on to him," said the rabbi. "How about inviting the Segals, too, Miriam?"

"Fine. I'll call them," she said. "I'm sure they'd appreciate a home-cooked meal."

54

The letter came in Tuesday's mail. The Rabbi opened it and read, "Dear Rabbi Small: This is to notify you that the board of directors have voted to renew . . ."

Miriam, having heard the postman's ring, came in from the kitchen. "Anything?" she asked.

"Nothing much." And he held the letter out to her.

She tried not to show her relief and pleasure as she read. She even managed to sound cross as she said, "They certainly took their time about it." Then she laughed, "Oh, David, I'm so glad."

He grinned at her. "See, and I didn't have to do a darn thing either."

ABOUT THE AUTHOR

Harry Kemelman is the author of the eight best-selling *Rabbi* novels. He lives in the Boston area.

11   Allow at least 4 weeks for delivery.   TAF-72

There's an epidemic with 27 million victims. And no visible symptoms.

It's an epidemic of people who can't read.

Believe it or not, 27 million Americans are functionally illiterate, about one adult in five.

The solution to this problem is you... when you join the fight against illiteracy. So call the Coalition for Literacy at toll-free **1-800-228-8813** and volunteer.

**Volunteer
Against Illiteracy.
The only degree you need
is a degree of caring.**

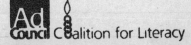

Ad Council · Coalition for Literacy

LV-1